A Storm
of
Infinite
Beauty

HISTORICAL ROMANCE

The American Heiress Series

To Marry the Duke
An Affair Most Wicked
My Own Private Hero
Love According to Lily
Portrait of a Lover
Surrender to a Scoundrel

The Pembroke Palace Series

In My Wildest Fantasies
The Mistress Diaries
When a Stranger Loves Me
Married By Midnight
A Kiss Before the Wedding—A Pembroke Palace Short Story
Seduced at Sunset

The Highlander Series

Captured by the Highlander
Claimed by the Highlander
Seduced by the Highlander
Return of the Highlander
Taken by the Highlander
The Rebel—A Highland Short Story

The Royal Trilogy

Be My Prince
Princess in Love
The Prince's Bride

Dodge City Brides Trilogy

Mail Order Prairie Bride
Tempting the Marshal
Taken by the Cowboy

STAND-ALONE HISTORICAL ROMANCE

Adam's Promise

A Storm of Infinite Beauty

A NOVEL

JULIANNE MACLEAN

LAKE UNION
PUBLISHING

Text copyright © 2023 by Julianne MacLean Publishing Inc.
All rights reserved.

Published by Lake Union Publishing, Seattle

www.apub.com

Amazon, the Amazon logo, and Lake Union Publishing are trademarks of Amazon.com, Inc., or its affiliates.

ISBN-13: 9781542036726 (paperback)
ISBN-13: 9781542036733 (digital)

Cover design by Caroline Teagle Johnson
Cover image: © plainpicture/Ableimages/Ben Miller / plainpicture;
© Varunyu / Getty; © Photo by Alex Tihonov / Getty

Printed in the United States of America

This book is dedicated to my daughter, Laura,
who is always in my heart.

When we contemplate the whole globe as one great dew drop, striped and dotted with continents and islands, flying through space with other stars all singing and shining together as one, the whole universe appears as an infinite storm of beauty.
—John Muir, *Travels in Alaska*

PROLOGUE

Valdez, Alaska
March 27, 1964

Twenty-three minutes before the earthquake struck, Valerie McCarthy was on her way to deliver a letter. She had poured all her heart and soul into it, aired all her youthful, pent-up passions and dreams. Her pen had flown across the page impetuously, expressing her deepest, most ardent desires. She was determined to try, one last time, to reach for the life she truly wanted.

The weather was crisp and cold that Good Friday evening, and the world felt strangely new to her. Gloomy gray clouds veiled the sky, yet the snowcapped mountains in the distance were cast in a heavenly light. An odd stillness hung in the air. Valerie's breath floated lightly in visible puffs as she pushed her baby carriage south along McKinley Street toward the city dock where the SS *Chena* was unloading supplies. Valerie would meet the ship and place her letter into the proper hands—the hands of someone she could trust.

Quickening her pace, she pushed Cameron over bumpy patches of ice that caused the carriage wheels to rattle in the hush of the evening, but her sweet angel slept soundly and didn't fuss.

Finally, she arrived at the corner of Alaska Avenue in the center of town and turned toward the waterfront. She made her way onto the earthen causeway that led to the dock, toward the noisy roar of delivery trucks coming and going, horns honking, and men shouting in the distance. A group of young boys ran past her in a race to watch the unloading of supplies—a thrilling spectacle in a town with few televisions.

Valerie walked briskly. Her nose was running, but she had no tissues, so she sniffed and wiped the back of her wrist across her upper lip. She pushed Cameron past the Village Morgue Bar. A few men stood in the doorway, arguing good-naturedly about something. Valerie kept moving, then glanced toward the small-boat harbor, where her friend Jeremy sat casually on the shiny front bumper of a parked car—talking to Angie.

Valerie slowed. For a few tense seconds, she watched and wondered, with more than a little concern, what they were discussing. Then Jeremy stood and pulled Angie into his arms. Valerie sucked in a breath at the sight of their embrace because Angie was a married woman and this was not a good situation. They both knew it.

But Valerie didn't have time for this. Not today. Not when she was on a mission of her own. Forcing herself to look away, she pushed her carriage and started off again. She would see Angie the next day and speak to her then.

At last, Valerie arrived at the end of the dock, where longshoremen were unloading cargo from the ten-thousand-ton supply ship. Wooden pallets were lifted out of the hold on ropes and pulleys. A steady stream of workers carried smaller crates down the sloping gangplank.

The *Chena*'s cook stood at the rail, tossing oranges to local boys with their hands in the air. Valerie removed her woolen hat and waved at him.

"Hello! Excuse me! Are you Marcus?"

"I am!" he replied.

"I'm Valerie, a friend of Jeremy's. I have a favor to ask."

He pointed at the gangplank and walked the length of the deck to meet her. She waited for him to disembark.

"It's nice to meet you, Valerie," he said amiably as he stepped onto the dock and bent over the baby carriage. "And who is this little person?"

Valerie peeled back the blanket. "This is Cameron. He's three days old today. Sleeping soundly, as you can see."

"My word. That's a good-lookin' boy if I ever saw one. Congratulations."

Valerie tucked the blanket back around Cameron's ears.

"What can I do for you?" Marcus asked, straightening.

She removed her mittens, reached into her pocket for the letter, and held it out. "Could you post this for me, wherever you end up next? There should be enough stamps on the envelope to cover it."

Marcus stared at the letter for a few seconds. "Is there something wrong with the post office in Valdez?"

Valerie continued to hold the letter out. "In a way, yes, but it's a long story, and if you want to hear it, we'll be here all day."

He narrowed his eyes a little as he studied her, then accepted the letter and read the address on the envelope. "Wolfville, Nova Scotia."

Valerie gestured toward Cameron. "I have news to share with a friend back home."

Marcus nodded knowingly, slid the letter into his breast pocket, and patted it three times. "Have no fear. I will ensure its safe delivery."

She let out a breath of relief. "Thank you. Jeremy said you'd be helpful. I appreciate it very much." She pulled her mittens back on and moved to turn the baby carriage around. "I don't want to take up any more of your time. It's quite busy here." A noisy forklift drove past.

"Have a good weekend," Marcus said as he turned and strode back up the gangplank.

With a heart full of hope, Valerie pushed Cameron away from the *Chena*. She smiled up at a young father who carried his daughter on his shoulders and wondered what her own future might look like, now that her letter was on its way home. Her life, and Cameron's, might be quite different in a month or two.

When the small-boat harbor came into view again, Valerie slowed her pace to look for Angie and Jeremy, but they had gone. Where, she had no idea, and she couldn't help but worry about what they were up to. Nevertheless, she continued walking and stepped onto the causeway, telling herself that it wasn't her problem to solve. Jeremy and Angie were adults. She had Cameron to care for now, and all she wanted was to leave the clatter and commotion of the busy Valdez waterfront and take him home to the peaceful serenity of Wilderness Lodge.

She had just begun to dream about the rocking chair in front of the fire when a flock of seabirds swarmed into town from the cannery. They darted wildly in all directions over her head. Then a dog began to bark a few blocks away, and another galloped past her at full speed in the direction of the mountains. Valerie looked up at the sky. Was a storm rolling in?

Suddenly the ground began to shake. It shuddered like a jackhammer and shook every bone in her body. A thunderous roar from deep inside the earth drowned out the commotion on the docks behind her. As she clung to the handle of the baby carriage, her insides flared with alarm.

The shaking intensified, and the ground beneath her rolled a full foot in one direction, then two feet in another. Valerie could barely keep her balance.

"It's the Russians! We're being bombed!" a woman shouted from the sidewalk. She staggered into the center of the street while parked cars bounced up and down, rolled, and crashed into one another.

The boys who had caught the oranges on the dock dashed past Valerie and shouted, "It's an earthquake! Run!"

They were heading inland, away from the waterfront, so she followed as fast as she could, pushing Cameron in the unwieldy carriage over bumpy slabs of ice while the earth rolled like giant waves in the ocean. The swells made their way up the street, lifting houses and cars on rising crests, then dropping them into the troughs.

One of the boys stopped and looked back at the dock, his eyes wide with terror. Valerie stopped and turned as well.

The *Chena* was bobbing up and down like a plastic toy, its shrill horn blaring. The warehouses on the dock creaked and groaned. Within seconds, they began to break apart. Roofs caved in, and the buildings crumpled. Before Valerie could comprehend what was happening, the entire dock gave way and collapsed into the sea, taking everything with it—cars, trucks, buildings, and people. All of it sank into the bay and disappeared before Valerie's horror-struck eyes.

She knew she had to run but struggled to keep her footing as the road slanted to one side. Glass exploded out of twisting, contorting buildings, and telephone poles swayed back and forth like windshield wipers. Utility lines snapped and whipped across the pavement. The earth heaved and bellowed. Cameron began to cry.

A huge crack opened in the road in front of Valerie, and dirty black water jetted out like a fire hose. She pulled Cameron back, but the fissure closed as quickly as it had opened. She didn't know whether to go forward or back, but when she turned to look at the waterfront, the *Chena's* stern was rising on a huge wave until the ship was nearly vertical. She blinked with fright, paralyzed by the sight of the large brass propeller spinning slowly in the air. She stood a few seconds, dazed, until the 440-foot cargo ship came crashing down thunderously on whatever was left of the dock and the people flailing about among the wreckage in the churning waters. She had never seen anything like it, and she choked back a cry of despair.

The *Chena*, now adrift and out of control, was moving on its side at a terrifying speed toward shore, plowing through small boats and debris. It generated an enormous wave that began to rush into town. Valerie stood paralyzed, staring as it surged up Alaska Avenue.

Desperate to outrun it, she gripped the handle of the carriage and pushed with all her might, sprinting hard. The ground was still rolling, and the tidal wave roared like a beast on her heels. Her mind screamed with a frantic need to save herself and Cameron.

She ran past a building just as its concrete facade collapsed into rubble and sent a cloud of masonry dust into the air.

The dark wave was still racing into town, gaining on her. Pure survival instinct took over as she pushed Cameron farther inland.

Another deep fissure opened in front of her. The front wheels of the carriage plunged into it. Valerie tugged and wrenched at the handle, but the vehicle was stuck. She scrambled in a mad panic to rescue Cameron from the trapped carriage, to take him into her arms and keep running, but frothy, ice-cold water slammed into her and knocked her off her feet.

No! The wave sucked her under, tossed her up to the surface, and sucked her down again.

Cameron!

Something struck her in the head, and she went numb, her body weak and immobile in a black, silent void. There were no more thoughts or fears. Only darkness. Nothingness.

Then the nightmare resumed. Valerie was engulfed in cold. She broke the surface of the foaming water and gasped for air. She was thrown against a car wedged vertically in a deep crevasse. In that instant, the wave slowed and began to retreat toward the bay, but it had carried Valerie two full blocks into town.

Dizzy and disoriented, wet, and shivering, she found her footing and chased after the outgoing wave, sprinting toward the fissure where Cameron was trapped, still buckled into the carriage, she prayed. She ran faster than she'd ever run in her life, but when she reached the crevasse, the world turned white as her hyperfocused gaze darted left and right, searching. The carriage was gone.

She took off again, chasing the wave that had retreated into the bay and taken the *Chena* back out.

"Cameron!"

The docks and everything upon them had been sucked into the sea. But all she cared about in that moment was Cameron. Her frantic eyes searched everywhere. The earth was still shaking, but she was barely aware of it. Then another deep fissure opened directly beneath her, and before she realized what was happening, she dropped straight into it.

PART I

THE CALM

CHAPTER 1

Annapolis Valley, Nova Scotia
May 2017

It was blissfully quiet in the pink, hazy dawn. Not a single breath of wind disrupted the stillness. The only sound that morning was the steady tapping of Gwen's running shoes on the asphalt.

She arrived at the end of her paved driveway, slowed her pace, and walked in small circles to catch her breath and cool down.

The weeping willow in her front yard stood in graceful tranquility. Letting her eyes fall closed, Gwen inhaled the sweet fragrance of apple blossoms from the orchard across the street. Toward the east, the sunrise glowed over the distant ridge on the horizon. The valley was stunningly beautiful, and Gwen was astounded by a feeling of rapture. It had been a while since she'd felt such enchantment. Perhaps it was the endorphins from the run, mixed with the scent of spring blossoms that told her summer was on its way.

She was ready for it. It had been a long, cold winter.

Gwen turned and climbed her front steps, opened the door, and entered the house—a two-story colonial with cedar shakes, warped and weather beaten to a soft pale gray. On the inside, it had been lovingly restored with a tasteful mix of historical charm and contemporary styles, including all the latest conveniences in the modern kitchen. She and Eric had spent an entire year on the renovations before they'd moved into the house—though Eric hadn't been able to enjoy it for long.

Gwen stopped in the foyer and pressed the heels of her hands to her forehead. Why did she do this to herself? She had just been marveling at the sunrise and feeling hopeful for the first time in ages. Why did she have to spoil it by thinking about Eric? He was gone. She had to accept it. Their marriage was over, and she had to stop dreaming that he would eventually come back. It had been a full year since he'd left, so the time had come to accept things the way they were.

Closing her eyes and taking a deep, cleansing breath, Gwen forced herself to tuck those thoughts away. *You must think of something else.*

What time was it? There. She needed to get ready for work.

Gwen opened her eyes and ran up the stairs to turn on the shower.

~

A half hour later, Gwen was dressed for work in a rust-colored pencil skirt, a matching sweater, and black pumps. She stood in her quiet kitchen and poured coffee into a travel mug. Then she remembered something. Today was the twenty-third of May. She was supposed to meet with someone—an American writer who had sent an email over a week ago to inform her of his intention to visit the museum. He'd explained that he was working on a biography about Scarlett and requested access to the archives. He wasn't the first writer to visit the museum—there had been many over the years—but he was the first to have a six-figure contract with a major New York publishing house.

"Shoot," Gwen said as she snapped the cover onto her travel mug, grabbed her purse, and walked out the front door to her car.

~

The Scarlett Fontaine Museum was housed in a large Victorian mansion in the small town of Wolfville, Nova Scotia. It was the childhood home of Ms. Fontaine, a famous Hollywood movie star and fashion icon of the 1960s and '70s. Born as Valerie McCarthy in the Annapolis Valley in 1942, Scarlett had traveled to New York after high school to pursue her dreams of becoming an actress. After a year in Manhattan, she had moved to Hollywood, where she'd achieved fast success with a lead role in an Oscar-winning film that had launched a fifteen-year career and earned her two Oscars—one for acting and another for best song—before she'd retreated from the spotlight and moved to Switzerland, where she died in 1979.

"Good morning, Nora," Gwen said as she walked through the front door of the museum. Nora worked in the gift shop and sold tickets to visitors.

In the summer months, Gwen and a few student employees conducted guided tours, but it was only May. The tourist season hadn't yet shifted into high gear. Bus tours from the cruise ships didn't begin until June.

"I don't suppose you remembered that we're having a visitor today?" Gwen asked Nora.

She moved out from behind the oak counter. "The American writer."

"Yes. His name is Peter Miller." Gwen adjusted her purse strap over her shoulder. "I think I might have tried to block it out."

She'd googled this guy and discovered that he was a notorious Hollywood paparazzo who had sold hundreds of salacious photographs of celebrities to every tabloid magazine imaginable. He'd once been heralded as the "most limber and accomplished fence jumper" in the Hollywood Hills.

"What time are you expecting him?" Nora asked.

"Nine thirty." Gwen glanced at her watch and headed toward her office. "That gives me time to hide all the good stuff."

Nora laughed. "Should I charge him the regular adult price for a ticket?"

"Definitely yes," Gwen replied. "Then bring him straight to my office. I don't want him nosing around untethered before I meet him."

~

Gwen didn't like to think that she had an axe to grind, but members of the paparazzi weren't exactly on her list of favorite people. Poor Scarlett had suffered from the constant hounding of the press. There was even a full museum display upstairs that illustrated her struggles and explained her subsequent move to Switzerland to seek privacy. Gwen wondered what Mr. Miller would think about that display when he toured the museum.

She sat down at her desk, which overlooked the back parking lot and a tennis court that had once belonged to Scarlett's family but was now open to the public. On that morning, museum hours didn't begin until ten o'clock, so when a black Honda Accord drove in at nine thirty, she knew it was Mr. Miller.

She rolled her chair closer to the window and watched him get out and stretch. She'd already seen pictures of him online. He was handsome, in his midthirties, with dark hair. Today he wore a black leather jacket, blue jeans, and sneakers with mirrored sunglasses. He was visibly fit, no doubt from all the exercise chasing celebrities in the streets or climbing trees outside of hotel-room windows.

He reached back into the car and withdrew a black canvas laptop bag, which he slung over his shoulder. Then he checked his phone and started walking while texting.

Gwen rolled her chair back to her desk and finished typing an email while she waited for Nora to show him in. A moment later she knocked on Gwen's open door. "Mr. Miller's here."

"Thank you," Gwen replied, closing her email program.

When Mr. Miller walked into the office, he no longer wore his jacket. Nora must have hung it up for him. He wore a crisp, white-collared shirt with the sleeves rolled up to the elbows.

Gwen stood to shake his hand over the desk. "I'm Gwen Hollingsworth."

Nora quietly left and closed the door behind her.

"Peter Miller." He stepped back. "Thanks for taking the time to see me. It's pretty thrilling, actually, to finally be here." He glanced around the room at the high ceilings, oak-paneled walls, and antique light fixtures.

"Thrilling?" Gwen replied.

"Yes. To see the town and house where Scarlett Fontaine grew up. It's like stepping into the past."

"I suppose it is. Please have a seat." She gestured toward the wing chair that faced her desk and sat down as well.

Peter set his laptop case on the floor and made himself comfortable.

"I'm eager to hear about the book you're working on," Gwen said, taking charge of the meeting. "But I should be up front and warn you that I'm very protective about Scarlett's memory. She was a private person at heart, and the last thing she would have wanted was a trashy tell-all about her personal life."

Peter inclined his head. "Is that what you think I'm writing?"

She leaned back in her chair, realizing she'd probably just insulted him by calling his work trash. But wasn't that the most accurate word for the sorts of pictures he took?

"Well, I'm not sure," Gwen said. "In your email, you called it a biography, but I did google you. You've never written a book before. Your publishing credits include much . . . let's just call them *shorter* works. And just so you know, I'm not a fan of the paparazzi."

"I prefer the term freelance photojournalist," he told her, then carefully studied her eyes for a moment. "But what matters here is that you don't seem to have faith in my credentials."

"Unless it's just a picture book you're working on?" Gwen asked, hitting below the belt.

"Nope," he said. "It's a real book with real words, correct grammar, and a table of contents. It will even have an index." He held up a hand. "But don't worry. No offense taken."

Gwen rubbed the back of her neck. "I'm sorry. I didn't mean to sound patronizing."

"It's fine. I'm used to it. I get it all the time."

"Do you?" she asked. "And that doesn't bother you?"

He glanced out the window and shrugged. "I try not to worry about what other people think of me."

"Well, that's obvious," Gwen replied. "Otherwise, you wouldn't point your telephoto lens into their backyards."

He met her gaze, and his eyes turned cool. "Touché."

They were quiet for a moment, and Gwen felt like they were sizing each other up. Peter sat forward, rested his elbows on his knees, and clasped his hands together.

"I think we might be getting off on the wrong foot here," he said, after a pause. "It's obvious that you care about this museum and Scarlett's memory or reputation—whatever you want to call it. I get that. You have a vested interest, and I know why, because I googled you as well."

Gwen folded her hands across her lap and watched him sit back in his chair. "Did you." It wasn't a question.

"Yes. I know that you're related to Ms. Fontaine and you're the sole heir to her enormous fortune, which is currently in the hands of your parents."

Gwen hated it when people thought they knew everything about her just because of something they'd read on the internet.

"That's true," she told him, choosing not to reveal her more personal kinship with Scarlett, her first cousin once removed, whom she had never even met because Scarlett had died before Gwen was born.

But Scarlett's music had gotten Gwen through some of the worst times in her life. Especially over the last two years.

"But let me assure you," Peter continued, "I'm not out to write anything salacious or trashy. I'm just hoping to do some good, solid research here and get permission to include some of the photographs from the museum's collection. Pictures from Scarlett's early life. Images that haven't been published before."

"I see," Gwen said.

"If it helps you to know my background," he went on, seeming determined to win her over, "I have a master's degree in twentieth-century history from Stanford, and during my undergrad, I minored in American lit."

Gwen's head drew back slightly. "I have to admit—that's a surprise. How in the world did you end up as a tabloid photographer?"

He glanced out the window. "I needed to make a living somehow. But enough about me." He looked at her. "What matters is that I have a book deal that requires me to put my research skills to good use, finally, which is why I'm sitting in your office right now, Ms. Hollingsworth, pleading for mercy." He grinned boyishly, and Gwen sensed he was a charmer who usually got what he wanted from women.

"Call me Gwen," she said coolly.

"All righty, then. Gwen. Let's cut to the chase. I'm here because I need your help."

Gwen was beginning to feel impatient. "I can certainly give you a tour of the museum, if you'd like, but the exhibits are pretty self-explanatory. You might prefer to look around on your own. You'll see Scarlett's gowns and jewelry and memorable costumes from her films. Upstairs, you'll find her bedroom and other rooms that have been restored to how they were when she lived here. Beyond that, you're welcome to conduct your research in the archives, which is also upstairs. We have a summer student looking after the collection. It's organized by year, starting from Scarlett's childhood all the way to her death in '79."

Peter's brow furrowed with a slight frown, as if he thought Gwen was trying to hide something from him. "What about the year she spent in New York?"

"What about it?" Gwen replied, too quickly. Her legs were crossed, and she started to swing her foot.

"I've never been able to find much information about that time in her life. No letters or anything."

"That's because not much happened," Gwen said with a casual shrug. "She went there to get her acting career off the ground, and she was estranged from her family. Her father didn't approve of the fact that she had run off to become an actress, and he expected her to fail. That's why she didn't write any letters—because she wasn't having any success. But then she packed up and went to Hollywood and . . . well, you know the rest."

Peter continued to look at Gwen as if he knew something she didn't.

"What?" she asked. "Obviously, if you're writing a biography, you know all of this. Or at least I hope you do. It's on her Wikipedia page."

"Yes, I'm familiar with all that," he said. "But I've done a bit of detective work, and what I really want to know, and the reason I flew all this way, is to ask if she ever spent time in Alaska."

Gwen's foot began to swing a little faster. "Not that I'm aware of. Why?"

He reached for his laptop case on the floor, unzipped it, and withdrew a file folder. "I stumbled across something a few months ago. I was watching a television documentary about the Alaska earthquake in 1964. Are you familiar with it?"

"Um . . ."

"It was the second-largest earthquake of all time," he explained, "after the Chilean quake in 1960. It registered nine point two on the Richter scale."

"No kidding." Gwen stared at the file folder on his lap and waited for him to show her what was inside. "What does that have to do with Scarlett?"

Her heart began to race because she was considered the world's foremost expert on Scarlett Fontaine. Gwen was also the dedicated caretaker of her incredible legend. What could this tabloid photographer possibly have discovered that Gwen didn't already know?

At last, he withdrew a photocopy of an article in an old newspaper and handed it across the desk. Gwen read the headline at the top of the page.

POWER OUTAGE CONTINUES

"Not the main article," Peter said, pointing at the sidebar, which contained a photo of a young man smiling and holding a baby. Gwen read the caption out loud.

"Joyful reunion in Valdez: A baby in a carriage was found floating on debris from the tidal wave that destroyed the city docks. The infant was rescued from the sea and safely returned to the distraught mother, who had been injured in the quake."

"Look carefully at the woman in the hospital bed," Peter said.

Gwen squinted at the grainy black-and-white photograph and felt an explosion of heat in her belly.

"It's Scarlett," Peter said. "Don't you think? If it isn't, then she must have a twin or a doppelgänger."

By now, Gwen's pulse was galloping. She couldn't speak for a few seconds. She held the photo at arm's length to get a better sense of the young woman's features. "It certainly does look like her. But it can't be."

"Why not?" he asked. "I've been digging everywhere, and I've never been able to find a single record of Scarlett Fontaine or Valerie McCarthy in New York in 1964. And then I saw this. It was a total fluke. I was watching TV one night . . ."

Gwen shook her head and handed the photo back to Peter. "It's not her because she never had any children."

"Are you sure? Maybe that's why she left home when she did—because she was pregnant. Maybe her family sent her away to have the baby and put it up for adoption. It happened all the time back then. And you know how strict her father was."

"Yes, but it can't be Scarlett," Gwen insisted. "Someone in the family would have known about it."

"And kept it secret," he argued. "That was the whole point of sending unwed mothers away to have their babies—so that no one would find out."

Gwen sat for a moment, considering it. Then she let out a breath. "Let me see that again." She took the picture and read the caption a second time. "It doesn't mention the woman's name. Was there not a follow-up article on another day?"

"Nothing," Peter replied. "I searched through all the local papers for weeks afterward. She was never identified, and neither was the man."

Gwen slid the photo back into the file folder and reclined in her chair. "Well. This is certainly interesting." She gazed across her desk at Peter. "Is this why you got the book deal? Because the publisher believes you might have uncovered a scandalous family secret that would shock the world and create a bestseller?"

Peter inclined his head. "Scarlett Fontaine was America's sweetheart. She was a flawless, innocent Hollywood princess who could do no wrong. You have to admit it's a bombshell."

Gwen tipped her head back and looked up at the ceiling. "I knew it. What did I say before? A trashy tell-all."

"No," he insisted, shaking his head. "That's not my intention at all."

"But how can this be good for Scarlett's memory?" she asked, meeting his gaze again.

"No one's perfect," he replied with a shrug.

Gwen pinched the bridge of her nose. "Part of me wants to ask you to leave, but I know you'll just walk out of here and write whatever you please about Scarlett, as long as it sells books."

"That's not true," he argued. "I'm here to do research. I'm looking for facts, and I'll be citing every source."

Gwen nodded with a feeling of defeat. "Okay. As I said, you're welcome to search through the archives, but I guarantee you won't find any references to Alaska. If there was something there, I would know about it."

"Because you know everything?" he asked, with a note of challenge in his voice.

Gwen didn't back down. "I just don't want you nosing around town, stirring up gossip, and starting rumors about Scarlett. She's a national treasure."

"I know that."

"Can you at least keep me informed about what you find?"

"Of course," he said. "But this is your town, and you know it better than I do, so I could use your help. As long as you remember that it's *my* story. I discovered it. And I would be very displeased if you scooped me and posted about this on the internet before my book comes out."

Gwen leaned forward on her desk. "I promise not to do that, as long as you promise me something in return."

"What would that be?"

She gestured toward the file folder. "First of all, I'd like a copy of that photograph."

He pulled it out and handed it over. "You can have this one. I've got others. But please keep it to yourself."

"I will." She set it down on the desk. "Second, you'll give me first dibs on any primary sources you uncover that prove your theory. I'd like them for my collection." She was already imagining a new exhibit to go along with the release of his book—if his theory turned out to be true. Which she still wasn't convinced would be the case.

"It's a deal," Peter replied. "Is that it? Anything else?"

"Not that I can think of."

"Good." He slipped the file folder back into his computer case and stood up. "Now I think I'll tour the exhibits."

"Sure," she replied. "And when you're done, I'll take you to the archive room. Our summer student will be here at ten. Her name is Susie, and she can help you find anything you need."

"Excellent." He reached into his back pocket for his phone. "Let's add each other to our contacts so we can text. I'll let you know if I find anything super juicy in the collection."

"I guarantee you won't," she said. "And please don't say *super juicy*."

His eyes lifted from his screen, and he chuckled. "You're very protective of Scarlett, aren't you?"

She chose not to answer that question as they traded phones and input each other's numbers.

A moment later, he was making his way toward the door, where he stopped and faced her. "Where's a good place to go for lunch?"

Gwen sat down and rolled her chair closer to the desk. "This is a university town, so there are all sorts of places on the main street. It's about a ten-minute walk from here."

"Great. Would you like to join me later? We could talk shop."

"Sorry, I can't. I have somewhere I need to be."

"Okey dokey." He walked out and closed the door behind him.

When Gwen was certain he was gone, she picked up the phone on the desk and dialed her parents' number, because this was major. They definitely needed to know about Peter Miller. Gwen was also going to suggest that they talk to their lawyers as soon as possible.

CHAPTER 2

Gwen waited all morning for Peter to pack up and leave for lunch. When she finally heard his footsteps tapping down the main staircase and saw him heading out the door, she grabbed her purse and drove straight to her parents' house.

They lived a few miles outside of town on a sprawling hilltop estate that overlooked the lush green valley below. Gwen pulled into the driveway, got out of her silver Mercedes-Benz, and walked up the stone steps. Her mother, Anne, was outside on the covered veranda, seated in her favorite white wicker chair, reading a glossy magazine.

"Hi, darling," she said, rising to her feet. "I still can't get over this. Do you think it's true about Scarlett—that she had a baby?"

"I don't know," Gwen replied. "And please remember to keep this just between us. Have you told Dad yet?"

"No," Anne replied. "He's teaching classes all afternoon. I didn't want to distract him, so I thought I'd wait until he got home. Did you bring the picture?"

"Yes, I have it in my bag. Let's go inside."

Anne opened the screen door, and Gwen followed her into the kitchen at the back of the house. She set her bag down on one of the stools around the large kitchen island and withdrew the newspaper clipping.

"It's kind of grainy," Gwen said as she handed it over.

Her mother peered through the lower portion of her progressive lenses. "My word. It does look like her." She read the caption below the photo, then handed it back to Gwen. "If it's true, it certainly is a bombshell, like you said. I don't know what to think."

Gwen slid the photo back into her bag. "Me neither. I just wish I could look into this on my own. It feels like it should be a private family matter."

"Nothing's private about Scarlett," her mother replied. "On the upside, maybe this fellow has some more information that he hasn't shared with you yet. I hope you were friendly with him." She gave Gwen a sidelong glance.

"Of course I was," she replied, indignant. "I gave him full access to the archives, and I told him that he could stay as long as he liked."

Her mother washed her hands at the sink. "Do you want something to eat or a cup of coffee?"

"I just had lunch at my desk," Gwen replied, "but I'd love a coffee."

While her mother switched on the Keurig machine, Gwen sat at the kitchen island and gazed out at the swimming pool. She thought about who in the family had known Scarlett best. Gwen's mother and Scarlett were first cousins, but they were two decades apart in age and had only met once when Anne was twelve and completely starstruck. Scarlett had no siblings. Gwen's grandmother, however, had been Scarlett's favorite aunt. They'd always kept in touch.

"Grandma Mary never said anything to you?"

"Nothing," her mother replied, "which makes me think she couldn't have known."

"That's why I don't see how it can be true," Gwen said, "because Scarlett was close to Grandma Mary and left her entire fortune to her. There was nothing in the will for a biological child."

"Maybe Scarlett wanted to take that secret to her grave," her mother suggested as she filled Gwen's coffee cup. "Or maybe the child died at some point. That would keep things simple from a legal standpoint, but it doesn't solve the mystery."

"About what happened in Alaska?" Gwen asked.

"Yes. I mean, obviously there was an earthquake," her mother added, "and a baby was rescued from the sea. It's an unbelievable story, even for a normal person."

"Scarlett was normal," Gwen reminded her.

"No, she wasn't. She was one of the most famous, most photographed, recognizable women in the world." She handed Gwen her coffee.

"Yes, but she was normal on the inside," Gwen insisted, though she couldn't possibly know for sure. Maybe that's what was so unsettling about all this. Gwen had always felt that, as the museum curator, she knew Scarlett intimately and better than anyone. But perhaps that wasn't the case at all. Perhaps everything she believed was pure conjecture.

She sipped her coffee. "If it's true, it raises a lot of questions. Like, is that the real reason Scarlett left home? Did her father make her feel ashamed or force her to put her baby up for adoption? Maybe she blamed him for whatever happened to the child and that's why they never spoke again."

Anne sat down at the island and laid her hand on Gwen's forearm. "Are you okay? I'm sure this situation must touch a nerve."

Her mother's words cut through Gwen's surface composure and landed in the dark inner hollow where her grief lived. Gwen's grief was quiet most days, but suddenly she was back there . . . in the hospital bed holding Lily, gripped by an agony no mother should ever be subjected to.

Tears stung her eyes, and she choked back the urge to cry. She didn't have the heart for this. Not today, when she needed to focus on what was happening at the museum.

Unable to meet her mother's gaze—because if she did, she would surely fall to pieces—Gwen reached for her phone and checked the screen for notifications. She swiped up a few times, awaiting the sweet mercy of distraction.

"I'm fine," she finally said, her voice shaking a little. "I'm thinking about the fact that we might have a relative out there somewhere."

Her mother understood that she needed a moment to mend and recover. Anne sat quietly, giving her that space.

Gwen set her phone down and turned her thoughts outward. "What would he or she be to us? First cousin twice removed?"

Her mother shrugged. "I have no idea." She pondered the situation, then set down her coffee cup. "But we should probably talk about the elephant in the room."

"Elephant?"

"Yes. Aren't you worried about a stranger coming out of the woodwork and demanding half the family fortune?"

Gwen clenched and unclenched her left hand. "As if there isn't more than enough to go around. The truth is I'd welcome that, because most of the time I feel guilty about getting everything after you're gone. It's too much for one person. And it's a huge responsibility."

"The museum, you mean?"

Gwen sipped her coffee. "No, not that. I love the job. I'm talking about the fortune." She paused, having some trouble voicing the next few words. She had to take a breath first. "I don't have any children to leave it to, so what will happen after I die? Who will look after Scarlett's memory?"

Her mother touched her knee. "You know our lawyers have anticipated every possible scenario. It will all be taken care of."

"Yes, but no one would care about the museum like I do," Gwen said. "It's personal for us because we're family."

"Don't be so sure that no one else would care. Scarlett was a beloved icon. She was adored by the whole world."

"And yet she died alone."

Gwen promptly dropped her gaze. Again, she couldn't look her mother in the eye, because her mother knew everything about her trauma in the delivery room and exactly why this situation was touching a nerve.

With a quick shake of her head, she checked her watch. "I need to get back to work, but first I need to ask . . . are you sure there wasn't anything else left behind when Grandma Mary passed? That Scarlett didn't have a private diary or some letters that she hid somewhere? Do we still have any of Grandma Mary's personal effects or anything from Scarlett's parents?"

"There's nothing," her mother replied. "Scarlett's father left everything to Mary, who left it all to your father. He knew the value of Scarlett's personal belongings and made sure it all went to the museum."

Gwen sighed with defeat. "Will you be sure to ask Dad about that when he comes home? Show him the picture and see if he can think of anything or if he knows of some unopened boxes somewhere. I'd want to go through them."

"I will," her mother replied. "Can you leave the picture with me?"

"Yes. I made that copy for you, but don't share it with anyone. I promised Peter that I wouldn't scoop him, and I want to keep him on our side and make sure he trusts me so that he shares what he finds."

"Understood."

Gwen finished her coffee, stood up, and carried the empty cup to the dishwasher. "I have to go. I don't want to leave him to his own devices for too long." She gathered up her bag and walked out the door.

~

When Gwen returned to the museum, Peter was browsing in the gift shop, talking to Nora. As soon as he spotted Gwen walking in, he set down the souvenir glass he'd been examining and made his way toward her in the wide entrance hall. "Do you have a minute?"

"Yes," she replied.

"Good, because I have some questions." He gestured toward the stairs. "Could we go up to the archive room?"

"Sure. Just let me get rid of my things." Gwen walked to her office, hung her coat on the coat-tree, and locked her purse in the desk before following Peter up the wide staircase.

"Gorgeous woodwork in this home," he said as he ran his hand up the polished oak banister. "Scarlett was a lucky young lady, to grow up in a house like this."

Gwen glanced at the enormous family portraits on the wall. "It depends how you define *lucky*. She certainly had everything in terms of material possessions and social status, but her father wasn't exactly a warmhearted fellow."

"The intimidating town judge," Peter replied, "laying down the law and handing out sentences every day, especially to his teenage daughter."

"He was very old school," Gwen agreed. "Incredibly strict."

"Not entirely surprising," Peter said, "given his career choice. He was a military man originally, wasn't he?"

"Yes. A lieutenant colonel in World War II."

Gwen and Peter walked past some museum visitors and entered the archive room at the back of the house. It was brightly lit by fluorescent lights on the ceiling and sconces on white walls. Susie was at her desk, working at the computer. Gwen suggested she take a break. Then she followed Peter to the largest worktable, where he was going through a banker's box full of items from 1963.

Gwen glanced at his open laptop. "How's it going so far?"

"Very well," he replied. "It's an incredible collection. There's so much to study. I've booked a week in a hotel, but I might extend it to two because I wasn't expecting to find so much about Scarlett's film career and her life in Switzerland." He paused and let out a breath.

"But right now, I need to stay focused on the Alaska element, which is everything prior to 1964. Do you know if any of her friends from high school might know something?" He withdrew Scarlett's 1963 yearbook from the box.

"They're all in their seventies now," Gwen explained, "and those who still live in the area have already shared quite a bit with the museum. Some have been interviewed on camera. The recordings are in the boxes from the later years, post-1995."

"Good to know," Peter said. "I'll need to look at those."

"You're welcome to," Gwen replied, "but as I've told you, I've seen them all, and there's no mention of Alaska."

His gaze swept across the rows of tall storage shelves. "Maybe you weren't looking for the right clues when you watched those interviews. Maybe there's something there, if we look at it through a different lens."

Perhaps he was right. Perhaps Gwen needed to look at everything again with fresh eyes.

Peter flipped through the yearbook from Scarlett's senior year and opened it to the drama-club section. "What about this girl?" He pointed at a photo of Scarlett with a friend on the high school gymnasium stage. They stood next to each other, arms linked together, cheek to cheek. "What's with the poem that Scarlett wrote here?"

Gwen examined the photograph. "That's not a poem. Those are song lyrics. She started writing music when she was sixteen. And this girl was one of Scarlett's best friends. That's her yearbook, actually. She was kind enough to donate it."

"Does she still live in town?"

"No," Gwen replied. "She moved to Manitoba years ago. But this one lives in Canning." She flipped the page and pointed at another photograph from the same school play.

"Were they close?" Peter asked.

"Somewhat. Scarlett was friendly with everyone. That was her charm. She wasn't one for cliques."

Peter seemed to be thinking about something. "How far is Canning from here?"

"About a twenty-minute drive."

"Would you mind calling her? Maybe you could set up an appointment for me to talk to her?"

"I'll give it a try," Gwen said. "And you're right. I should probably look at everything with fresh eyes. There could be something here."

Peter gestured toward the shelving units, which took up half the room. "I'd welcome the help."

A sudden sense of purpose flooded into Gwen's mind, and it was a welcome sensation—because she'd been in a low-spirited rut for a long time.

"Let me go downstairs and make that phone call," she said. "Then I'll come back up and join you. And I'll have Susie set up the A/V equipment in the parlor downstairs so we can watch the interviews."

"You're amazing," he said as he sat down at the table. "Thank you."

"Just doing my job."

But Gwen's work at the museum had never been just a job to her. It was part of her identity. It was in her blood, quite literally. And it was the thing that had kept her going when everything else was falling apart.

CHAPTER 3

Gwen didn't realize what time it was until the windows in the archive room grew dark. Nora and Susie had left the museum at five, and Gwen had promised to lock up. Now it was past seven, and her stomach was growling.

Seated at the large worktable, directly under a fluorescent light, she leaned back in her chair and stretched her arms over her head. Peter, who was working at the opposite end of the table, glanced up.

"Ready to call it a day?"

"Not really. My mind is churning with questions, especially about Scarlett's year in New York."

"Her *alleged* year in New York," he reminded her.

Gwen nodded. "There really isn't any proof, is there?" She thought about how skeptical she'd been that morning when he'd first presented the photograph. She felt differently now.

"Not that I've ever found," he said, "and believe me—I have left no stone unturned."

Gwen let out a sigh. "I do believe you. And now I'm hungry. How about you?"

"I've been famished for the past hour, but I didn't want to interrupt your flow."

"Because you thought I'd want to quit and lock up?" she asked.

"Do you?" He sat back and watched her expression.

"No. Because I'm supposed to be the expert here, yet I've been missing a puzzle piece all these years, and I never even realized it."

He folded his arms across his chest. "Is it too much to hope that I've won you over with my brilliant historical discovery?"

She chuckled softly. "I don't know about *brilliant*. Lucky, for sure. And yes, I confess that you have my attention. And I still want to watch those interviews before we visit Mrs. Dion tomorrow."

Her stomach growled again, and Peter sat forward. "How about I spring for a pizza?"

Gwen tossed her pencil onto the table. "Sounds good. Let's order one."

Peter reached for his phone, and she gave him the name of a local shop. After he placed the order, they gathered up their belongings and left the archive room. Gwen locked the door behind them and followed Peter downstairs to the front parlor.

"Can I do anything to help?" he asked as she turned on the flat-screen television that Susie had rolled into the room before leaving for the day.

"No, just make yourself comfortable."

She searched for the DVD with interviews from 1995 and slid it into the machine, then joined Peter on the sofa. Together, they watched the raw footage from the first interview with a woman who had once been the family's housekeeper. She described Scarlett as a friendly, intelligent young girl who loved to perform. She was always dancing and singing and copying the choreography from *Guys and Dolls* and *Gentlemen Prefer Blondes*.

A half hour later, the doorbell rang. Peter got up to tip the pizza-delivery man while Gwen turned off the television. Then they moved to the dining room to eat at the large mahogany table.

"This is very nice," Peter commented, looking up at the crystal chandelier. "You know, this house is not what I expected. I thought it would be 1950s or '60s decor, but it's very Victorian."

"Like I said, her father was old school in every way."

While they ate, they talked about Scarlett's death in Switzerland, which had shocked the world in 1979 because she was only thirty-six years old, still young and beautiful, and no one had known she was ill. For years, the tabloids had speculated that she was still alive and living secretly abroad. Even today, the occasional report of a sighting somewhere in the world went viral on the internet or made it to the front page of a tabloid.

Peter reached for a second slice of pizza. "I find it interesting that Scarlett's life is often described as tragic because of her early death and the fact that she died alone in a foreign country. But as a family member and a woman, do you consider her life tragic?"

Gwen sipped her water. "I never thought so before today. I mean, of course any death is tragic, especially at a young age, but I wouldn't have said her whole life was tragic. Quite the opposite. She followed her dream and broke free from her controlling father and achieved incredible success professionally. She wrote music that will live forever. I have no doubt that she derived a great deal of satisfaction and fulfillment from that, from being able to pursue her art. So no, it wasn't all tragic. It was a life well lived, in my opinion."

He wiped his mouth with a napkin. "But you said you never thought it was tragic before today. You feel differently now?"

Of course she did. How could she not?

Gwen took a few seconds to formulate her answer, sipped her water, and cleared her throat. "If Scarlett had a baby, that means she was separated from her child. Either the child died or she gave it up, and that changes everything, because a woman never gets over something like that. On top of it all, she chose—or was advised—to keep her pregnancy a secret, so she couldn't confide in anyone or share her pain. That's tragic all on its own."

"I agree," Peter said. "And that's what made me want to write this book. Her life seemed like a dream in so many ways, but there was a real woman behind all that success. A woman perhaps with a broken heart. Yet she achieved great things regardless. That makes her stronger than anyone knows."

Gwen took a breath and let it out slowly. She thought of her own small, brokenhearted life, constantly clouded by the shadow of her grief and loneliness. Day after day, it was the same. She never veered from her familiar routine, perhaps for some sense of control or security—or to avoid letting go of what she had lost.

Lily. Her marriage.

She went home to an empty house, cooked supper, watched television, or caught up on some reading. She kept busy so that she wouldn't think about the horror of what had happened to Lily or miss Eric and surrender to the temptation to look at his Facebook page and see what he was doing with Keri, the new woman in his life.

Nights were hard. She couldn't bear to imagine him sleeping beside Keri, holding her close, intimately and lovingly, like he used to hold Gwen. Sometimes she would lie awake and picture him making love to Keri and wonder if they were doing it at that very moment. Jealousy would rip into her gut like a dagger, and she would pound the mattress with her fist. She would wish terrible things on them both.

But most nights, she would lie on her side, hugging his pillow and blaming herself for driving him away with her perpetual grief and gloom. She would think of all the times she had shut him out, and she would feel nothing but regret. Those were the nights she would long for him in the empty spot in bed beside her and wish she could go back and do everything differently. Loneliness would keep her awake, haunting her until she got up and did something like wash dishes or watch a late-night talk show.

Gwen was always relieved to see morning light in the window so that she could get up, go for a run, and head off to work. Perhaps she liked the same old routine because something new would require her to move on from the old, and she wasn't ready for that. Or maybe she was afraid of it. Afraid of another fresh disaster and the pain it would bring, all over again.

"What do you think of that?" Peter asked, and she realized she hadn't responded to his theory about Scarlett being stronger than anyone knew.

Perhaps it was time for Gwen to be stronger too. Or make an effort to invite change into her life.

"Yes," she said, redirecting her thoughts to the conversation. "And people do think she had a charmed life. She made everything look so easy with that dazzling smile, but it couldn't have been all sunshine and roses. Not if she was forced to give up a child."

Peter finished eating and leaned back in his chair. He regarded Gwen closely. "Do you have children?"

She balled up her napkin and tossed it onto the plate. "I hate being asked that question. And I don't mean that in a rude way—it's just that . . ." She stopped and couldn't seem to finish the thought.

"It's none of my business," Peter said.

"No, it's fine." She waved a hand through the air and tried to detach herself from the discomfort of sharing her story with others. "It's just painful to talk about, and it makes things awkward sometimes. People get uncomfortable, and they don't know what to say to me."

He sat patiently, waiting for her to explain.

"I had a baby," she finally told him. "But she only lived a few hours."

"Oh, God," he quickly said. "I'm so sorry."

"Thank you." After a pause she managed to continue. "It was a difficult labor, and when she was born, they realized something was wrong." Gwen paused again. "It's not easy to talk about," she told him a second time.

"You don't have to."

"No, I should. I need to learn how to face it and not just bury it all the time." She swallowed hard and gripped the armrests on the chair.

"She had something called hypoplastic left heart syndrome. It's a congenital defect where the left side of the heart is severely underdeveloped. They rushed her to surgery and tried to save her, but . . ." Gwen forced the words out of her mouth. "She didn't make it."

"I'm so sorry," Peter said again.

She met his sympathetic gaze. "At least I got to hold her before things went wrong, and for a moment, the world was perfect."

They both sat quietly at the table.

"You were right," he said in a low voice. "It's hard to know what to say." After a lengthy silence, he asked, "How long ago was that?"

"It's been two years," Gwen explained. "But on top of losing my baby, my marriage fell apart. A casualty of the grief and my reluctance to have another child because there would be an increased risk of the same thing happening again. But Eric wanted to try, and we just couldn't seem to agree on anything. So now, I'm trying to move on. No choice really."

She had no choice because Eric had left, and now he was seeing someone else, which made it less likely that they would ever work things out.

Peter looked down. "This news about Scarlett must hit close to home. You're probably cursing me right now, wishing I hadn't come and told you about this."

"No," Gwen firmly replied. "I mean . . . it opens a wound in a way, but it feels good to be sitting here, working late. I haven't felt this kind of focus or energy in a long time. It also makes me feel a closer connection to Scarlett, to know that she might have had a baby that she had to give up. I understand that kind of pain. And of course I want to find out what happened to the baby—if there was one."

"We have our work cut out for us." Peter stood and closed the pizza box.

"Feel free to take those leftovers back to your hotel," Gwen suggested, deliberately changing the subject. "Where are you staying?"

"The Old Orchard Inn. Gorgeous views of the valley."

"For sure."

They cleaned up the mess, carried the plates to the kitchen, and returned to the front parlor. Gwen picked up the remote control and joined Peter on the sofa, where they watched the full interview with Joan Dion, who was Scarlett's close friend from high school. Mrs. Dion was expecting them for lunch the following day, and Gwen was exceptionally eager to talk to her.

CHAPTER 4

Gwen sat in the passenger seat of Peter's rental car, her purse on her lap, her attention on the passing landscape outside the window. The apple blossoms in the orchards were in full bloom, and the sky was a brilliant cornflower blue. She couldn't help but recollect many days like this, early in her marriage, when she and Eric had gone for long drives past charming farmhouses from bygone eras and freshly plowed fields that would provide acres of sunflowers and grains by summer's end. They would hold hands in the car and talk about what kind of house they wanted to buy and how much land they would need for flower gardens and tomato plants.

She turned and glanced at Peter behind the wheel, which only made her miss Eric more. She wanted their old life back, even though she was angry with him for his abandonment and there were days when she felt that she could never forgive him for starting a relationship with another woman.

Peter touched his foot to the brake as the steep North Mountain loomed ahead of them, and Gwen glanced at the clock on the dashboard.

"We're almost there," she said, bringing herself back to the present. "Slow down, and turn onto that dirt road just coming up on the left."

He made the turn, and they bumped and bounced over potholes. Soon they emerged into a clearing where a century-old farmhouse stood among willow trees. It was painted red with white trim, and the steep forested mountain behind it was a stunning backdrop.

Peter pulled the car to a halt, and they got out of the vehicle. "It's so quiet here," he said. "I don't think I've ever experienced silence like this in my entire life."

"Maybe you should get out of the city more," she helpfully suggested.

"You're definitely right about that."

He shut the car door, and they made their way to the front porch. Peter was about to knock when Joan appeared at the screen door. Her gray hair was swept into a loose chignon reminiscent of the beehive days, and her paisley dress was formal, with a high buttoned collar and malachite brooch.

"I heard you pull in," she said. "I hope you're hungry."

"Oh, Joan, you didn't need to make a fuss." Gwen stepped into the warm country kitchen. A pitcher of lemonade was set on the table beside a two-tiered plate of white-bread sandwiches cut in triangles. The room smelled of freshly baked apple pie.

"What's the fun in life if you can't make a fuss for company?" Joan replied.

Gwen introduced Peter. "This is the man I spoke to you about on the phone. He came all the way from California."

Joan shook his hand. "It's a pleasure to meet you. Gwen tells me you're working on a book. I hope I can help."

"I hope so too," he replied cordially.

They sat down at the table, and Joan poured lemonade into three tall crystal tumblers, then invited Gwen and Peter to help themselves to the sandwiches while they made small talk. Peter told her about the book he was writing and spoke about his education at Stanford. It was conspicuous to Gwen that he neglected to mention his career as a tabloid photographer. She chose not to mention it either.

Eventually they arrived at the subject that had brought them to Joan's home: her childhood friendship with a future Hollywood screen legend.

"We watched your interview last night," Gwen said. "The one you did for the museum opening?"

"Oh, yes. But I don't know what I was thinking, wearing that horrid pink dress."

Gwen smiled. "I thought you looked lovely. But most importantly, you were very well spoken. It's a valuable piece of history, Joan."

She waved a hand as if it were nothing.

"But the real reason we're here today," Gwen continued, "is to ask a few questions about the year before Scarlett—or Valerie, rather—left for New York. You see . . . we've come across something that suggests she might not have gone to New York. That she might have gone somewhere else."

"Where?"

Gwen studied Joan's expression and searched her eyes for a sign that she might already know the answer, but Joan appeared genuinely surprised.

"We think she spent some time in Alaska," Peter told her. "Do you know anything about that?"

Joan fiddled with the large gemstone pendant she wore as a necklace. "No, nothing. Though we didn't keep in touch after she left for New York, not until years later, after she'd starred in a few films and wrote to me, just to say hello. You have those letters in the museum, don't you?"

"Yes, we do," Gwen replied. "And we treasure them. But we think that she might have had some reason to leave Nova Scotia when she did. She had a falling-out with her father, as we all know."

"He didn't approve of her becoming an actress," Joan replied with a note of disapproval herself. "He considered it beneath Valerie and . . . well, he was very straightlaced."

Gwen sat forward slightly. "Do you know if Valerie was involved with anyone the summer before she went away? Did she have a boyfriend?"

Joan chuckled frostily. "All the boys liked Valerie. The minute she walked into a room, the rest of us became invisible."

The edge of jealousy was obvious, and Gwen glanced at Peter.

Joan sat forward, seeming eager to share at least one small morsel of gossip. She spoke in a hushed voice. "But she *was* involved with someone the summer before she left. We didn't see much of her."

"Do you know who it was?" Gwen asked with sudden heightened interest.

"No. I didn't know his name. But we all guessed it was a seasonal farmworker. Her father would have disapproved of a boy like that, which is probably why she kept it secret from everyone, even her friends. Knowing her father, he would have driven the boy out of town at gunpoint, or at least in handcuffs, in a manner of speaking."

"That's unfortunate," Peter replied, glancing briefly at Gwen.

"You're sure you never met this boy or heard his name?" she asked. "Did any of your other friends know?"

Joan shook her head. "I'll be honest. We were all cross with her that summer. It felt like we didn't matter to her anymore, that she didn't care about us, so we stopped being friends."

"Ah," Gwen replied. "I didn't know that. I always thought everyone loved Valerie. I'm glad you're telling me this."

Joan fiddled with her earring. "Well, it didn't seem right to say bad things about her when she'd become so famous. That's not what people want to hear."

Peter reached for a rolled asparagus sandwich. "Did she try to resolve things with you before she left?"

"No. She left without saying goodbye, and I didn't hear from her again until many years later. I think she was just lonely in that flashy

Hollywood life, and she was longing for home and the people who knew the real Valerie. Not Scarlett, the movie star."

"But no mention of a boyfriend?" Peter asked again. "Or a heart-break before she left Nova Scotia?"

"No. She just wanted to hear about her old friends, what we'd been up to. I told her I was happily married to a wonderful man," Joan said proudly.

"I'm sure she was happy for you," Gwen replied.

An awkward silence ensued, and Joan offered a slice of pie and made a pot of tea. They spent the rest of the visit discussing the upcoming Apple Blossom Festival, which Peter knew nothing about. Gwen promised to fill him in on what to expect in the coming days—concerts, a parade, fireworks.

A short while later, they said goodbye to Joan, got into the car, and drove off.

"That was illuminating," Gwen said. "You weren't tempted to show her the newspaper clipping?"

"I was afraid to," Peter replied. "I had a feeling that the minute we left, she'd call everyone she knew, and my book would no longer be relevant. My publisher wouldn't be pleased."

Gwen glanced out the window and sighed.

"What's the matter?" Peter asked. "You don't sound happy."

"I don't know. This just feels wrong."

"In what way?"

She turned to him. "I feel like such a busybody right now, nosing into other people's personal lives. Part of me thinks we should just leave the past buried, like Scarlett obviously wanted it to be. She would absolutely hate this."

"You know I can't let it go," Peter replied emphatically.

Gwen let out a breath. "No, of course not. Because it's not in your nature to respect other people's boundaries or privacy."

"That's a bit harsh, don't you think?" he asked. "Especially when you admit to being just as eager as I am to find out the truth."

She gave him a look. "Actually, I don't think it's harsh at all. Are you even aware of the distress you inflict upon celebrities? How they feel harassed? Imagine if someone followed *you* around all the time with a camera in your face or chased your car. Not to mention the cruel things you guys print about them, commenting about their weight gain or making fun of their outfits."

"Hey, I never wrote that stuff," he said defensively. "I just took photos."

"Which is what made it possible for *others* to write it," she said.

They drove for a while without talking, and it wasn't until they reached town that Peter spoke. "You're right, Gwen, and I don't know why I'm arguing with you about it. I'm just making excuses, I guess. If it makes any difference to you, I do feel guilty about some of the work I did. Very much so."

She waited for him to elaborate.

"I especially hated selling pictures of celebrities with their kids. It always felt sleazy, so I stopped doing that. And there was one night I was sitting in my car outside a certain celebrity's house because of a tip I'd gotten that she was dating an A-lister. I was determined to break that story because I really needed the money."

"What for?"

"Hospital bills for my mother. My dad got in a bad car accident and needed long-term care, which wasn't covered by their insurance."

"I'm sorry to hear that."

"Thank you. But regardless of why I needed the money, I still felt like a stalker."

"Did you get the photo that night?" Gwen asked.

"I did," he replied. "And it paid well, but I felt horrible about what I had to do to get it." He glanced at her. "That's why I wanted this book deal—so that I could get out of that racket. But maybe it's no different, being a biographer. It's still an exposé of someone's private life."

Gwen considered that. "I disagree. Books are important, and if they're well researched and you're writing the truth, they're important records of historical figures. Photographs are important too, under the right circumstances. And Scarlett deserves to have a comprehensive book written about her life, so I appreciate what you're doing. I think I'm just too close to everything—a bit emotional about it since I saw that newspaper clipping. I'm sorry. I was a bit judgy back there."

"Don't be sorry," he replied. "I deserved it. I was the lowest of the low."

She inclined her head in a casual manner, hoping to lighten the mood. "I wouldn't go that far. There are worse things a person could do for a living."

"There's always something worse, isn't there." Peter pulled into the museum parking lot and drove around to the back, then shut off the engine. "Thanks for today."

Gwen gathered up her purse and removed her seat belt. "I should be the one thanking you—for suggesting we talk to Joan. And for driving."

"It was my pleasure."

She opened the car door and got out. "Now, I'm going inside to make a few phone calls."

"To whom?" he asked, leaning across the console.

"A few more of Scarlett's friends from high school," she replied. "Someone might know something. And then I'll call the museum in Valdez, Alaska. With your permission, I'd like to email a copy of the newspaper clipping and see if anyone has any record of it or if they know the name of the young man who rescued the baby. If he's still alive, he might know something. I'd crop Scarlett out of the photo, of course."

"That would be helpful," Peter said, seeming surprised.

"I could also try and track down the photographer. Have you tried that?"

"I did, but he passed away in 1982, so that was a dead end. And I was hesitant to ask the Anchorage newspaper about the photograph because I didn't want to tip my hand. If someone recognized Scarlett, they might republish it, and again, my book would no longer be groundbreaking."

"I understand." Gwen glanced toward the tennis court, then made a move to shut the car door. "Will I see you inside?"

"Probably not. I'm going to head back to the hotel and write for a while. I'm a bit behind."

"All right. I'll see you later."

When she returned to her office on the ground floor, members of the International Scarlett Fontaine Fan Club were just stepping off a double-decker bus from Halifax. Before she knew it, the museum was packed. She was grateful that Susie had the tour under control because she wanted to make those phone calls and contact the museum in Valdez right away.

~

The following morning, Gwen sat down at her desk, switched on her computer, and opened her email. A steady flow of messages flooded her inbox. While she scrolled down, scanning for anything urgent and quickly deleting junk mail, she sipped coffee in her travel mug. Then she caught a name. Douglas Warren—the curator of the museum in Valdez. She rolled her chair closer to the screen and read his reply.

> Dear Ms. Hollingsworth,
> I received your message and the image you sent. I'm afraid I don't recognize the young man in the photograph, but I've only been living in Valdez since 1996. I have therefore taken the liberty of reaching out to some residents who survived the earthquake in 1964

and continue to reside here. If any of them can identify the man in the picture, I will most certainly let
you know.

Best, Douglas

A car pulled into the back parking lot just then. Gwen rolled
her chair to the window and looked out. It was Peter, just arriving. A
moment later, he appeared at her door. "Good morning."

"Good morning," she replied, sitting forward. "How did you make
out last night?"

"Good. I got some writing done. Then I spent the rest of the evening creating a Scarlett Fontaine playlist."

Gwen's eyebrows lifted. "A playlist?"

"Yes." He sauntered into her office. "I was intrigued by that poem
she wrote in the yearbook, which you said wasn't a poem but song lyrics.
So I was up until midnight, listening to all her songs in chronological
order, according to when she wrote them."

Gwen knew every song of Scarlett's, but she'd never listened to the
whole catalog in order. "And?"

He moved to the upholstered chair in front of her desk and sat
down. "It was enlightening. You could see changes in her way of thinking, her moods, and what seemed to matter to her on a grander scale as
time went on. I don't think I truly understood Scarlett Fontaine before.
But now, looking at the music . . . I don't know how to explain it, but
listening to everything she wrote for hours on end was like some kind
of spiritual experience."

"I know the feeling," Gwen told him. The music Scarlett had written at the end of her life had been Gwen's saving grace in her darkest
moments after losing Lily and then Eric. It was the only time when
Gwen had felt glimmers of hope that there might be light in her life
again, one day.

"I don't think I was on the right track with my book before," Peter continued. "I wouldn't have been able to do it justice. And it's not just the lyrics, which I want to talk to you about. It was the way she married the lyrics with the melodies. No wonder those songs are classics. She should be up there with the greats like Cole Porter or Andrew Lloyd Webber. Or the Beatles."

"I've always thought that," Gwen replied, feeling somewhat electrified. "Her fans come here, and they remark about how gorgeous she was or what a wonderful sense of style she had. I have a whole display about the songs she wrote, but people are more interested in the superficial things—like her ball gowns and the characters she played in her films." Gwen drummed her fingers on the armrest. "It's because she's a woman, you know. That's why she didn't receive proper recognition for contributing to the soundtracks of her films. The studios only wanted to promote her beauty."

Peter slowly nodded.

"If you ask me," Gwen added, "her music is her greatest achievement. That should be her true legacy—or at least be equal to everything else."

"I agree." Peter sat forward. "So I want to talk to you about the lyrics. I took notes last night, and I think there might be some clues about Alaska. If you have a few minutes this morning, come upstairs, and we can talk about it."

"I'll do that," Gwen replied. "But I have something to share with you as well." She reached for her mouse and clicked to open her email program. "I heard back from the museum curator in Alaska. His name is Douglas Warren, and he said he would reach out to some local residents who survived the quake and still live in Valdez. Someone might be able to identify the man in the photograph."

"That would be amazing," Peter replied.

They looked across the desk at each other. Neither of them seemed to have anything more to say, but the air between them seemed alive with exhilaration.

It became awkward suddenly, so Gwen dropped her gaze, and Peter glanced at his watch. "Is now a good time for you to come upstairs?"

"I just have a few things to finish up here first." Feeling oddly flustered, Gwen reached for her purse. "Susie's not in today, so I'm going to trust you with the key." She removed it from her key ring and handed it across the desk. "You can give it back to me later."

"Thanks," he replied as he stood. He picked up his laptop case and gave her a friendly smile. "I'll see you in a bit."

"For sure." She nodded, then sat back and watched him walk out of her office.

~

"Come and see this," Peter said as soon as Gwen entered the archive room.

She moved closer to a coiled notebook on the table that was full of handwritten notes, scrawled hurriedly.

"This is the theme song from the film *Last Look at You*, which came out in 1969. Read the third verse, after the bridge."

Rivers of ice from mountains to sea
Thunder resounds without rain
The eagle will soar, and the earth will roar
And always, love will remain

"Those images sound like Alaska," Gwen said. "*The earth will roar.* That could be an earthquake."

He flipped forward a few pages. "And how about this one? This was a song she wrote in 1974. It was recorded by a female jazz singer who turned it into a mainstream hit. Almost no one is aware that Scarlett wrote it."

Gwen bent over the notebook. "She wrote a lot of songs that were sold to popular recording artists. That's the bulk of her estate—the royalties from her original songs that are still recorded by new artists today."

Gwen read the lyrics to the jazz piece.

The dark endless night, the return of the light
Forever remember the rock and the ice

"Alaska has only four hours of daylight in the winter," she said. "Days get longer in the spring."

Peter tapped his finger on the open notebook. "I've noticed she often writes about the sea in a way that makes it seem violent, like a murderous villain. It makes me wonder if it's a metaphor for something. Maybe the boyfriend was abusive?"

"Interesting theory," Gwen said. "But many of her ballads are uplifting love songs."

"True. But just as many are about heartbreak."

Peter reached for another book on the table. He must have brought it with him, because it wasn't part of the museum collection. "Back to Alaska and the violent sea . . . I've been researching the earthquake, and there were a hundred and fifteen deaths in Alaska, which is quite remarkable considering the strength of the quake and the damage it caused. But guess where the greatest loss of life occurred." He opened the book to a page he had marked with a yellow sticky note and showed Gwen a black-and-white aerial photograph of a devastated town. "Valdez, Alaska. But not because of the quake. Most of the people died when the docks collapsed on the waterfront."

Gwen squinted to look more closely at the picture. "No kidding."

"And check this out," Peter continued. "Do you see this glacier behind the town? The whole town was built on the loose sediment from that glacier, and when the shaking started, the ground liquefied under the docks, which caused an underwater landslide, taking the docks with it. Most of the people on the docks fell into the sea, and the displacement of all that earth and the structures caused a tidal wave that swept into the town. Doesn't that sound like a lot of Scarlett's lyrics?"

Gwen took hold of the book and studied the old photographs. "It does. And the newspaper clipping said the baby was rescued from the sea. Maybe she was on the docks when they collapsed."

"That's what I'm thinking as well," Peter said.

Gwen pondered all this and made a face. "I hate to challenge your theory, but she was also writing music in Switzerland up until the year she died. I often thought that the references to mountains and snow were inspired by the Swiss Alps, but maybe you're right. Maybe it was Alaska."

"And guess what they called Valdez," he added. "Little Switzerland. There was even a hotel in Valdez called the Switzerland Inn."

Gwen turned to Peter, perplexed. "Do you think that's why she went to Switzerland? But why not back to Alaska?"

"Maybe she wanted to be reminded of it but couldn't go back there because people would have recognized her and made the connection to her being there in '64."

Gwen set the book down and wandered toward the storage shelves. She chewed on her thumbnail as she considered the facts. "It doesn't really make sense. If she lived in Valdez, wouldn't someone have sold a story about her to the tabloids or bragged about how they knew her once? In all these years, no one ever did that."

Peter sat down at the table. "That's definitely a fly in the ointment. Unless she was only there for a short time, maybe just passing through?"

Gwen faced Peter. "She took a stage name when she went to Hollywood. She would have been Valerie McCarthy in 1964. Not Scarlett Fontaine. But still . . . people don't often forget beautiful faces." Gwen looked up at the storage boxes on the top shelves. "Suddenly I feel like I need to rethink every impression and opinion I ever had about her. Start from scratch and get to know her all over again."

"My feeling is that she wasn't as easy to read as everyone thought," Peter said. "Or as happy. She was famous for her smile, but when I listened to her entire body of work last night . . ." He paused. "There was something melancholy about it all. There's also anger beneath the surface of everything. It's subtle, but it's there if you read between the lines. But those ballads she wrote in Switzerland, at the end of her life?" He pressed his fist to his chest. "They're so beautiful. The love hits you right here. It's hard not to weep when you listen to those melodies."

Touched and surprised by Peter's romantic interpretations, Gwen turned to him. "I feel the same way about those songs."

A spark of memory took her back to moments when she'd sat at her daughter's grave, listening to Scarlett's music, surrendering entirely to her grief . . .

"Gwen?" Peter said.

She realized she had turned away from him. She was now facing a colorful framed painting on the wall—a meadow of wildflowers—while her eyes stung with tears.

Peter laid his hand on her back. "Are you okay?"

"Yes. I'm sorry." She blinked the tears away.

"Don't apologize." He briefly rubbed her shoulder before giving her some space and returning to the open books on the table.

Watching him, Gwen realized that perhaps she needed to rethink her initial impressions of Peter as well as Scarlett. He was more moved and affected by the music than she had expected, and he'd been very caring and sympathetic just now.

"I'm glad you came here," she said openly. "And that you trusted me with the picture you found."

"I'm glad too." He tidied the books spread out on the table. "I'll probably spend the whole day here, if you don't mind, going through the rest of the collection."

"Of course. That's fine." Gwen hesitated before leaving, then spoke impulsively. "Do you have dinner plans tonight? I'd like to talk more about all this. If you're free."

He looked up at her, and his mouth fell open slightly. "Yes, I'm free. I'd like that. What time?"

She told him when and where, and he wrote it down in his notebook.

When she walked out of the archive room and was closing the door behind her, she discreetly glanced back at him. He was watching her too, but they both looked away before the door clicked shut.

CHAPTER 5

Gwen arranged to meet Peter at Le Caveau, the fine-dining establishment at Grand-Pré Wines. When she called for a reservation, the restaurant was fully booked, but the hostess made room for her, as always, because she was a regular patron and a neighbor. Her property bordered the winery on the high side of the vineyard.

Gwen drove home from work, parked her car, and went inside to change out of the office attire she'd been wearing all day. She kicked off her black pumps, ditched the pencil skirt and blazer, and slipped into a sweater and a comfortable maxi skirt with flat sandals—a necessity if she planned to walk home across the vineyard after dark.

A short while later, as she reached the winery's cobblestone courtyard, her cell phone rang. She checked the display and saw that it was Eric.

Gwen stopped in her tracks. The air around her seemed to swirl upward. Eric hadn't called in months. They'd agreed it would be best if they cut the cord completely, because every time they talked, they argued or cried. She knew it was best, but it didn't stop her from missing him and wondering what he was doing with Keri at any given moment.

She took a deep breath before she answered. "Hello?"

"Hi," he said. "It's me." The sound of his voice caused her heart to thump a little faster. "I hope I'm not catching you at a bad time."

"No, I'm just heading into Le Caveau." She thought of all the times they'd eaten there during their home renovation. They used to call it "their place" in the same way that most couples had a song.

"Le Caveau?" he replied. "The scallops and the cream sauce . . . do they still have that on the menu?"

"Of course." She hoped he was missing their regular table. That would at least suggest that their time together still meant something to him. "I'll probably order it tonight."

"Just like always." She recognized the note of nostalgia in his voice and felt a pleasant mingling of relief and happiness.

"Are you meeting someone?" he asked.

Was he curious if it was a date? It wasn't, but her pride demanded that she play it coy. "It's no one you know." She stepped onto the wooden deck that surrounded the wineshop. "What's up? I haven't heard from you in a while. How's Keri?"

It was important that she sounded at ease with the situation, because again: her pride.

"She's good." Eric paused. "That's the reason I'm calling, actually. It's been getting kind of serious lately, and I thought we should talk about that."

Oh, God.

"All right," Gwen replied hesitantly, checking her watch. She was now five minutes late for her reservation. This was definitely going to put a damper on dinner.

Eric exhaled into the phone, and she wished he would just spit it out, whatever it was.

"Keri's been hinting at rings lately," he finally explained, "whenever we walk past a jewelry store."

"Really?" Gwen swallowed uneasily. "You've only been dating for six months."

"I know," he replied. "We haven't been together very long, and she's quite young."

Young. Yes. Gwen knew exactly how old Keri was, because when Eric had started seeing her, Gwen couldn't help herself. She'd looked her up on social media. As it turned out, Keri was fresh out of college, and her Instagram page consisted of not much except sexy kissy faces and her holding up cocktails—and an odd obsession with toe cleavage. Eric was thirty-five and ran his own construction company. He'd had a whole life with Gwen before they'd separated. They'd gone to the same university, backpacked across Europe, gotten married, bought a house, renovated it, gotten pregnant, had a baby . . .

"Young isn't such a bad thing," she said, clinging to her composure. "We were young when we started dating."

"Yes, but . . . I can't help but wonder if . . ."

He stopped abruptly, and Gwen pressed the phone tighter against her ear, as if that would make him finish the sentence more quickly. "Can't help but wonder what?"

"If you and I gave up too soon," he said. "Everything fell apart so fast. Maybe we shouldn't have been so quick to throw in the towel."

A warm evening breeze lifted a lock of Gwen's hair, and she closed her eyes, relishing the moment—because these were the words she had dreamed of hearing ever since Eric had moved out.

But today, he'd called her because he was getting serious with another woman and he was feeling confused. The last thing she wanted to be was a shoulder to cry on if he was simply having cold feet.

"Let's not forget," she said, "that you were the one who wanted to separate. I never wanted that. I was happy with the status quo."

"Happy?" Eric replied. "That's not a word I would use to describe the situation. Neither of us was happy, and you know it."

Tension twisted through her body, because here they were, doing it again. It was the same old argument, like a broken record.

Yet he was not wrong. She could see that now. The past year, living alone, had given her a clearer perspective on how they'd behaved toward each other after the loss of Lily.

"You're right," she said with a sigh of surrender. "We weren't happy. But we'd just lost a child. I'm not a psychologist, but I'm pretty sure my unhappiness was warranted, given the circumstances."

"But you wouldn't talk to me," he argued. "You'd disappear into the bedroom in the middle of the day, and you wouldn't come out. It was like you blamed me for what happened."

"I didn't blame you," she insisted. "You blamed yourself—we both blamed ourselves—so you were projecting your feelings onto me. And I stayed in the bedroom because every time I came out, you were pushing me to cheer up. You kept insisting that I just needed to stop moping around the house. You treated me like I was a crybaby who wouldn't get up and simply dust myself off."

Eric was quiet for a moment while Gwen's heart pounded with frustration and regret. Why did they always end up arguing? Why couldn't they just admit their mistakes and let it go? Figure out a way to get back to what they once were and simply love each other?

Of course, she knew the answer. She was still angry with him for leaving her when she needed him most. And she was hurt by his relationship with Keri. Gwen remembered all too well when he had first begun dating Keri—a much younger woman who smiled and laughed all the time and wanted to go dancing and drinking until three in the morning on Saturdays and rent electric scooters to zip around the city on Sundays. And post everything on Instagram, of course. At the time, Gwen had not had the emotional energy to compete with that, so she hadn't bothered to fight to get Eric back. That didn't mean she hadn't been completely heartsick over it.

Eric cleared his throat and spoke softly. "Maybe I wasn't the best husband. I should have been more patient. I'm sorry. I do regret that."

His words caught Gwen off guard. This was the first time Eric had ever acknowledged his part in the breakdown of their marriage. Mostly, he'd blamed Gwen's grief for their troubles.

But now he was calling to tell her that his girlfriend was hinting at marriage. Did that mean their marriage was truly over?

"I'm not sure what you want me to say," Gwen murmured sadly, standing on the wooden deck in front of the wineshop, looking down at people seated at outdoor tables, enjoying dinner under the trees. "Or why you called. What is it that you want exactly?"

Perhaps he was just trying to be kind and give her some closure before he asked for a divorce.

Eric groaned, sounding frustrated with himself. "I don't know. Maybe I'm just looking for advice."

Advice?

"You know me better than anyone," he continued. "I want to know what you think I should do."

"Um . . ." She shook her head and tried to make sense of this conversation. "I'm not sure what you're asking me."

"Advice about Keri," he explained. "What should I do? Should I keep dating her? Or not?"

Gwen's stomach clenched with disbelief, and she covered her forehead with a hand. "Seriously? I can't tell you what to do, Eric. It's your life, and you're a grown man. You'll have to figure that one out on your own." She turned and started walking toward the restaurant. "I'm sorry, but I have to go. My reservation was at seven, and you know how I hate being late for things."

"I remember," he said.

"I'll talk to you later." Gwen ended the call and hesitated at the bottom of the stairs, waiting for her heart to quit pounding before she entered the restaurant.

A moment later, the hostess led Gwen to the table where Peter was seated and waiting. As luck would have it, it turned out to be her regular table with Eric. After the phone call just now, it was jarring to see Peter sitting there.

"Hi," he said, rising to his feet, his blue eyes smiling. "I was getting ready to send out a search party."

Gwen sat down across from him and hung her purse on the back of the chair. "Sorry I'm late. I had to take a phone call. I was outside in the courtyard for the past ten minutes."

"Nothing wrong, I hope."

Gwen reached for the glass of ice water that was waiting for her. "It depends on how you look at it. It was my husband, Eric."

Peter reached for his water as well and took a sip. "You mentioned you were separated. Is everything okay?"

"Yes," she replied, "but it was strange. I haven't spoken to him in months, and suddenly he wants my advice about his love life."

Peter shook his head as if someone had tossed water in his face. "That seems odd."

"I know," she replied. "It sounds completely inappropriate when I say it out loud. The whole conversation was kind of upsetting, actually." Gwen pointed at her glass of water. "I think I might need something stronger than that."

He slid the wine list toward her, but Gwen didn't need to read it. She'd eaten there so many times that she had the entire menu stored in her head.

"Would you like to share a bottle of white?" she asked. "Have you tried the Tidal Bay yet? It's local, made here at the winery. They call it 'Nova Scotia in a glass.'"

"The server mentioned it," Peter replied. "She told me it pairs well with the scallops."

"It does. You'll love it." Gwen placed the order, sat back, and took a deep breath.

"We were talking about your husband," Peter said encouragingly.

"Yes. And I'm not sure what to think right now. He said the woman he's been dating wants to get engaged, and that's what he wanted advice about. They've only been together for six months, and she's young. Like . . . twenty-two."

Peter's lips formed an O, and he slowly whistled. "And he's not sure? I wonder why."

Gwen propped her elbow on the table and rested her chin on her hand. She stared at the small vase of flowers and imagined Eric cooking dinner for Keri. Talking about having children one day. Had they ever discussed that? She couldn't bear to think about it.

"How do you feel about him getting engaged to someone else?" Peter asked.

Gwen took her elbows off the table and leaned back. "I'm not sure. He brought up the reason why we separated, and he apologized for how it all went down. That was a shocker because up until now, he's always blamed me for pulling away, when really, I think he was having just as much trouble dealing with the grief as I was. He just handled it—or mishandled it—in a different way."

"Grief over your daughter . . . ," Peter said, making sure he understood.

"Yes. Eric thought I was going to be depressed forever. He said I was like a dark cloud hanging over his life, when he wanted to be happy and start living again." Gwen sipped her water. "Hence the twenty-two-year-old sociology major who wants to go dancing all night and speed cycling the next day and fly to Jamaica to go kitesurfing."

Peter's eyebrows lifted. "You don't like water sports?"

Gwen chuckled. "I love the water. I just didn't want to organize vacations in general when I had just buried my firstborn child."

"Understandable." Peter leaned forward and spoke gently. "I'm sorry you went through all that."

Something tugged in Gwen's chest, but then her shoulders relaxed, and she let out a breath. "Thank you. I appreciate that. But let's not talk about this anymore. I don't want to think about Eric right now."

The waitress arrived with the wine, uncorked the bottle, and poured. She then took their dinner orders. After she left, Gwen glanced around at other people in the restaurant enjoying their meals. Then Peter, across the table from her.

"You know a lot about me," she said, "but I know nothing about you, except that you're a photographer."

"Was a photographer," he said. "Now I'm a writer."

He offered no more than that, so she asked, "Married? Kids? I see you don't wear a ring."

He turned his hand over and looked at it. "No, but I recently came out of a five-year relationship."

She was surprised to hear this—that he'd been in a committed relationship. The moment he'd walked through her door, Gwen had taken him for a man who enjoyed his freedom. From what she understood, he worked all hours of the day or night, staking out homes of celebrities, waiting outside their gates. Gwen imagined him living in a small apartment with a mattress on the floor. Other times, she imagined that he made buckets of money as a paparazzo and lived in a glitzy penthouse apartment, which he used as a babe magnet. But a five-year relationship? That was not something she'd envisioned.

"Can I ask what happened?"

"We were living together," he explained, which squashed the playboy persona. "And everything was fine for the first few years. From the beginning, she said she had no interest in getting married. She thought a marriage certificate was an unnecessary slip of paper that represented a dying institution that made money for lawyers, since so many marriages end in divorce. But then something changed, and she started suggesting that I was a commitment-phobe and she was wasting her best years on me. Anytime I reminded her that she had told me from the beginning that she didn't believe in marriage . . . well, that just proved her point— that I didn't want to commit and that's why I was with her in the first place. By time that time, I was so frustrated by the constant arguments that

I wouldn't have married her if she'd dragged me down the aisle by the scruff of my neck." He frowned a little. "She looked at me with such contempt. So we broke up, and I moved out."

Gwen found herself riveted. "That must have been rough."

"Yes, but that's just my side of the story. I'm sure she has a totally different take on it, and when she tells the tale, I'm the villain."

Gwen tipped her head back and sighed. "That's always how it goes, isn't it. I'm sure I'm the villain in Eric's story too. I mean, when you think about it, when a relationship ends, there's always disappointment for both people, and we tend to focus on our own heartache or anger. It's easier to believe that none of it is your fault and that you're the victim, instead of taking responsibility for the mistakes you made too."

"Agreed," he said. "Sometimes I wonder why people want to get involved in a relationship in the first place. Statistically, most of them are doomed from the start."

Gwen's shoulders slumped a little. Maybe she was just a hopeless romantic, but deep down, she still wanted to believe in love and marriage. Her parents, after thirty-five years, were still happy together. They were best friends, and her father still looked at her mother as if she were the most beautiful creature on earth.

The appetizers arrived—they'd both ordered the scallops—and Gwen was grateful for the diversion. She didn't want to talk about relationships anymore, especially their failed ones. Besides, that wasn't why she'd invited Peter to dinner. They were here to discuss their shared interest in Scarlett Fontaine's lost year.

Peter brought up one of Scarlett's early films in which she'd played a young European princess who became a nurse during World War I. They talked about her performance and how that character had shaped her image for the rest of her career. Scarlett often chose roles where she faced life-and-death situations and behaved heroically. She never played a villain or a misfit.

"Was it all an act?" Peter asked. "Was she really as perfect as she seemed in her films? In real life, she never had a deep and lasting relationship with anyone, and she died alone. Maybe she had issues."

"I've often wondered that," Gwen replied. "She lost her mother at a young age and had a controlling father. Maybe she wasn't capable of trusting a man. On the other hand, maybe she wanted to be in control of her own life. There's nothing wrong with a woman who chooses not to get married. That takes self-confidence and independence, especially in the previous century, when women were groomed to become wives and mothers. They were brought up believing that they needed a man to provide for them. I like to think that she was fulfilled by her career and her music and that was enough for her."

Gwen finished her last scallop and dabbed the corner of her mouth with the napkin.

"There's no way I'm going to disagree with you about that," Peter said.

She chuckled. "That's good, because no one would question her life choices if she were a man. No one would suggest that she had emotional issues."

"You're right. An older man who doesn't marry is considered an eligible bachelor. But a woman is called a spinster. What's that old saying? She's put on the shelf?"

Gwen was rather enjoying this debate. "I don't know what happened in Alaska," she said, "but based on what I do know, I think Scarlett chose what she wanted for herself—and she was strong and independent. The ultimate feminist. She moved to Switzerland to get away from the annoying, intrusive press and photographers who wouldn't leave her alone. No offense."

"None taken."

"And just because a woman is alone doesn't mean she's lonely," Gwen added, needing to believe that for herself. "Scarlett had her most productive songwriting years in Switzerland, especially that final year. She was pouring her heart and soul into her work. She was busy creating up until the very end. I doubt she would have wanted to be confined to a kitchen, washing dishes and doing laundry for a man who went out into the world, doing his own thing. Not unless he was supportive of her doing her thing, which not all men would have been back then. It was a different time."

Gwen regarded Peter steadily across the table, her pulse beating with an intense drive to discover the answer to the burning question: Did Scarlett die happy? Fulfilled? Or was she forever afflicted with grief over the loss of her child?

Their dinner arrived, and Gwen took a whiff of her rainbow trout, served with jasmine rice and poached parsnips. The waitress offered fresh-ground pepper.

She and Peter chatted about other things while they ate, and afterward, when the waitress came to clear the table, Peter got up to visit the restroom. While he was gone, Gwen picked up her phone and checked her emails. She scrolled through the most recent unread messages and saw a reply from Douglas Warren, the museum curator in Valdez. She tapped the message and began to read.

> Dear Ms. Hollingsworth,
> Regarding your inquiry about the young man in the photograph, I am delighted to report that I heard back from a woman in town who remembers him. I have a name for you and some additional information that you might find useful. Give me a call and I'll relay it to you.

He provided his phone number at the museum, and Gwen immediately checked the time. It was 8:15 p.m. in Nova Scotia—therefore only 3:15 in Alaska. He was probably still at his desk.

Peter returned to the table and sat down. "Fancy a dessert?"

"No," Gwen replied hastily. "Let's just get the bill."

"Okay." He regarded her with uncertainty.

Gwen signaled to the server. "I just got an email from the museum curator in Valdez, and he has a name for us."

"No kidding."

She passed her phone across the table. "Read his note. We can call him as soon as we leave here."

The waitress brought the bill, and Peter insisted on paying. Then they walked out of the restaurant and stepped into the radiant pink glow of the sunset. Outdoor tables, lit with candles, stood on stone patios beneath vine-covered trellises. There was a low murmur of laughter and conversation.

"This is a great spot," Peter said, stopping to look. "You must come here a lot."

"I do, mostly because I live just over there, on the other side of the vineyard." She pointed. "I walked here."

Peter turned toward the grapevines, silhouetted against the purple sky. The moon was just beginning its rise. "I can drive you home if you like, since it's getting dark."

"Not necessary," Gwen replied. "I've crossed this vineyard a hundred times in the dark. I'll use the flashlight on my phone."

He considered it for a few seconds, then shook his head. "At least let me walk with you. I need to make sure you get home safely."

"That's very gentlemanly of you, but honestly, this is a safe place. The only threat is the blackflies."

"Well, there you go." He spread his arms wide. "If there is a known threat, I must walk you home."

With a light chuckle, Gwen surrendered. "All right. But let's make that phone call first."

She led him up the flagstone steps, and they paused, away from the noise of the outdoor restaurant, while she searched for Douglas's phone number in the email. Peter stood patiently at her side while crickets chirped in the grass. She swatted at a few blackflies, then dialed the number and held the phone between them. It rang twice on the speakerphone before someone answered.

"Douglas Warren."

Gwen locked eyes with Peter, and she felt a jolt of energy between them. "Hi, Douglas. It's Gwen Hollingsworth from Nova Scotia. I read your email. Thanks so much for looking into this for me. I appreciate it."

"No problem," he replied.

"I should tell you that I'm here with someone who is writing a book that might reference the earthquake. You're on speakerphone. Is that okay?"

"It's fine," Douglas replied. "And if you're looking for information about the quake, I'm your man. I know everything there is to know, and I have an extensive collection here. Whatever questions you have, just ask, and I'll do my best to help."

"That's wonderful. Thank you so much. We might want to take you up on that offer. We're still in the early stages of our research."

She didn't want to reveal what they were truly working on, and Peter seemed to agree, because he gave her a thumbs-up.

"Good stuff," Douglas replied. "So here's what I can tell you about the man in the photograph. His name is Jeremy Mikhailov, and he was born and raised in Valdez."

Gwen's blood sparked with excitement. "Could you spell that name for me?"

Peter whipped out his phone to take a note as Douglas spelled Jeremy's last name and shared more information. "The person I spoke to said he was a well-known character in town, always getting into trouble with the law. Half the town loved him, while the other half loathed him or feared him."

"He sounds like a criminal," Gwen suggested, meeting Peter's speculative gaze in the hazy white glow from her cell phone. The crickets grew louder, and the blackflies were becoming a nuisance. They both waved their hands around until Gwen gestured that they start walking to escape them. She led the way onto the wide grassy walking path through the vineyard.

"It depends who you're talking to," Douglas replied. "Some folks said he had a heart of gold, but he was, factually speaking, a petty thief. From what I understand, you were fine as long as you didn't cross him. If you did, he'd threaten to burn your house down."

Peter and Gwen shared a look as they walked through the fading light.

"But he rescued a baby," Gwen said. "That must have made him into a hero."

"You would think so," Douglas replied. "But I'm afraid I don't have any record of that. There was a lot of chaos in the days after the quake. Power was out, and the whole town had been designated as unsafe. People were evacuated. And lots of people were heroes that day, in all sorts of ways, so Jeremy got lost in the shuffle, I imagine."

"I understand," Gwen said.

"All I can tell you is that Jeremy left Valdez after the quake and never returned. The woman I spoke to heard that he'd been spotted in Juneau a few years later, up to his old tricks, stealing motors off fishing boats or breaking into people's sheds in the winter to steal a shovel or whatnot. That's all I have for you, I'm afraid."

Gwen glanced at Peter. "Thank you, Douglas. This has been very helpful. We'll be in touch if we need more information about the earthquake or anything else."

"Very good. You have my number."

They said goodbye, and Gwen ended the call.

"That was interesting," Peter said.

"It certainly was. I wonder if Jeremy still lives in Juneau."

"You would think if he'd rescued Scarlett Fontaine's baby and returned it to her, he would have made that public over the years or bragged about it to someone."

"Yes," Gwen replied, trying to make sense of it. "Unless we're both imagining this entire thing and that's not even Scarlett in the picture."

"But it has to be," he said. "I have a feeling."

"I do too."

They continued along the path until they reached the road on the far side of the vineyard. It was dark by then, and the sky was full of stars.

"Would you like to come in?" she asked as they approached her house. "Maybe if we google Jeremy, we'll get lucky."

"Sure."

She led Peter across her front lawn and up the steps to the covered veranda, where she unlocked the door and stepped inside. She turned on the lamp in the foyer and kicked off her sandals. "Come through to the kitchen. Would you like a drink? A glass of wine or something else? I have twelve-year-old scotch and some beer—or coffee, if you prefer."

"A beer would be great."

She fetched two bottles of Keith's from the refrigerator and twisted off the caps. "Let's go into the den and turn on the computer."

He followed her to her cozy little workspace off the kitchen, which had been a primary focus for her during the restoration. She'd made sure it had a full wall of floor-to-ceiling bookcases opposite the fireplace, which was original to the house.

"This is an incredible home," Peter said, looking around at the thirteen-foot ceilings and historic millwork. "What year was it built?"

"Around 1783," she replied. "We tried to keep as much of the original elements as possible when we renovated, but obviously we updated the kitchen. That was a total gut job."

"You did great with it," Peter replied as he wandered toward the bookcase. "You know . . . you can tell a lot about a person by looking at the books they hold on to. I see you like fiction."

"I do. I like to read the big bestsellers just to see what all the fuss is about, but I like nonfiction too. Historical biographies, and—please don't judge me—I like self-help books." She pulled an extra chair close to the computer.

"No judgment here." He bent to a lower shelf and pulled out a book. "Is this your yearbook? You went to the same high school as Scarlett?"

Gwen swiveled in her chair to face him. "Yes, I did."

He flipped through it. "Are you in here?"

Gwen stood and approached him. "Let me see." She flipped through it as well and found a picture of herself backstage, in costume, during the final performance of the high school musical. "That's me there." She pointed.

He looked carefully at her standing arm in arm with a group of cast members. "Following in Scarlett's footsteps?" he asked with a look of amusement.

Gwen chuckled softly. "Not at all. I was far too shy. I wouldn't even have tried out if it weren't for my music teacher, who encouraged me to at least try out for the chorus." She turned the page. "That's him there. Mr. Thornby. He was great."

She flipped to another page, where she found Eric's graduation picture. "And that's my husband."

Peter bent his head to look more closely. "You were high school sweethearts?"

"Yes. He was my first love. I thought we'd be together forever." The inescapable heartache rose back to the surface, so she closed the book and slid it back on the shelf. "Enough about that. I don't want to be maudlin." Itching to change the subject, Gwen returned to the desk and turned on the computer. "Let's see what we can find out about Jeremy."

Peter sat down beside her, and Gwen started googling. She typed Jeremy's full name, along with the word *Juneau*. A Facebook page came up.

"Goodness," she said, sitting forward and squinting at the profile picture of an older man in a small motorboat. "Is that him?"

"Could it be this easy?" Peter asked, sitting forward as well. "Can you zoom in on him?"

It was a private Facebook page for friends only, but Gwen was able to enlarge the picture. "It's hard to tell, but he's the right age, and how many Jeremy Mikhailovs can there be in Juneau, Alaska?" She turned to Peter. "What should we do? Send him a message?"

"Let's give it a try."

Gwen let her fingers hover over the keyboard while her belly swarmed with butterflies. "I'm not sure what to say."

They both thought about it, and before Peter had a chance to offer any suggestions, she began to type.

Hi Jeremy. We don't know each other, but I found a newspaper clipping about the Good Friday Earthquake in 1964, and I'm wondering if it's you in the picture. It shows a young man who rescued a baby from the sea in Valdez. If it's you, could you let me know? I'm doing some research about the earthquake, and I'd love to talk to you about it.

"Does that sound okay?" she asked Peter.

"It's perfect."

She hit send, and they waited a few seconds. Nothing happened, so they sat back and stared at the screen. She folded her arms. "Maybe he never goes on Facebook."

"That's a possibility." Peter slid her a glance. "It's hard to be patient, isn't it?"

Another minute passed, and nothing happened, so they did some more googling but found nothing outside of the Facebook page.

"Maybe we'll hear from him tomorrow," Peter said. "Maybe he's out fishing, or maybe he's a morning person." He picked up his phone and tapped the screen. "Do you have a speaker with Bluetooth? We could listen to some of Scarlett's music while we wait."

"Yes, I have a speaker over there."

Before she had a chance to rise from her chair, her computer chimed with a notification. She grabbed hold of the mouse and clicked on Messenger. "He replied."

She and Peter read the message together.

Are you with the press? If you're a reporter, I don't want to talk to you. Piss off.

Gwen sat back and laughed. "Good heavens! I wasn't expecting that."

Peter laid his hand on her back, between her shoulder blades. "Tell him you're not with the press—that you're from Wolfville, Nova Scotia, and it's a personal matter. If he knew Scarlett back then, he might have known where she came from."

Gwen typed the reply and hit send, and they waited. Jeremy responded immediately.

I don't answer questions on the Internet.

"He's skittish," Peter said.

"I'll suggest that we talk on the phone." Gwen quickly keyed the message along with her cell number.

Jeremy's reply appeared immediately.

No way.

She and Peter stared at the screen for a few seconds, then turned to each other. "Are you thinking what I'm thinking?" Gwen asked.

"Probably," he replied.

"We need to go there," she said.

"Yes." Peter pointed at the keyboard. "Tell him that you'll be visiting Juneau this weekend. See if he'll agree to meet with you in person."

"Should I tell him I'm related to Scarlett?" she asked.

Peter thought about that for a moment. "If he knew her back then, he would know her as Valerie."

"That's right." Gwen sat forward on the edge of her chair and thought carefully about how to form a reply. Then she began to type.

> I understand. You don't know me. But would you consider meeting me in person? I plan to be in Juneau on Friday, and I would love to talk to you about my mother's cousin, Valerie McCarthy. They were close, and I'd like to know more about the time she spent in Alaska. My family has questions, and no one seems able to answer them. Would you be willing to help us and share what you know? I promise I'm not a reporter. I'm Valerie's first cousin, once removed.

"That's good," Peter said.

Gwen clicked send and felt an adrenaline rush while they waited for Jeremy to respond.

A moment later her computer chimed again, and a message appeared.

> Meet me at The Alaskan Hotel bar. Friday at 5 PM. And you better not be a reporter.

Gwen responded instantly.

> I promise I'm not a reporter. I'll see you Friday.

She hit send and turned to Peter. "A hotel bar? That's a bit worrisome."

"I'll go with you," he said. "I'll hang out at a table in the corner."

Gwen shook her head with disbelief. "This is amazing. He obviously knows something."

Peter sat back. "Judging by his messages, I don't think he'd be keen to talk to either of us if he knew about the book."

"True," Gwen replied. "But I don't want to lie to him. I want him to trust me. To trust *us*."

"He will."

"I hope so. I also hope he's not a serial killer."

They sat for another moment, letting it all sink in.

"We should book flights," Peter suggested. "I could be ready to fly out tomorrow."

"Me too." She logged on to the Air Canada website. "Window or aisle?"

"Aisle."

"Perfect, because I prefer the window." Gwen began to fill in the online reservation form while she marveled at the fact that they were finally going to speak to someone who actually knew Scarlett in Alaska. And God willing, that someone might also know what happened to her baby.

PART II

THE STORM

CHAPTER 6

Valdez
September 1963

On the final approach to Anchorage, after a long and exhausting trip across the continent with multiple connections in the US, the view from the aircraft was both frightening and awe inspiring. Valerie McCarthy pressed her forehead to the window and gazed down at rugged mountain ranges, lush green forests, and the rich blue waters of Cook Inlet. The sky was blue, and the sun was shining. Visually, it was spectacular, but this was unfamiliar territory, and she felt as if she might as well be flying to the moon.

Sitting back, she gripped the armrests. Her knuckles turned white as she fought the urge to cry, because she needed to stay strong and get through the next seven months. After that, she would pick up the pieces of her unfortunate life and start over. It was the only choice. When this ordeal came to an end, she promised herself she would forget what had happened back home and make her own way in the world. She would follow her heart and make all her dreams come true.

Valerie returned her attention to the window and watched the slow descent. Suddenly they were zooming close to the ground, mere feet above the runway. She braced herself for the landing and whatever might lie ahead.

~

Shortly after the plane touched down in Anchorage and made its way across the tarmac, Valerie gathered her belongings. A man named Frank Brown—an old wartime friend of her father's—was supposed to meet her inside the airport and drive her to Valdez. Her father had assured her that Mr. Brown was a trustworthy fellow, but that was not a word she would use to describe her father, so she had no idea what to expect.

She was seated at the back of the cabin and had to wait for everyone to deplane ahead of her, which seemed to take forever. Finally, she lugged her heavy tote bag up the aisle. When she reached the exit door, she was struck by a shockingly cold wind that blew her dark hair in all directions. Carefully, she descended the steps, gripping the rail, and entered the airport, where she proceeded to the baggage claim area to meet Mr. Brown. She had no idea what he looked like. Her father didn't know much either. They hadn't seen each other in almost twenty years.

"Valerie McCarthy?"

At the sound of her name, she turned toward a giant of a man with a bushy beard and mustache, a wool cap, and heavy brown boots.

"Yes, that's me." Her mind flooded with relief. "Are you Mr. Brown?"

"Yep." His words were clipped. "It took you long enough to get off the plane. We need to be getting on the road. It's a six-hour drive back to Valdez."

Six more hours?

"I'm sorry about that," she replied. "I was at the very back of the plane."

His broad shoulders rose and fell with an exasperated sigh. "I suppose that couldn't be helped. Do you have a suitcase?"

"I have two, along with my guitar," she replied. "It looks like the bags are coming now."

They waited in awkward silence.

Valerie spotted her guitar case, marked *Fragile*, and ran quickly to collect it. Then she pointed out her suitcases to Mr. Brown, who picked up both bags and carried them outside to a blue Chevy Nomad station wagon parked at the curb. A woman got out of the passenger seat.

"This is my wife, Carol," Mr. Brown said as he loaded Valerie's suitcases into the back of the car.

Carol wore a boxy brown coat and a woolen skirt with sensible black walking shoes. "Welcome to Alaska." She looked at Valerie from head to foot.

Grateful to hear the word *welcome* from these strangers who had agreed to take her in, Valerie said, "I appreciate you coming to fetch me. I had no idea it would be such a long drive."

"We make a trip to Anchorage a few times a year," Carol explained, "for medical appointments and such, so it was no problem to work you in to those plans. Hop in. I made sandwiches for the drive home, and you'll find a bottle of root beer on the seat."

Valerie got into the car and breathed a sigh of relief to be on her way somewhere with people who seemed to have everything under control.

But did they know why she had been sent to live with them? Were they aware that she was eight weeks pregnant and without a husband? Had her father been forthcoming about that?

~

Five minutes into the drive, Valerie fell into a deep slumber. When she woke, it felt like not a moment had passed, but suddenly gigantic mountains loomed on each side of the highway. Their sharp, snow-covered peaks seemed to touch the sky.

"Where are we?" she asked groggily. "And how long was I asleep?"

Carol glanced over her shoulder. "You've been sleeping for hours. We're at Thompson Pass. On the homestretch now."

Mr. Brown drove around the bend, and a massive river of solid ice came into view, sliding downward between two mountains.

Valerie sat forward and craned her neck to look up. "Is that a glacier? I've never seen one before."

"It's the Worthington Glacier," Mr. Brown informed her, "and you'll soon get used to seeing them. You'll need to learn about them too. Your father told me you were good in school. Good at memorizing things."

Valerie stared apprehensively at the back of Mr. Brown's partially balding head. "Yes, but what will I need to memorize?"

She met Mr. Brown's dark gaze in the rearview mirror. "The script for the *Wanderer*."

Valerie chewed her lower lip. "Um, I'm not familiar with the *Wanderer*. Is it a play?"

Carol slapped her husband on the shoulder. "You didn't tell her when she got off the plane, did you!"

"Tell me what?" Valerie asked hesitantly.

Carol turned in her seat. "We got you a job. You'll be working at Wilderness Lodge and helping out with the boat cruises for the rest of the tourist season until winter comes. You'll narrate the tour and memorize the information. They'll probably get you to work in the dining room as well. When the season ends, you'll clean the lodge. You'll be living there too."

Valerie's breath came short. "Wilderness Lodge? I . . . I thought I would be living with you in town. My father said—"

"It doesn't matter what your father said," Mr. Brown snapped. "He asked us to look out for you and make sure you were taken care of, and that's what we intend to do. But you can't stay with us. We don't have the space."

"I see."

Valerie wondered again if they knew why she had been sent to Valdez. Perhaps that was the real reason they didn't want her living in their home. Perhaps, like her father, they were ashamed of her terrible secret.

~

Wilderness Lodge stood five miles outside of Valdez at the end of a long dirt road that passed along the base of the Chugach Mountains. It was an enormous log cabin with forty guest rooms and a restaurant that operated during the spring, summer, and fall seasons. It also had its own private dock with a seaplane and a tour boat called the *Wanderer*.

It was past ten o'clock when they arrived, but the sun was just setting as Mr. Brown drove into the parking lot. Eager to stretch her legs after the long journey from Anchorage, Valerie got out of the car. While she waited for Mr. Brown to open the back, she took in the view of the bay and the enormous mountains on the opposite side. She breathed in the fresh, pine-scented air and listened to the water lapping up against the hull of the boat, which bumped gently against the dock.

Mr. Brown pulled both her suitcases from the back of the station wagon and carried them toward the front entrance of the lodge.

Inside, the lobby was rustic, with a high cathedral ceiling of knotty pine logs. The focal point was a gigantic stone fireplace with a moose head and antlers over the mantel. Bearskin rugs adorned the plank floors, and the furniture was upholstered in red plaid.

Mr. Brown strode to the reception desk and tapped the bell vigorously three times. An older lady hurried out of the back office. She wore her long gray hair in a ponytail and was dressed in a nubby wool sweater and faded jeans.

"Frank. I didn't expect you for another hour," she said.

"We made good time on the road," he replied. "Didn't stop for anything."

"Well, you must have set a world record," she replied. "Welcome back. And this must be Valerie." She slid her eyeglasses low on her nose, just like the strict schoolteacher Valerie remembered from second grade.

Valerie's belly was rolling with nervous knots, and she couldn't seem to look the woman in the eye. All she could do was stare at the floor.

"Welcome to Valdez," the woman said. "I'm Maud Wilson."

Valerie glanced up briefly and nodded.

"She slept most of the way from Anchorage," Carol explained, trying to be helpful.

Maud moved out from behind the reception desk. "Don't you worry, sweetheart. We'll get you situated. I have a room all ready for you. Are you hungry?"

"She just finished a sandwich I made," Carol told her.

Valerie was beginning to wonder if she'd ever be able to speak for herself.

"Frank, if you wouldn't mind taking her bags to the end of the hall," Maud said. "Room number twenty."

Valerie suspected the rooms in this place didn't come cheap, and her stomach tightened. "I'm not sure what arrangements my father made," she said, "but I can't really afford to pay for—"

"Room and board are free," Maud told her. "As long as you pull your weight here, we'll be glad for the help."

Valerie nodded gratefully and followed Maud and Mr. Brown down the long hallway. "I'll do my best."

"I'm sure you will," Maud said. "But no one expects a thing from you tonight. You'll need a good sleep to recover from the trip. You came a long way. Best not to overdo it too soon, or you'll want to leave us before you even give us a fair chance."

They reached the end of the hall, and Maud opened the door to the room that would be Valerie's for the next seven months. Like the rest of the lodge, it was rustic, with knotty pine walls, a pine dresser, and a brass bed with a colorful handmade patchwork quilt. Valerie looked down at the braided rug and across the room at a framed painting of a man standing in a shiny sunlit stream, fishing.

"This is wonderful," she said, her sleepy eyes settling on the bed. "Thank you."

Mr. Brown stood in the doorway with his hands in his pockets. "We'll be off, then. I'll come out to check on you once a week, or I'll send my son, Joe." Mr. Brown spoke with a note of warning. "He's a cop."

Valerie couldn't make her mouth work. All she could do was look away as Mr. Brown turned and walked out.

Maud approached Valerie. "I'll leave you to get settled. And if you're still hungry, you can eat in the dining room tonight, free of charge. I'll introduce you to Henry, the chef. After that, you'll eat with us. The dining room is just for guests."

"Who is *us*?" Valerie asked.

"My husband and me. We live in the house out back. You'll meet Blaine tomorrow. He'll take you out in the boat and get you trained for the tours. In the meantime, unpack those suitcases, and I'll come check on you in half an hour."

Maud walked out and closed the door behind her with a gentle click.

Silence descended, and Valerie stood immobile, feeling lost and homesick. But she couldn't go back. Geographically, this place might as well be a fortress with fifty-foot walls, because she had no money and therefore no freedom to travel anywhere.

Suddenly Drew's face appeared in her mind, and she felt as if her whole life was imploding. It was his fault she was here. She wished she had never met him.

CHAPTER 7

Valdez
1963

The *Wanderer*—a recently refurbished ferryboat from Seattle—had been purchased by Maud and Blaine Wilson when they'd built Wilderness Lodge in 1958, one year after Alaska gained its statehood. Alaska, the Wilsons believed, was a land of opportunity, a chance for new beginnings. It was an undiscovered gem for nature lovers, unspoiled and untapped in the tourism industry. Thinking progressively from a business perspective, they sold their Port Orchard home and gave up the so-called rat race to embark upon a new life among whales, eagles, sea otters, and bears.

The first five years of operation had been a rousing success. Visitors came from all over the world to experience the pristine beauty of Prince William Sound, where porpoises frolicked in turquoise waters that reflected jagged mountain peaks and where glaciers broke off into the sea with dramatic and thunderous force—a spectacular sight and sound to behold.

Three times a week, the *Wanderer* made daylong trips from the sheltered, ice-free waters of Valdez, along the wooded shores of the towering, misty fjord—to watch whales break the surface and flip their tails before they dove back down to the depths. To spot bald eagles soaring overhead. To marvel at the crystal-blue magic of the massive Columbia Glacier.

On Valerie's first day, she woke early—her body clock not yet adjusted to the time zone on the Pacific coast. She tiptoed in her nightgown out of her room to the dark, quiet lobby and found a book to read called *Travels in Alaska* by John Muir. She read for two hours before the sun came up.

Later, when the day began for guests in the lodge, she got dressed, pulled on her wool coat, and walked up the narrow gravel path to the little house on the hill, hidden in the trees. She was expected there for breakfast at seven o'clock.

She knocked on the front door, and Maud answered. "Good morning." She invited Valerie inside, where the smell of bacon and toast induced a ravenous hunger. Valerie followed Maud to the kitchen.

"Have a seat," Maud said. "I hope you like your eggs scrambled."

"I like eggs any style. Thank you."

The back door swung open, and a tall muscular man with wild white hair and a bushy mustache kicked the dirt from his boots before stepping inside.

"This is my husband, Blaine," Maud said. "Blaine, this is our new girl, Valerie, all the way from Nova Scotia."

He stopped and stared. When he spoke, his voice was deep, smooth, and smoky. "I must be dreaming. You, my dear, are the answer to our prayers. Welcome." He removed his coat, hung it on a hook by the door, and then rubbed his hands together on his way to the breakfast table.

"Can I do anything to help?" Valerie asked.

"Don't worry about a thing," Maud replied. "I've got it all under control. Just take a seat, and I'll serve you a plate."

A moment later they were all seated and digging into a hearty breakfast, sipping on strong coffee.

"Has Maud told you what you'll be doing today?" Blaine asked.

Valerie swallowed a crispy fried potato and wiped her mouth with a napkin. "She said I'll be going out on the boat with you?"

"That's right," he replied. "The tour starts at ten, and we have eight passengers booked. I'll take you down to the dock after breakfast and tell you what to do, show you the ropes—literally—and teach you the safety protocols. I have a notebook with a narration about the history of Valdez. Lots of stuff about the gold rush and the Russian occupation. You can read from it today, but have it memorized for next time."

"I can do that," she said. "I'm used to memorizing lines. I was in the school play three years in a row."

He sat back and spread his arms wide. "Perfect! And tonight, Angie will train you in the dining room."

"Who's Angie?" Valerie asked.

"She's our little lifesaver," Blaine replied as he shoveled a forkful of eggs into his mouth. "She's been working for us, off and on, since we built this place." He picked up a slice of bacon and dipped it in ketchup. "But she's a married woman now and starting a family."

Valerie cleared her throat. "She's expecting a baby?"

"Yes. That's why we're so glad to have you here to take over when she needs to quit. She's expecting next March."

Oh, God. They had no idea why Valerie was there.

Blaine reached for his coffee. "She's Frank Brown's daughter-in-law. I thought maybe, since you're an old family friend of the Browns, you might already know her."

Valerie shook her head while a case of nerves caused her mouth to go dry. "I only met Mr. Brown for the first time yesterday. I'd never even heard of him before a week ago."

Maud and Blaine exchanged a look of confusion. Then Blaine sat back and recovered his easygoing nature. "Well, no matter. You're here now, and we're grateful to have you. It's not easy to staff the lodge over the winter months."

Valerie struggled to remain calm. "I'm grateful to be here, but . . . I'm not exactly sure if Mr. Brown told you everything about me. I don't want to put you in an awkward position where you're . . ." She paused. "What I'm trying to say is that I don't want to keep any secrets from you. And if you don't want to keep me on after what I'm about to tell you, I'll understand."

They both stared at her questioningly.

"Not keep you on?" Blaine slapped his open palm on the tabletop and sent the cutlery bouncing. "Are you mad? We opened a bottle of bubbly when Frank called to tell us that you were coming."

A lump formed in Valerie's throat, and she was overcome with humiliation.

Maud reached across the table and squeezed her forearm. "Spit it out, sweetheart. It can't be that bad."

"But it is." Valerie recalled her father's words when she had told him.

"How could you bring shame on me like this? Thank God your mother isn't alive to see you sink so low. I can't even look at you."

The next morning, he had booked her a flight to Anchorage and ordered her to pack her bags. He'd said she could come home when it was over—when she had given her baby up for adoption—and they would never speak of it again.

Valerie lifted her gaze and regarded Maud and Blaine in turn. "I'm here because I'm expecting a baby. I'm eight weeks along."

Maud's face went pale, and Blaine frowned. They sat for a moment, speechless.

"The father?" Maud finally asked.

Valerie shook her head. "He doesn't want anything to do with me."

Maud rubbed Valerie's shoulder. "I'm sorry, sweetheart. Who was he . . . if you don't mind my asking? A boyfriend? Or just someone you . . ."

"I loved him," Valerie told her resolutely. "And I thought he loved me too, but I was so stupid. It was only a summer fling to him." She said nothing more, because if she kept talking, she might cry, and last night she'd promised herself that she would never cry another tear over Drew.

Maud tucked a lock of hair behind Valerie's ear. "That must have been difficult for you."

Valerie nodded silently. "It was. But I meant what I said before. I'd understand if you didn't want to keep me on."

The Wilsons exchanged a look of disbelief. "Don't be daft," Maud said. "We want you here, and we'll take each day as it comes." Then Maud balked. "But are you having morning sickness? Maybe the tour boat isn't such a good idea."

An unbearable sadness swept over Valerie, and her throat tightened around a jagged lump. It was the first time, since the moment she'd realized she was expecting a baby, that anyone had expressed concern about her well-being, either physical or emotional. Up until that moment, she'd been standing strong, like a rock, coping as best she could. But Maud's kindness caused something inside her to melt into an exposed puddle of gratitude.

"No morning sickness," she replied. "At least not yet."

"Maybe you're one of the lucky ones," Maud said. "I wasn't so lucky myself. I was sick every day for three months."

"You have children?" Valerie asked, still fighting tears.

"Three boys. All grown up and living happy lives in the Lower Forty-Eight. They like to visit and go fishing in the summer. Maybe you'll meet them if you're still here then."

A quiet moment passed. The big clock on the wall ticked steadily, and the kitchen faucet dripped into the copper sink. Valerie sat back and felt a surprising sense of comfort and calm.

Blaine pushed his chair back and clapped his hands together. "Enough chitchat, ladies. We have a boat tour to prepare for. You have much to learn, Valerie. We should get going."

Valerie turned to Maud. "Can I help you clean the dishes?"

"What a sweetheart you are to offer. But I'll take care of this, and you can help me tomorrow when there's no boat cruise."

"It's a promise." Valerie stood up, pulled on her coat, and followed Blaine to the dock.

~

On Valerie's first day of training aboard the *Wanderer*, she stood on the deck of the boat, in the shadow of towering mountain peaks, and watched banks of ocean mist roll seaward. She inhaled the sharp, salty tang of the sea and felt invigorated. When she'd boarded the plane in Halifax, her heart had throbbed with dread for the next seven months of her life. She'd deemed this time in Alaska as punishment and a prison sentence, with nothing to look forward to but boredom and loneliness. But Maud and Blaine had welcomed her into their home without judgment, and now Blaine was teaching her about safety protocols on a tour boat and describing Alaskan wildlife, glaciers, and waterfalls. Lonely and bored, Valerie was not.

Blaine had given her a warm slicker to wear. It was bright yellow with a sturdy hood and the Wilderness Lodge logo embroidered on the left breast pocket. He showed her where the life jackets were stored and went through a safety drill, twice. Later, while she sat at the stern, practicing the script for the narration, a bald eagle swooped from the top of a tall Sitka spruce and caught a fish in the water, close to shore. The sudden splash startled Valerie. She dashed to the rail to watch the eagle drag the fish onto the beach and kill it. He spread his large wings and took to the air, clutching the fish in his talons, and feasted upon it on the top of the tall spruce tree.

"Did you see that?" she asked Blaine when he emerged from the bridge.

"I did," he replied, seeming amused by her astonishment.

Shortly before ten o'clock, passengers began to arrive for the tour. Some were guests of the lodge, while others had come from the Hotel Valdez in town or the Switzerland Inn.

By the time they cruised out of the quiet, picturesque fjord, bordered by dense evergreen forests at the base of the mountains, a light misty rain began to fall. It did nothing to dampen the spirits of the passengers, who were well dressed for foul weather and delighted by the sight of two magnificent humpback whales making their way toward open water. The whales rolled gracefully at the water's surface, then dove down to the deep with a final wave of their enormous tails.

After that, the *Wanderer* cruised merrily along through the gray mist toward the highlight of the journey: the grand Columbia Glacier.

As they drew near, Valerie stood on the top deck with the rest of the passengers, marveling at the sight of the steep wall of jagged ice, two miles wide, threaded with jewellike strands of blue. Blaine cut the engine, and they drifted closer, listening to the impressive creaking and cracking of the massive frozen wonderland. After a time, a small section of the glacier broke off and fell heavily, cascading into the sea. It raised a cloud of white spray and a thunderous roar that caused everyone to exclaim in awe.

Later, during the return journey, Valerie joined Blaine at the controls. The tour was nearly over, and they were motoring back to the lodge in clear weather. "I can't believe what we saw today," she said.

"Even after hundreds of tours," he replied, "it never ceases to amaze me. I hope you'll like it here."

"I like it so far. It's not at all what I expected."

"And what was that?" he asked.

Valerie shrugged. "I don't know. More snow, I guess. The weather's not that different from home, but the mountains . . . we don't have those in Nova Scotia. Our version of a mountain is a molehill compared to what you have here."

Blaine gave her a sidelong glance while he steered the boat closer to shore. "I don't want to scare you, but in the winter, Valdez gets more snow than any other city in Alaska. It's the snowiest place in the USA. It's kind of a badge of honor for us."

"Well. I'm glad I brought my woolly mittens." Valerie grinned at him.

An unexpected roar of an outboard motor sent her pulse racing, and she looked out the side window at a small black skiff racing alongside the tour boat. It overtook them and veered recklessly into their path, fishtailing until the driver spun around and circled back.

"Who is that?" Valerie asked.

Blaine shook his head disapprovingly. "That's Jeremy Mikhailov. He's just showing off. But if he keeps that up, one of these days he's going to get himself killed."

Valerie left the bridge and moved to the port side, where Jeremy was standing up in his skiff, speeding past them and waving. A few of the passengers waved back, but some of them grumbled with scorn. Valerie watched until he grew distant, heading back toward Valdez.

She returned to the bridge. "He's gone," she told Blaine. "Does he do that often? Chase your boat and cause a ruckus?"

"More often than I would like," Blaine replied, glancing down at her. "He's a troublemaker, for sure. Half the people in this town would warn you to keep your distance from him."

"And the other half?"

Blaine shook his head again. "The other half thinks he's harmless and has a heart of gold. Maybe they just feel sorry for him."

"Why?"

Blaine hesitated. "Because he's been dealt some bad cards. Doesn't have a good family life."

Valerie thought of her own less-than-perfect life back home and understood how it could knock you around.

"And what do *you* think about Jeremy?" she asked.

"I think the jury's still out on that. Which is why we prefer to stay on his good side."

"What happens if you don't?"

Blaine slowed the engine as the lodge came into view and steered the boat closer to shore. "Let me tell you a story. Three years ago, I was driving into town and saw him limping on the side of the road. I pulled over, and he told me he had crashed his motorbike, so I drove him back to the spot, loaded the bike onto the back of my truck, and drove him home. Two days later, he showed up at the lodge with a brand-new set of hedge clippers to thank me for what I did."

Blaine shifted to a lower gear, slowing the boat as they approached the dock, where Maud was waiting to tie the lines.

"That sounds like a nice gesture," Valerie replied, confused by Blaine's hint of aggravation.

"Maybe," he said. "Or maybe not. Because the following week, I'm at Pinzons, enjoying a beer, and the owner of the cannery tells me that he had his hedge clippers stolen out of his shed. He had just bought them, brand new, in Fairbanks the week before."

"Oh dear," Valerie replied. "Did you tell him about Jeremy's gift?"

Blaine let out a dejected sigh. "No. It caught me off guard, and I guess I didn't want to get the kid into trouble. He was so proud when he gave me the clippers, and when we thanked him and expressed our appreciation, his face lit up with . . ." Blaine paused. "I don't know. I guess that's why he gets away with so much. He can be so eager to please. He's like a child sometimes, desperate for a kind word. So I kept my mouth shut."

"You never told anyone?"

"No, but I quietly returned the clippers to John's shed the next day so that it looked like he just misplaced them."

Valerie looked up at Blaine's profile. "That was nice of you."

"Was it?" he replied. "Or maybe I was just trying to avoid Jeremy's retaliation. Maybe that's the problem around here. People are afraid of him, so he gets away with things he shouldn't get away with. Heaven help you if you call the cops on him. He might throw a brick through your front window the next day."

The *Wanderer* bumped up against the dock, and Blaine asked Valerie to go outside and toss the lines to Maud.

"How was the tour?" she called out.

"Spectacular!" Valerie replied.

As soon as Blaine cut the engine, the distant roar of Jeremy's motorboat caught her attention. She turned and scanned the water for him, but he was nowhere to be seen. The outboard motor went silent, and she suspected he had disappeared into a cove somewhere.

She decided she would do her best to avoid Jeremy Mikhailov, because she had enough problems in her life. She couldn't afford to make any more mistakes, and the last thing she needed was trouble.

CHAPTER 8

Juneau
May 2017

Gwen and Peter checked in to separate rooms at the Alaskan Hotel, a Victorian-style landmark in Juneau's downtown historic district, built during the Alaska gold rush.

Gwen entered her room using the key provided by the front desk clerk. She laid her carry-on suitcase on one of two narrow twin beds, then glanced around at the furnishings and carpet beneath her feet. The room was clean, and the linens were fresh, but there was something that felt haunted by ghosts from another century.

A knock sounded at her open door, and she jumped.

"Sorry," Peter said from the doorway. "I didn't mean to frighten you."

She laughed. "I was just imagining ghosts appearing after dark. Please come in."

He entered and looked around. "It's quite a place, isn't it?"

"Sure is. I can't wait to see the bar. I'm picturing saloon girls and red velvet fainting couches. Funny that Jeremy suggested it."

"Why do you say that?" Peter asked.

She unzipped her suitcase and found her makeup and toiletries. "I don't know. I guess I imagined meeting him in a biker bar or a pool hall on the outskirts of town."

Peter remained just inside the door. "We have four hours until he arrives. Want to get a bite to eat? We could try the Red Dog Saloon. It's close by."

"That sounds appropriate, and I'm hungry. Just give me a few minutes to freshen up."

Her cell phone rang just then. "Shoot. I hope it's not Jeremy calling to cancel." She dug her phone out of her purse, checked the display, and saw that it was Eric.

Gwen stared at the screen for a few seconds, feeling fixed to the spot. The last thing she wanted was to hear that he'd decided to get engaged after all and she needed to call a lawyer because he wanted to start divorce proceedings.

Perhaps, in coming to Alaska, she'd wanted to escape that part of her life for a while—to stick her head in the sand, essentially, because the thought of losing Eric for good made her feel sick to her stomach.

"Is everything okay?" Peter asked, breaking the spell.

"It's Eric."

Peter took a slight step back, his eyes losing the spark from only seconds ago. "I'll let you take that. Come and get me when you're done."

She nodded and finally answered the call. "Hello?"

"Hey," Eric said. "I was just about to leave a message."

"Sorry," she replied, closing the door behind Peter. "The phone was at the bottom of my purse," she lied.

"Ah." He paused. "So . . . what's up?"

Gwen made a face. "What do you mean, *what's up?*" She moved to the small bed and sat down. "You're the one who called *me*."

"I know," he replied. "I just called to say hi. And ask how you're doing."

She ran her finger over the stitching on the bedspread and felt a tugging sensation in her chest, because it was nice to hear his voice—and he didn't sound like he wanted her to call a lawyer. "I'm fine. How are you doing?"

"I've been better," he replied.

He left it at that, which gave her no choice but to take the bait.

"Why? What's going on?"

Eric sighed dejectedly into the phone. "I don't know. Life's been so weird lately. Do you ever feel like everything is flying off the rails?"

"I'm familiar with the sensation," she replied. "But you're being cryptic. You've called me twice this week after months of radio silence. Talk to me."

He was quiet for a moment. "I want to. But could we meet for dinner tonight? I'd rather talk in person."

A mixture of curiosity and frustration caused a tightening in her belly. For months after he'd walked out on their marriage, she had sat by the phone wishing he would call and apologize and beg to come home. She'd wanted that more than anything in the world and would have taken him back in a heartbeat because he was her best friend and soulmate.

On top of that, she'd been raised to believe that marriage was for life. She'd never imagined herself as a single woman again, not after she'd walked down the aisle and said, "I do." And she'd loved being married. She and Eric had been happy together. They'd shared all the same dreams. It had been a beautiful life until one of those dreams had suffered a sudden, tragic death.

It wasn't until Eric had started dating another woman that she'd forced herself to accept their separation and focus on other things, mostly her work. But most days, she still longed for Eric to leave Keri and finally come home to her so that they could work things out.

"I can't get together tonight," she told him bluntly. "I'm in Alaska."

He laughed, as if she were joking. "What?"

"No, seriously. I'm in Juneau."

Ten full seconds passed before he responded. "What are you doing there?"

Gwen walked to the window and pulled the curtain aside to look down at the street. "I'm helping a friend with research on a book."

"Who's the friend?"

Not sure how to answer, Gwen let the curtain fall closed and returned to the bed.

"Is it the same person you were meeting at Le Caveau the other night?" Eric asked.

"Yes, actually," she told him. "His name is Peter."

There was another lengthy pause.

"Are you seeing each other?" Eric asked.

There it was. He was jealous. Gwen heard it in his voice.

She couldn't deny that it was satisfying. At the same time, she was annoyed, because it was none of his business who she was with, and he had no right to act as if she owed him an explanation or confession. Not after the past six months with Keri on the scene.

"I told you he was a friend," she replied honestly.

"But you flew to Alaska together?"

"Yes, we just arrived."

"Are you in the same hotel? Is he in the room with you right now?"

Gwen laughed with disbelief. "It's none of your business, Eric! But no, he's not here."

She could just imagine Eric pacing around his living room, dumbfounded, shocked that Gwen wasn't sitting home by the phone anymore. And where was Keri? Gwen certainly wasn't going to ask.

"You're right," he said. "It's not my business. I'm just surprised—that's all. I didn't know you were . . ."

"Didn't know I was what?" she asked. "Having a life?"

She waited for him to respond, but he seemed lost for words.

"Gwen . . ."

The sound of her name on his lips took her back ten years, and something inside her softened.

"What do you want?" she asked, forcing herself to remain grounded in the present.

A car with a bad muffler drove by on the street.

"I called because I want to talk about us," Eric said. "I feel like the past year was some kind of . . . I don't know . . . a bad dream or hallucination or a spell of temporary insanity."

Her throat went dry. "What are you saying?"

"I'm saying that I think we both lost it a little. We went crazy . . . in different ways."

But Gwen had never felt that she had gone crazy. She'd always believed her grief was normal. It would have been crazy *not* to be affected by what happened.

"You gave up on us," she said. "You deserted me when I needed you most."

"I know."

"In sickness and in health," she continued. "Isn't that what we promised each other? But you were quick to bail when life got tough."

He didn't argue. "You're right. I see that now. I've had time to reflect."

"While you were banging Keri?" The words shot out of her mouth like a bullet, and she didn't regret it.

"I deserve that," he said.

"Yes, you do."

For several seconds, neither of them spoke. Gwen sat on the small twin bed in the Victorian hotel, waiting for her husband to tell her, once and for all, what he truly wanted.

"Maybe we could get together when you get back," he carefully said. "Just to talk, if you're willing."

Gwen covered her forehead with her hand. "I don't want to talk about you and Keri."

"No, of course not. I don't want to talk about that either. I want to talk about us and everything that went wrong. I know I've made mistakes, and I'm sorry. That's why I called. That's what I wanted to say to you. And there's still so much more I want to say. You didn't deserve what you got. I was a bad husband."

Again, her hardened heart softened, and her anger cooled a little. "I appreciate that. And you weren't all bad. We were happy. Before."

"Yes. And I can't tell you how much I miss what we had. It's finally hitting me that you aren't a part of my life anymore, and it feels . . . it just feels so wrong. Like I've lost my best friend."

Gwen flopped back on the bed. "I don't want to have this conversation when you're in a relationship with another woman."

"I hear you. But what if I ended it? Do you think then we could . . . I don't know . . . talk more and see how things go?"

She sat up, alert and hyperfocused. "Are you suggesting that we give our marriage another try?"

"Maybe," he replied. "I'm not sure."

It galled her that he still didn't know what he wanted, that he might just be having cold feet with Keri and wanting to make sure he was doing the right thing.

"I can't talk about this right now," she said. "I'm on the other side of the country, and I have work to do."

"Research on that guy's book," he said, sounding miffed.

"His name is Peter, and yes. And just so you know, it's important to me. This book."

Eric let that sink in. "What's it about?"

She stood and walked to the sink in her room, looked at herself in the mirror. "I can't really share that with you. It's confidential."

"I see."

Finally, Eric capitulated with a sigh of defeat that she didn't believe for one second. First, it was too charming, spilling over with phony notes of "woe is me." She knew him too well. He believed he was going to win her back because he knew how devastated she had been by their separation. He knew how badly she'd wanted to stay married and work it out. He now assumed that things were still the same.

Perhaps they were. Or could be. She wasn't sure. But she didn't want it to be that easy for him. He deserved to grovel a bit. And she deserved that too.

Gwen turned away from the mirror. "I'll call you when I get home, okay? Next week sometime. We'll talk then."

Eric's voice changed after that. He didn't sound quite as confident or triumphant. "All right. Have a good time in Alaska. Don't get eaten by a bear."

"I'll try not to. Now I really have to get going."

Gwen ended the call and went straight for her toothbrush and makeup bag, because she didn't want to dwell any longer on her failed marriage. Her stomach was growling, and the Red Dog Saloon was calling her name. And Peter was waiting for her, patiently, in the next room.

~

"He actually said that?" Peter asked as he dipped a french fry into ketchup. "He told you he would end it with . . . what's her name again?"

"Keri," Gwen replied. "Yes, that's what he said, though he didn't commit to it. He just said 'what if' he ended it."

"It sounds like he wants to make sure all bases are covered before he does anything rash."

"That's how I took it as well," Gwen replied. "He doesn't want to burn both bridges and have no way off the dreaded island of solitude."

The piano player started a new tune. He plunked jauntily at a Billy Joel song, saloon-style.

"Is that 'My Life'?" Peter asked, turning toward the piano.

"I believe so. I love Billy Joel."

"Me too."

They sipped their beers and watched a couple of tourists walk through the swinging saloon doors and gape at the thick carpet of wood chips on the floor.

Gwen dipped another french fry in the ketchup. "I need to confess something," she said. "I didn't hate it when I told Eric I was in Alaska with a friend." She made air quotes around the word *friend*. "He sounded shocked. I think he expected me to always be there, sitting at home, just waiting for him to come back."

"But here you are, living your life," Peter stated.

"Yes. I love what we've been working on. I haven't felt this excited about anything since . . . well . . . since I was pregnant. Life's been pretty dreary since then, but this is the opposite of dreary."

"It's been exciting for me too."

Gwen glanced at the time on her phone. "One hour before we meet Jeremy. Maybe we should talk about a game plan. Like how I should introduce myself and what questions I should ask him."

The server arrived to clear away their plates, and they ordered coffee. Then they went over everything they knew and, more importantly, everything they didn't know.

A half hour later, they returned to the Alaskan Hotel, and Gwen changed into jeans and sneakers. Not that she expected to be running anywhere. At least she hoped that wouldn't be necessary. But one could never be too sure with a former delinquent. She was glad Peter would be nearby to keep an eye on things.

CHAPTER 9

Valdez
1963

In the days following Valerie's first boat cruise in Alaska, where she'd watched humpback whales frolic and witnessed the calving of the mighty Columbia Glacier, the weather turned. At first, soft misty rain turned cold. By the end of the week, a thin film of ice covered the windshield on Blaine's truck in the mornings, and he had to scrape it off before heading out to run errands in town.

It was a busy time. Valerie helped Maud with housekeeping duties. She changed linens and cleaned bathtubs. In the evenings, she waited on tables in the dining room with Angie Brown, Frank's daughter-in-law, who was great fun to work with.

Valerie had no regrets about revealing her secret to Maud and Blaine that first morning, as it established an instant trust between them. She felt as if she had known them all her life, like a favorite aunt and uncle. They were good people—compassionate, nonjudgmental, and forgiving of others' mistakes, whether it was a small error in the boat-tour narration or a stolen set of hedge clippers. Blaine and Maud wanted only to see each person in their orbit succeed in some way.

Valerie felt fortunate. Emotional pressures were easing. Sometimes she found herself standing on the dock, staring at the tall mountain peaks with a sense of reverence, feeling grateful for her fate in this remote, unfamiliar place. She felt surprisingly at home, more at home than she'd ever felt in her father's house.

She had no desire to go back there. The only things that tugged at her heart were thoughts of Drew and the terrible fight they'd had when he had broken up with her. She had been angry and told him she never wanted to see him again. But whenever his face materialized in her mind, a feeling of intense loss and desolation swept over her, and she had to force herself to turn away from it. It was confusing to be missing him, especially at night, and easier not to think of him at all.

In the mornings, it was simpler. There was enough activity to engage her mind and stir her creativity. The sky, the water, the wind, the whales, and the *Wanderer*, as it sliced through waves on its way out of the fjord . . . all of it was like a symphony. With or without Drew, Valerie was inspired. The music kept her going.

~

It had been two weeks since Frank Brown had dropped Valerie off at the lodge. She was outside, sitting on an Adirondack chair at the water's edge, enjoying a short break before dinner hour, when a police cruiser pulled into the parking lot, its rubber tires crunching heavily over the white gravel. Valerie turned in her chair and watched the driver get out. He wore a black winter jacket and held a police cap in his hand. After placing it on his head, he looked up at the front of the lodge as if he were examining it for structural defects.

Valerie walked up the sloping lawn toward the front deck, which stretched the full length of the A-frame portion of the building. "Hi," she said, and he turned.

"Hello." They met in the parking lot, and he extended a hand to shake hers. "You must be Valerie."

"I am." The first thing she noticed, besides the fact that he had a firm handshake, was how handsome he was. He had a strong jaw and a straight nose. His eyes were hazel with flecks of yellow. He was at least six feet two.

He stepped back and removed his cap. "I'm Joe Brown. Angie's husband. My father drove you from the airport."

"Yes," she replied. "He mentioned you might come by to check up on me."

The corners of Joe's mouth curled up in a small grin, and he chuckled. "That's one way of putting it. You'll have to excuse my father. He doesn't exactly have a way with words. If Valdez had a welcoming committee, he wouldn't be welcome on it."

Valerie relaxed a little and smiled. "He was fine. It was good of him to drive all that way to meet me. I appreciated it."

Neither of them seemed to know what to say next, so Valerie invited Joe to follow her onto the deck.

"Now that we've established that I'm not with the gestapo," Joe said, "I'm actually looking for my wife. She left a note saying she'd be working tonight, but I don't see the car."

Valerie checked her watch. "Her shift starts at five. It's only four thirty."

"Is it?" He checked his watch as well. "You're right." He turned toward his cruiser in the parking lot. "She should be here any minute, then."

"Yes. She's always early."

Joe scanned the front yard and glanced back at the parking lot.

"Would you like to come inside to wait?" Valerie asked, feeling suddenly awkward.

"No, I can't stay." He strode to the deck railing and leaned over it to look around the side of the building. Then he returned and placed his hat back on his head. "I don't suppose you've noticed any suspicious characters lurking around here?"

Valerie inclined her head with curiosity. "We have guests who are always lurking—if that's what you mean."

"No, that's not what I mean. Do you know Jeremy Mikhailov? He's a local."

"I know of him," she replied. "He was riding alongside the tour boat last week in a small skiff. But I've never actually spoken to him, and I haven't seen him since."

Joe squinted at the mountains on the far side of the bay. "If he comes around, be sure to let me know. He can be a problem for some people, and he's dangerous. I thought I saw him heading out this way earlier."

Valerie shrugged. "Honestly, I haven't seen him."

Joe scanned the yard again. "Right, then. I should get going. When Angie arrives, tell her I'll see her at home later." He turned and walked down the steps.

Valerie strolled to the edge of the deck to watch Joe get into his car and drive off.

As soon as he was gone, something made a noise under the deck. There was an obvious rustling and thumping, and Valerie backed away from the railing, fearing it was an oversize rat or a small bear.

"That was close," a voice said, and she let out a breath of relief as a human emerged and rose to his feet before her—a young man with curly brown hair, looking disheveled as he brushed dead leaves off his jacket and his shabby blue trousers. "Thanks for covering for me. I owe you one."

"I wasn't covering for you," she replied. "I didn't even know you were there."

"You didn't see me crawl under?"

"No," she said. "When was that?"

"I don't know. Right about the same time Joe got out of his car. It's pretty tight under there. I was on my belly the whole time with my cheek in the dirt, right under you, listening to every word of your conversation."

Valerie bristled and struggled to remember what she had said when Joe asked all those questions, because clearly this was the infamous Jeremy.

"It's not polite to eavesdrop," she said.

"I didn't have a choice." He spoke defensively, bordering on heatedly. "Even if I stuffed cotton in my ears, I could still hear you. You were standing right on top of me."

"And whose fault was that?" she asked and suddenly realized how ridiculous it was to argue with him. "Never mind. You must be Jeremy. I'm Valerie." She stuck out her hand, and he stared at it, as if he had no notion of polite etiquette, but then he shook it.

"I know who you are," he said. "Angie told me all about you. You're the new girl from out east."

Valerie's eyebrows rose a fraction. "You're friends with Angie?"

Valerie had worked two shifts with Angie, but she hadn't mentioned Jeremy, even though Valerie had confessed quite a bit about her own life and had mentioned seeing Jeremy on the tour.

"Angie and I go way back," he explained. "I've known her since fifth grade."

"I see." Valerie was still struggling to get a handle on this. "But you're not friends with her husband?"

Jeremy wagged a finger at her. "Now who's being nosy?"

Valerie felt a rush of unease at the smart-alecky look in his eye.

"I'm only joking." He scratched the back of his head. "Joe takes after his father. He doesn't think too much of me, but that's okay. I don't think too much of them either."

"Why is that?"

"Because Joe's a knucklehead. So is his dad."

Valerie was curious to know more, but she was also hesitant about encouraging any sort of intimacies with Jeremy. Blaine had warned her about him, and she needed to be careful and get through the next seven months without any snags.

A car pulled into the lot.

"There she is," Jeremy said. He leaped off the deck and jogged across the lawn to meet Angie.

Valerie watched from a distance as they spoke. After a moment, Angie glanced back at Valerie, who felt suddenly like a voyeur, spying on them. She turned and looked across the water.

A moment later, Angie approached, and Jeremy disappeared into the forest.

"You finally met Jeremy," she said as she walked up the steps with her heavy tote bag slung over her shoulder.

"I didn't know you two were friends."

Angie rolled her eyes a little and headed toward the main door of the lodge. "I try to be his friend, but he doesn't make it easy."

Valerie followed Angie inside and across the lobby to the dining room. "What do you mean?"

Angie set her bag inside a cupboard behind the reception desk and removed her coat. "He doesn't know how to steer clear of trouble. I wish he would just grow up and get a job and stop acting like a thirteen-year-old."

Valerie followed her into the kitchen. "How old is he?"

"Same age as me. Twenty-four."

Valerie lowered her voice. "I thought he was younger than that. He's not very big."

"He's five feet six and skinny as a rake," Angie remarked. "He used to get picked on when we were kids. Maybe that's why he grew up to be such a rabble-rouser."

Angie and Valerie donned their serving aprons. Henry, the head cook, was chopping carrots on the counter by the stove. "Salmon special tonight," he called out. "Lemon-dill cream sauce and garlic mashed potatoes."

"Sounds delicious," Angie said. "We have the best chef in Valdez, right here."

He waved his big knife at her. "And you are the best girl in Valdez named Angie."

They laughed, and Valerie and Angie set to work dressing the tables with white tablecloths and candles.

"Jeremy said you've known each other since fifth grade," Valerie mentioned.

"Yes. That's when my family moved here from Arizona, and he's been loyal to me ever since." Angie unfolded a tablecloth and floated it onto a table. "But that's mostly because of my mother. She worked in the grocery store, and one day, Jeremy was caught outside with a candy stick. Joe's father was a cop back then and dragged him into the store by his coat collar to report his crime to my mom, who assured Frank that she'd given the candy to Jeremy. She didn't, of course, but from that day forward, he would have done anything for her. And for me too."

Valerie fetched a tray of cutlery rolled in cloth napkins. She began to place them on the tables. "Blaine told me it was best to stay on Jeremy's good side. But that doesn't seem right—that people should be afraid of provoking him. Already, I feel like I'll be walking on eggshells every time I see him."

"Don't worry—you'll be fine," Angie said dismissively. "You work with me, and you work for Blaine, and Jeremy would do anything for that man. He'd give him the shirt off his back."

Valerie still wasn't entirely convinced she could throw caution to the wind where Jeremy was concerned. There was a look in his eye that gave her the willies.

"But he wouldn't do that for your husband?" Valerie asked. "Because Jeremy didn't seem too eager to talk to him today. That must be awkward if the two of you are friends."

"Not really," Angie replied as she rolled more napkins around cutlery. "Jeremy doesn't move in our social circles—or any social circles, for that matter. So it's not as if I hang out with him. We just talk sometimes if we bump into each other."

Valerie carried another tray of cutlery to a table. "I'm not sure if I should tell you this," she said, "but Joe was here looking for you earlier, and he seemed to be looking for Jeremy as well. He warned me to be careful around him. He used the word *dangerous*, and he said that if I saw him lurking, I should let him know right away."

Angie let out a huff of frustration. "No, don't do that. Joe just needs to relax about Jeremy. He wouldn't hurt a flea. And I'm allowed to have friends. I can talk to whoever I want. It's not like there's anything going on between us."

Valerie paused and turned toward Angie. "Is that why Joe doesn't like him? Because he thinks there's something going on?"

Angie groaned. "Oh, God, who knows? It's not true at all, and I'm sure Joe knows it, but he likes to beat his chest and act possessive. It's more about appearances, in my opinion. And his ego. He doesn't want anyone seeing his wife talking to another man—especially the one who's like a bothersome little horsefly he can't swat away." She gave Valerie a look. "That's what I mean about Jeremy not knowing when to quit. He enjoys taunting Joe. Joe would drag him off in handcuffs if he could catch him. But Jeremy's like a slippery little fish. It drives Joe insane." She laughed softly at the thought, and Valerie wondered if Joe might have good reason to be suspicious of Angie's friendship with Jeremy.

"How long have you and Joe been married?" Valerie asked.

"Two years, but we've been together since eleventh grade."

"It must be nice to be with the person you love," Valerie said.

Angie regarded her with sympathy. "You miss him, don't you? That boy you left behind in Nova Scotia?"

"He's the one who left *me*," Valerie reminded her. "And I'll never forgive him, not as long as I live."

She was still trying very hard to forget him.

Angie began to light candles on each table. "Well, I, for one, am glad you're here. It's nice to have someone my age to talk to. This is a small town, and everyone knows everyone's business, and when your husband is the local cop, it's even worse. Sometimes I'd like to just pack my bags and leave. I could sneak onto one of the supply ships and hide out in the hold. Become a stowaway, all the way to Seattle, and start fresh. Like you're doing here."

Valerie was surprised to hear Angie say such a thing. She was married and expecting a baby in the spring.

"But this is only temporary," Valerie told her, wanting to steer the conversation away from babies on the way. "I'm not here forever. Next summer, I'll make my way to New York or Hollywood. I want to be an actress or a singer. Or maybe both."

Angie sighed dreamily. "I wish I could go with you. But knowing Joe, he'd probably hunt me down and drag me back by the hair."

Valerie stopped what she was doing. "But he's good to you, right? He wouldn't ever hurt you?"

"Oh no. It's nothing like that," Angie assured her. "That was just an expression. He gets jealous sometimes, but his bark is worse than his bite. It's only because he's crazy in love with me." Angie nudged Valerie and winked, then looked around the dining room to make sure everything was in order. "It makes me a lucky woman because he's the best-looking man in Valdez."

"And you are the prettiest girl," Valerie said with a smile.

Angie laughed. "Until you arrived." She tossed a napkin at Valerie, who caught it in the air.

"That's a matter of opinion. And it's irrelevant anyway, because I won't be here for long. A year from now, no one will even remember who I was. I'll be like a little cloud of dust that just . . ." She waved her hand through the air. "Disappears like magic."

Angie chuckled. "I love how you talk. You need to play your music for me sometime. I bet your songs are amazing."

"I'm still working on them," Valerie replied reservedly. "I'm not ready to perform for anyone yet."

"You could at least play me something on your guitar. Do you know 'Up on the Roof' by the Drifters? I love that song."

An older couple walked into the dining room and asked if it was open for dinner yet. Valerie glanced at the clock on the wall. "We open in five minutes, but I can seat you now, if you like."

Valerie fetched two menus from the reception desk and invited them to follow her to the table with the best view of the water.

~

Later that night, after the dining room closed, Valerie retreated to her room and picked up her guitar. As soon as she strummed a minor chord, a memory came to her. It was vivid and fragrant, and she was immediately transported back to one of those hot summer afternoons when she and Drew had walked with their guitars to the abandoned hunting shack in the forest. Song sparrows had chirped in the trees, and the air smelled of fresh pine. They'd sat cross-legged on the floor, facing each other, while Drew played a catchy riff he'd composed the night before. Valerie had followed with a vocal that came out of nowhere, lyrics inspired by his complex chord progressions.

Together, that afternoon, they were creatively charged and passionate about music and life. They'd made love for the first time, moved by the lyrics and melodies they'd composed. After that, and for the rest of the summer, they couldn't keep their hands off each other. The only time they hadn't been wrapped in each other's arms was when they were playing their guitars.

Valerie had never known such bliss. She'd thought they'd be together forever, writing music and traveling the world like a couple of hippies.

How could it have ended the way it had? She didn't have the answer, and when she thought of those idyllic days in the forest, her heart ached with sorrow.

～

Valerie had a hard time falling asleep that night and woke several times. Shortly before dawn, Drew walked into her room with his guitar and sat on the foot of the bed. He began to play a few clumsy, dissonant chords and was having trouble putting the notes together. He wouldn't ask for Valerie's help. He ignored her completely, even when she tried to offer a helpful suggestion.

Suddenly, light flashed over his head like an exploding star. Valerie woke from the dream and sat up. She half expected Drew to be sitting there, still plucking ineffectively at the guitar strings, but she was alone in her room, incapable of alleviating her anguish.

CHAPTER 10

Valdez
1963

In the dining room the following night, after the last guest had paid the bill and walked out, Angie approached Valerie. "Is everything okay? You haven't talked much tonight."

Valerie felt instant remorse. "I've been thinking about Drew. Remembering things. I've been angry with him since I came here, but last night I couldn't stop thinking about how happy we were before it ended."

Angie gathered up the tablecloths for the laundry basket. "What happened between you two, anyway?"

Valerie looked down at the floor. "I don't even know where to begin. We had an incredible summer, and he told me he loved me. But at the end of August, right before I was supposed to leave for school, he broke up with me."

Angie tossed another tablecloth into the laundry basket. "Did he tell you why?"

"Yes, but it made no sense," Valerie replied, "because everything was fine the day before. Or at least I thought it was, but maybe it was all a lie. Maybe he was just using me, looking to have fun for a summer, and I got serious too fast and scared him off."

"What could scare him if he was in love with you?"

Valerie remembered their final days together. "I started talking about taking a year off from school so that we could travel around the world and write music. My father would have lost his mind if I'd left town with a boy, unmarried, especially a boy he didn't approve of. In the end, Drew acted just like my father. He said it wasn't a good idea, that I was being childish and irresponsible. He basically decided what was best for me—the traditional route that a good girl should take—and I hated that. He also suggested I was just using him to rebel against my father. He said we should end things, and I stormed off after telling him I never wanted to see him again." She spoke bitterly about what she was thinking. "Sometimes I wonder if my father knew about us and offered Drew money to leave me. I wouldn't put it past him."

"Maybe you're better off without him," Angie said, "if he was just like your father or if he accepted a bribe to stay away from you."

"Maybe. But now I think I was just upset and it's my fault we argued like we did. I couldn't see his point of view."

Angie swept the floor under one of the tables while Valerie lifted the chairs to rest upside down on the tabletop.

"Here's what I don't understand," Angie said. "If you were supposed to go away to school, what are you doing here?"

The exhaustion from Valerie's sleepless night got the better of her. She plunked herself onto a chair and pressed the heels of her hands to her forehead.

Angie set the broom aside, sat down beside her, and squeezed her shoulder. "What's wrong? It can't be that bad."

"It is," Valerie replied.

Angie sat patiently, waiting for Valerie to elaborate.

"I might as well tell you," she finally said, looking up. "Because you're going to find out anyway . . . when I start to show."

Angie sat back. "Oh. I see."

"Are you shocked?"

"A little. But I guess . . . not really. Now that I think about it."

"Please don't tell anyone," Valerie pleaded. "It's supposed to be a secret. That's why Frank sent me here for the winter when the lodge will be closed. No one will see me."

"Do the Wilsons know?" Angie asked.

"Yes, I told them the first day. They were kind about it." Valerie narrowed her gaze. "I thought maybe Joe knew about it and he might have told you."

"No. I don't think he knows anything. And it doesn't surprise me that Frank is keeping it secret. He used to be a spy in the war. Or so he claims."

Valerie's eyebrows shot up. "You're joking. I had no idea."

Angie relaxed in the chair, and they sat in silence, thinking about everything.

"What are you going to do when the baby comes?" Angie asked.

"Put it up for adoption. That's why my father sent me here. He said he would make all the arrangements, and then he expects me to come home and go to university as planned, as if it never happened."

"What about Drew?" Angie asked. "Does he know?"

"No, and that's what's keeping me awake at night."

"But why didn't you tell him?"

Valerie thought back to the day she'd learned she was pregnant. It had felt like her life was over. "He left the valley after we broke up," she explained, "and I didn't know where he went. I couldn't reach him, and after a while I gave up trying, or maybe it was my pride. The last thing I wanted was for him to think I was trying to trap him. Then I panicked. I told my father about the baby because I was terrified that he would find out anyway, that my doctor might tell him."

"He can't, you know. That's confidential medical information."

Valerie shrugged. "It's a small town. And my father knows everyone."

Angie propped her elbow on the table, rested her chin on her hand. "It's your life, but if you ask me, I think you should try and find Drew. Even if he says he doesn't want the responsibility of a child and he agrees about an adoption, at least you'll know, and you won't feel like you kept something from him. You won't always be wondering 'What if?'"

Valerie looked up at the ceiling and exhaled. "You're right. And I think I'll always feel guilty if I don't tell him. Someday our child might want to know who his real parents are. It wouldn't be fair not to put Drew's name on the birth certificate." Valerie bent forward and rested her head on the table. "I don't know how I got myself into this. We were being so careful. At least I thought we were."

"That's how it happens," Angie replied. "I wish there was something I could do to help you. When are you due?"

Valerie sat up again. "March twenty-eighth."

"I'm due March tenth, so at least we'll be going through this together." She reached for Valerie's hand. "That's something, isn't it? Maybe we can help each other. Have you been having morning sickness?"

"Not at all," Valerie replied. "What about you?"

"A bit, but it usually passes by noon. That's why I'm glad I work evenings in the restaurant."

They talked about other symptoms of pregnancy and shared their knowledge of what was to come.

"I'm glad I met you," Valerie said. "It's good to have someone to talk to."

"I'm glad I met you too," Angie replied. "And don't worry. Everything will work out. Maud and Blaine are the best, and I'll be here for you. Call me anytime if you want to talk."

Gazing toward the dark windows that overlooked the water, Valerie recognized, for the first time, the intense fear that had caused her to hate Drew in the moments when her mood had swung in that direction. It wasn't just about their breakup. It wasn't her bruised ego or her sense of betrayal. It was something else, something more than heartsickness over a brief summer romance.

What if I tell him about the baby and he still doesn't want me? I'll be rejected again. Abandoned.

Perhaps that was the heart of it. Perhaps that was why she'd agreed to come to Alaska when her father had suggested it. She'd packed her bags and taken off without a fight because her fear was a monster inside of her, and it stretched all the way back to her mother, who had died and left little Valerie alone in the world with a father who was incapable of love.

Valerie's cheeks grew hot. "I think I'm afraid to admit that I still love him because he hurt me, and I don't want to be hurt like that again. It's easier to tell myself that I hate him."

Angie regarded her with sympathy. "But maybe he loves you too, and he hasn't been able to reach you either."

Valerie laid her hand on her flat belly and imagined what it might look like in six months' time. "Maybe I'll write a letter to Drew and send it to his parents' house," she said tentatively. "I don't have their address, but I know their names and the town they live in, so if I send it to general delivery, it might reach them, and they could pass it on. A letter might be better anyway. I'll be able to get all my thoughts down properly. I'll tell him the truth about where I am and what's happening, and I'll leave it up to him to decide what he wants. Whatever it is, I'll accept it. Maybe that's all I need. A sense of closure."

Angie stood up to finish sweeping. "I can mail it for you. I'll take it straight to the post office."

"Would you? That would be helpful. Thank you."

"And if he wants to be with you," Angie added, "you might want to start saving your tip money now to pay for your flight home, because I doubt your father would buy you a ticket."

"Definitely not," Valerie replied.

Feeling apprehensive, she stood and busied herself with preparations for breakfast in the dining room the next morning.

Later, after Angie shut off the lights and went home, Valerie returned to her room to think about that letter. She stayed up until three in the morning, getting all her thoughts down on paper and recopying it multiple times to make changes.

The next night, Valerie handed the sealed envelope to Angie, and for the first time since the end of the summer, she allowed herself to nurture a quiet, cautious hope.

CHAPTER 11

Valdez
1963

With Valerie's letter tucked into her coat pocket, Angie drove through the darkness, back to town. One of her headlights was on the fritz, so she clutched the steering wheel with both hands and squinted to stay focused. She would need to tell Joe about that broken light as soon as she got home. He would take care of it, because he pulled people over for safety infractions like that every day. It wouldn't do for his wife to be driving around town with a defective headlight.

But that wasn't the only reason she was clutching the steering wheel. Feeling unsafe in a moving vehicle reminded Angie of the misery that had descended upon her life after the death of her sister in a car accident. It had wrecked her sense of security forever, and she'd had severe bouts of anxiety ever since, knowing that life could be lost in an instant. It could happen to anyone—or to someone else whom she loved. Someone like Joe or her parents, who had moved back to Arizona, and now her baby.

Angie touched her foot to the brake pedal as she rounded a curve, while the weak beam of her single headlight shone on the road. Oh, the stress of these dark curves . . .

When her sister had died, Angie had done her best to console her parents, but nothing could take away their pain. Angie was not a mother yet, but being pregnant, she now possessed a deeper understanding of her parents' grief. All along, she'd thought their emotional withdrawal and their move back to Arizona was because they loved Shana more, but maybe that wasn't the case. Maybe there was no cure for the loss of a child. No possible solace, not even the existence of the remaining child.

At least Angie's pregnancy had brought new happiness into their lives. Her father had started woodworking again. He was building a cradle, which he planned to ship to Alaska soon. And Angie was finding comfort in her new friend, Valerie. Their conversations reminded her of treasured moments with Shana, who had always been open about her romances and heartbreaks.

It had been a long time since Angie had had a friend she could confide in. It had been almost seven years since Shana's car went off the road. Angie was more than ready for a close friendship. In fact, she wanted it quite desperately.

~

Angie walked through her front door and found Joe asleep on the sofa. Dirty dishes were piled next to the sink, and a record was skipping on the turntable.

"You're late," Joe said groggily. He sat up while Angie moved to switch off the record player. "Where were you?"

"At work," she replied with a ripple of disappointment when she noticed four empty beer bottles on the coffee table.

He grumbled as he stood. "The dining room closes at nine, but it's past ten. Why are you so late?"

Angie explained quickly. "I stayed to talk to Valerie, the new girl. She's in a bit of a pickle."

That little nugget of information seemed to rouse Joe. He walked to the kitchen table, pulled a cigarette out of the half-empty package, and struck a match to light it. "What's going on with her?"

"She misses her boyfriend back home," Angie said as she moved to the front closet and hung up her coat. "They had a fight and broke up before she came here, and she didn't tell him where she was going. She didn't say goodbye."

Joe went to the fridge for another bottle of beer. Angie wished he would just have a soda, because he had such a hard time waking up in the mornings when he'd been drinking, and it was up to her to get him out the door.

"I wouldn't be too pleased if you left town without saying goodbye," he said with a note of disbelief that a woman could do something like that.

Angie returned to the kitchen and filled the sink to wash the dishes.

"What's she going to do about it?" Joe asked, puffing on the cigarette.

Angie faced him. She didn't think he knew about Valerie's pregnancy, but she couldn't be sure. And since his father was old friends with Valerie's father, Angie had to be careful about what she revealed. She didn't want to betray her new friend. "Nothing," she replied with a shrug. "She's just sad and needed a shoulder to cry on."

She turned away from Joe and loaded some plates into the soapy water. Joe stood behind her, smoking. After a while, he extinguished the cigarette in the ashtray and slid his hands around her waist. He kissed the back of her neck.

"You smell good." His voice was husky and low. "Coming to bed soon?"

Joe was certainly a charmer when he wanted to be, even after a few beers. His lips were soft and warm, and he knew exactly how to use his hands, even standing at the kitchen sink. With a light touch, he pushed her hair away from her neck and kissed behind her ear, which made her flesh tingle with desire. She turned, rose on her tiptoes, and wrapped her arms around his neck. They kissed passionately, and her body responded to his skillful advances.

"I'll be there soon," she said playfully, pushing him back. "Just give me a few minutes to finish up here."

One side of his mouth curled up in an eager grin, and he kissed her on the cheek before he sauntered out of the kitchen.

Angie watched him go and felt almost dizzy with yearning. She was one lucky woman.

~

The phone rang and jolted Angie awake. She sat up with a gasp, then immediately flopped back down because she was accustomed to this. Her husband was an officer of the law, and sometimes the phone rang in the middle of the night. It was nothing out of the ordinary and nothing to cause panic. Usually, it was a complaint about some local teens causing trouble down at the docks or someone who'd had a little too much to drink and driven their car into a ditch.

Joe was out of bed in an instant, padding naked across the floor to the phone in the kitchen. "Joe Brown speaking."

Angie lay on her back, blinking up at the ceiling, listening.

"Not again," he said with annoyance. "At least we know where he is. Did he break the lock?" There was a pause. "No problem. I'll check it out when I get there. Don't do anything else. Just sit tight. I'm heading out now." Joe hung up the phone and returned to the bedroom.

"What's going on?" Angie asked. She sat up and tugged at the covers to keep warm in the midnight chill.

Joe switched on the overhead light and opened the closet. He reached for his trousers and pulled them on. "Jeremy's sleeping in the Jacobsons' shed."

Angie glanced at the window. It was pouring rain outside. "His parents probably locked him out of the house again. You're not going to arrest him, are you?"

Joe shrugged into his shirt. "I might, because breaking and entering is a crime. You know that."

Secretly offended by his condescending tone, she said, "But if he's got nowhere else to go and he's not hurting anyone . . ."

"Sure," Joe said mockingly. "It's totally fine. Until he makes off with Mr. Jacobson's lawn mower and sells it in Seward on Friday."

"But he hasn't taken anything, has he?" she countered. "He's just sleeping in there."

"He won't be sleeping when I burst through the door." Joe buckled the belt on his trousers. "And if that lock is busted, you can bet your last dollar I'll be marching him straight into the station and charging him."

Angie forced herself not to say anything more, because no good could come from getting into an argument with Joe about the law, especially when it concerned Jeremy. Joe had once accused her of being biased, and there was some truth to that. But was it so wrong to take pity on someone who had been dealt a bad hand in life? Maybe all Jeremy needed was a leg up. If someone would only help him and give him a job that he could do, something he enjoyed, he might be fine. He only acted out when he felt desperate or threatened or backed into a corner.

She continued to sit up in bed while Joe shut the closet door and approached the bed.

"Go back to sleep," he said, "and don't take Jeremy's side in this. He gets away with too much around here, and it's people like you that encourage him."

"How do I encourage him?" she asked, indignant.

"When you help him get away with stuff," Joe replied. "You and half the people in this town are responsible for him never learning right from wrong. And when you make me out to be the bad guy . . ." Joe was about to walk out when he stopped, changed his mind, and bent to give her a kiss on the cheek. "I'm just trying to do my job."

"I know," she replied. "And I don't think you're the bad guy."

He touched his forehead to hers and spoke genuinely. "That's a relief, my love." He turned and grabbed his gun and holster off the dresser.

Angie listened to the sound of him leaving through the front door, stomping down the steps, and starting the police cruiser. After a few seconds, he backed out of the driveway and roared down the street.

Angie settled back under the covers, but she couldn't sleep. She dreaded the thought of Jeremy shivering in the cold inside the Jacobsons' shed.

What was he doing there in the first place? The last time she'd spoken to him, he'd said he had a mattress on the floor in his parents' garage. What could have happened?

CHAPTER 12

Rain pelted the windshield of the police cruiser, and the wipers snapped noisily back and forth.

"Does the shed have a window or a back door?" Officer Edwards asked as Joe drove to the Jacobsons' property, three miles outside of town.

"It has two windows," Joe replied. "One on each side and a double door at the front. Be ready to jump out as soon as I pull in, because Jeremy will try to make a run for it. He's a slippery little rascal."

Joe pulled into the Jacobsons' yard, skidded to a halt on the gravel with both headlights trained on the shed. He shifted into park, and he and Edwards got out with their batons.

The rain was coming down sideways, and the blustery wind whipped at Joe's heavy black slicker. The car headlights beamed straight at the front door of the shed, where the padlock was hanging open on the bracket. Joe wrenched the door open and shone his flashlight into the dark space.

Sure enough, there was Jeremy, huddled on the floor under a wide shelf containing automotive supplies. He was wrapped in an old carpet and held his hand up in front of his face to block the blinding glare from the flashlight.

"Didn't your mother teach you how to knock?" Jeremy asked, frowning at them.

"What are you doing in here, Jeremy?" Edwards asked. "You know you can't be breaking into people's sheds in the middle of the night."

"I didn't break in," he explained. "Mr. Jacobson never remembers to lock his door, so you can't charge me with anything."

Joe's gut rolled over with frustration, and he strode forward to grab Jeremy by his coat collar. "I can charge you with trespassing. Let's go." He wrenched him to his feet.

Jeremy stumbled as he was pushed toward the open door. "I appreciate this, Joe. You're actually doing me a favor. Winter's coming, and I'd be grateful for a warm bed and three square meals a day until spring."

Exasperation singed the corners of Joe's self-control. All he wanted to do was shake Jeremy until his teeth rattled, but he resisted the urge and squeezed Jeremy's coat collar in his fist, thrusting him outside. Jeremy fell onto his hands and knees in the driving rain while Joe reached for his handcuffs.

Jeremy coughed and sputtered. "Okay, okay," he blubbered, rolling onto his back. "I'll go with you this time." He held his hands up while he blinked into the rain that was striking his face. "How's Angie, anyway?"

The question was clearly meant to taunt Joe, but Joe had been down that road with Jeremy before, and he couldn't let himself get all riled up. That never ended well, so he clenched his jaw and didn't respond.

He glanced at Edwards. "Close the shed door, and lock it behind you."

Edwards fumbled with the padlock, which wasn't coming free of the bracket.

Before Joe had a chance to slap the cuffs on Jeremy, he leaped to his feet and shoved Joe backward, causing him to lose his balance. Then he darted across the grass toward the woods.

"Get him!" Joe shouted.

Joe and Edwards took off across the wet field. They swung their flashlight beams in all directions through the driving rain, searching for Jeremy. They splashed through puddles, and Edwards slipped on his heel. His feet went up, and he fell onto his backside.

Joe didn't stop to help him. He kept running toward the tree line with no idea which direction Jeremy had gone. It was pitch black in the dense, dripping forest. He stopped, breathing heavily, and shone the light left, right, and then left again. He stood still and listened . . .

Nothing. Only Edwards approaching from behind him.

"Be quiet!" Joe whispered. "Where did he go?"

They both stood motionless in the rain while the wind howled through the treetops.

"I don't hear anything," Edwards said.

"Shh. You go that way. He couldn't have gotten far."

They trod as quietly as possible into the dark forest, searching through the drenching weather and listening for the sound of footsteps running, escaping. But Jeremy had vanished. They hunted doggedly for at least twenty more minutes before they finally gave up and returned, soaking wet, to the police cruiser. They got in and removed their hats.

"I told you he was slippery," Joe said. "Why didn't you have my back?"

"You told me to close the shed door."

Joe turned the key in the ignition, but nothing happened. He tried again. Still nothing.

"The battery's probably dead," Edwards said matter-of-factly, "because you left the headlights on."

"No kidding." Joe rested his forehead on the steering wheel. "That rotten little sneak."

After a moment, he took a few deep breaths and watched the rain slide down the windshield.

Edwards spoke dejectedly. "The lights are on in the kitchen. I'll go and see if Mr. Jacobson has some jumper cables."

He didn't wait for Joe to agree or disagree. He simply got out of the car and ran to the front door. But Joe wasn't ready to move yet. He needed a moment to get his frustration under control and ride out the humiliation of this wretched night.

CHAPTER 13

Juneau
2017

Walking into the Alaskan Hotel bar was like stepping into a time machine.

Gwen arrived fifteen minutes early for her meeting with Jeremy Mikhailov and took a moment to inspect her surroundings—ornate late-Victorian woodwork, patterned wallpaper, stained glass, and red lightbulbs in the fixtures that harkened back to the location's history as a brothel at one time.

She chose a table close to the small stage, where the walls were papered with entertainment flyers. She removed her jacket and hung it on the back of her chair, then approached the young woman tending the bar. She wore a name tag that said Margie, and she was exceptionally pretty with long, wavy red hair.

"What can I get you?" she asked.

"A glass of white wine. Pinot grigio if you have it."

She seemed thrown. "Hmm . . . there might be an open bottle out back." She left the bar to check, but Gwen stopped her before she got too far.

"Never mind. I'll just have a beer. What do you have on tap?"

Margie listed off the selections, and Gwen chose a local beer. She carried it back to her table, dug out her notepad and pen, and set them in front of her.

The front door opened, and Gwen felt a pang of nervousness, but it was only Peter. He winked as he passed and went straight to a small table at the back. He removed his rain jacket, then approached the bar and ordered a beer.

Gwen sat alone, scrolling through emails on her phone, pretending to be reading them. But she was far too tense to focus on correspondence of any kind. She didn't know what to expect from Jeremy. Mostly she was afraid he wouldn't show.

The door opened again, and a small group of tourists in brightly colored rain jackets strolled in. They talked and laughed and were eager to try the peanut butter whiskey. Margie poured a row of shots.

Gwen kept her head down and sipped her beer, waiting and waiting. Eventually she looked at the time. It was 5:10 p.m.

By now she was convinced that Jeremy wasn't coming. She met Peter's gaze across the room and shook her head. She mouthed the words, "He's not coming," just as the door opened and an older man walked in. He wasn't tall, but he was fit and slender. He wore a navy puffer jacket with blue jeans and a gray scarf tied around his neck. His hair was gray, but there was plenty of it, thick and wavy.

Gwen laid her phone down and sat up straighter in her chair, but the man didn't look at her. He went straight to the bar and spoke to Margie as if he knew her well. She nodded and tossed her head in Gwen's direction, then poured him a glass of scotch, straight up.

At last, he approached Gwen's table. "Are you Gwen Hollingsworth?"

"Yes." Feeling overly eager, she reached out to shake his hand. "You must be Jeremy. It's nice to meet you."

He shook her hand, then set his glass on the table and shrugged out of his jacket. He draped it on the back of the chair and sat down across from her.

"You've come a long way," he said. "I'm going to go out on a limb here and guess that you don't have any other business in Juneau, except to talk to me."

"What gave me away?"

"Just a hunch," he replied. "But it sure took you long enough."

She sat forward slightly. "What do you mean?"

"It's been more than half a century since the quake," he said. "And your famous cousin has been gone for a quarter of a century. You're her family. Didn't you wonder what happened to her when she was here?"

It was a blatant accusation of not caring enough, but Gwen let it roll off her back because she was grateful for Jeremy's candor—and for the fact that he seemed to have a genuine understanding of the situation and Scarlett's lifelong estrangement from her family. Not to mention her desire for privacy. He must have known her personally, and he must have known her well.

"We didn't even know she spent time in Alaska," Gwen explained. "We thought she went to New York that year. It was pure luck that we stumbled across the newspaper clipping and recognized her."

Jeremy sipped his whiskey. "It's a wonder no one picked up on that before now. I thought for sure when she won that first Oscar that the gossip magazines would be calling, but no one ever did."

"Amazing," Gwen said. "But it's a grainy photograph, and you're the main focus."

"Lucky for her." He sipped his whiskey again.

Gwen sat forward. "Yes, because she valued her privacy, especially at the end of her life."

His eyes narrowed. "You talk like you knew her, but judging by the look of you, you couldn't even have been born when she passed."

"You're right. I never met her, but I wish I had. My grandmother kept in touch with her over the years, but that was Valerie's only connection to Nova Scotia after she left. She never came home again. Are you aware that I'm the curator of the Scarlett Fontaine Museum in Nova

Scotia? It's in the house where Valerie grew up. I manage the collection, so I guess you could say I'm a bit of an expert on her life."

He laughed at that. "No, you're not. No one is."

Gwen felt a chill of unease. "But you must know *something*," she said. "You're the only person on record who knows about . . . let's just call it the lost year."

He smirked. "I do know a bit about that." He said nothing more, and she wondered if he was intentionally drawing out the suspense and taking some pleasure in it.

"Can you confirm that she had a baby here in Alaska?" Gwen asked.

Jeremy regarded her with ire, and she worried that she'd pushed too hard and too fast.

Finally, he nodded. "I can confirm it. But it wasn't Scarlett Fontaine who had the baby. It was Valerie McCarthy, a nice girl in a bad situation."

Gwen frowned. "How bad?"

He shook his head at her, as if she should know about this. "Her father was a tyrant. He sent her away to put her baby up for adoption and—"

"I do know about that," Gwen said, interrupting him. "That he was very strict."

Jeremy sipped his whiskey. "Based on what she told me, she had no one when she came here. No one who cared about her."

"Not even the father of her baby?" Gwen asked.

Jeremy shook his head morosely.

"So . . ." Gwen sat forward and rested her arms on the table. "You were close to her? She opened up to you?"

"I wouldn't say we were close," he replied, "but she was an honest person, and we had a lot in common."

Gwen found that difficult to believe, because Jeremy was—according to Douglas Warren, the museum curator—a petty thief and feared by half the town of Valdez.

"How did you become friends with her?" Gwen asked.

Jeremy stared into his glass and swirled the amber liquid around. "She worked with a girl who was . . . let's just say she was a friend of mine."

Gwen picked up her pen. "What was her name?"

"Angie," he replied. "She worked with Valerie in the dining room at the Wilderness Lodge. They got to be good friends."

"What was her last name?"

"Brown."

Gwen wrote that down as well, but when she looked up, Jeremy's eyes had darkened.

"I don't like that you're taking notes," he said. "People have a right to their privacy. I don't even know what I'm doing here. I almost didn't come because Valerie asked me to never talk about what happened in Valdez. She didn't want it getting in the way of her career. She knew it would change the way people looked at her."

"She was probably correct about that." In a move to alleviate Jeremy's concerns, Gwen set down her pen. "This is why I appreciate you agreeing to meet me. And please remember that I'm her family. What I really want to know is if her child is still out there somewhere. That would make him or her a relative of mine, and for that reason, I'm emotionally involved."

Jeremy offered no response, so she rambled on. "But there's more to it than that. Scarlett—I mean Valerie—was a wealthy woman when she died. I can't help but feel that any child of hers is entitled to a share of that fortune."

His eyes narrowed with skepticism. "That's generous of you."

Gwen stopped talking. She took a breath and closed her eyes. "I'm probably saying too much. I'm sorry." She paused, then opened her eyes. "This is just so surprising to me, and I'm very grateful that you agreed to talk to me. There's so much I want to ask you. I don't even know where to begin."

He rubbed the back of his neck. "What do you want to know?"

She thought about Peter's book—but mostly the museum displays and archives. What she truly wanted most was the whole story, every detail of Scarlett's year in Alaska. And of course, she wanted to know about the child's father. Who was he? And what happened between them?

"I guess we should start at the beginning," she said. "How did you meet Valerie, and what was her life like in Valdez? Was she happy there?"

Jeremy shifted in his chair and sat up a little straighter. "The first time I saw her was on the water," he explained. "She was working for a man named Blaine Wilson, who owned Wilderness Lodge and a tour boat that took tourists out to see whales and glaciers."

"Wilderness Lodge . . ." Gwen resisted the urge to write it down.

"It was her first day working on the boat, and I was out fishing. I passed them on the water and waved at the tourists." He seemed lost in thought for a moment. "But the first time I talked to her, I was hiding from Angie's husband, Joe, who was a cop. He had it out for me, but Valerie was a nice person. She didn't give me away, and that wasn't the only time she helped me and Angie out."

"Tell me more," Gwen said. "I'd like to hear how Valerie helped you. The both of you."

He swirled his whiskey around again. "There was one night when Joe and Angie had a fight, and I'll never forget it." He tipped his glass up and finished his drink, then signaled to Margie for another. He didn't wait for her to bring it. He launched straight into the whole story of Valerie's year in Alaska. But mostly, it was about Angie.

CHAPTER 14

Valdez
1963

Valerie had been waiting for the right moment to talk to Blaine about something. She wasn't sure how to begin, but she had to get it off her chest. After she finished loading cans of soda into the cooler on the boat, she found Blaine in the bridge, writing something in his notebook. He closed it and set down his pen when she walked in.

"I have a confession to make," she said. "I've been feeling guilty about it."

He cocked his head. "I'm listening."

She wet her lips. "I'm grateful to have a job here, and I'm happy. I feel very blessed."

He frowned a little. "But?"

"No buts," she replied. "I love it here. But I feel like you should know that . . ." She paused. "I wrote a letter to my ex-boyfriend."

"Back home," he said, just to clarify.

"Yes. I wrote to tell him about the baby and to let him know that I'm open to whatever he might want. If it turns out that he wants to be a part of this . . ." She paused again. "I might go home. As soon as possible."

Blaine stared at her intently. "Is that what you want to do?"

"Well . . . it depends on what he says. If he writes back and says he still loves me, then yes, I'd do whatever it took to go home and be with him. Except that I don't have any money, and I'd hate for you to be left in the lurch with no one to help out over the winter. I don't want to just quit on you."

Blaine kept his gaze fixed on hers, and she noticed the deep lines at the outer corners of his eyes. It made him seem old and wise, content with the life he had chosen. "Sometimes you have to do what's right for you," he said, "and not worry about what others think."

She thought about Drew—those blissful summer days in the forest, the joy of their songwriting—and her stomach clenched with regret. "I'm probably just dreaming anyway. I don't know what I was thinking, sending that letter. He already made it clear he didn't want to be with me."

The boat bobbed up and down on the gentle swells, and Blaine gazed out at the mountains across the water, the wispy clouds, in constant motion, casting rolling shadows on the jagged peaks.

"Everything will work out for you," he said. "You'll see." He looked her straight in the eye. "And no matter what happens with that young man, you'll have a home here with us for as long as you want it. And in my opinion, if he doesn't write back immediately and tell you to come home, then he's not good enough for you. You're a special person, and you deserve the best."

Blaine's words, kind and free of judgment, tempered the self-doubt she'd been wrestling with for weeks. All her life, really. She found herself wondering where she would be today if she'd had a father who said things like that to her.

"One day," Blaine said, "when you look back on all this, everything will make sense, and you'll be glad for this experience. But for now . . ." He stood up straighter. "You just have to follow your gut and do what feels right. If you decide to leave us, that's okay. It'll happen the way it's meant to, and you'll figure it out. Time has a way of making everything come clear."

~

That afternoon, after a midday tour, Valerie sat on the wide wooden deck at the lodge, watching the *Wanderer* bob up and down on angry swells at the dock. The wind had come out of nowhere in the past hour, and the Alaskan flag was whipping noisily at the top of the flagpole.

She couldn't stop thinking about a sea otter they'd seen on the tour, floating on her back and feeding her baby on her belly. The passengers had rushed to the side to take pictures.

Valerie thought of her own baby and wondered what it might feel like to cradle him or her on her belly in that way. Would they even let her hold her baby in the delivery room if she planned to give it up for adoption? How painful would that be?

With a knot of uncertainty in her belly, Valerie imagined her letter making its way to Drew in Nova Scotia. What would happen when he learned that he was going to be a father?

She had so many questions and doubts.

"It'll happen the way it's meant to, and you'll figure it out. Time has a way of making everything come clear."

She hoped Blaine was right about that.

A car pulled into the parking lot. It was only four o'clock, not yet time for dinner guests to arrive. Valerie rose from her chair, strolled to the rail, and saw Frank Brown getting out of his car. She had forgotten what a big man he was.

"Just the person I came to see!" he shouted. He crossed the lot and climbed the steps, then stood with his hand on the post.

"Here I am," she replied, not knowing what to expect from this visit. He hadn't checked up on her as he had promised. Not once since he had dropped her off.

"You doin' okay?" he asked.

"I'm fine—thank you."

He stared at her for a moment, squinting a little. "Do you have everything you need out here?"

"I do. The Wilsons have been wonderful."

"Good." He dug into his pocket, pulled out a crumpled ten-dollar bill, and handed it to her.

"What's this for?"

"It's from your father," he replied. "He wants to make sure you're taken care of."

She accepted the money and stared at it for a few seconds. "Great. Ten bucks will fix everything."

Frank turned and spit over the railing. "He said you were a handful."

"I beg your pardon?"

"You heard me," Frank replied. "Your father said you were out of control—that you needed some discipline to get you back in line. I wasn't sure about letting you come out here to stay, because the Wilsons can be soft, but I figured it was far enough out of town that you wouldn't get into trouble. At least not any *new* trouble."

Resisting the urge to talk back, Valerie slipped the ten-dollar bill into her coat pocket. "Thanks for the money. I'll save it for a rainy day."

"Plenty of those in Alaska," he said, "until the snow flies. So don't expect to be going anywhere over the winter. We'll be getting some mighty big storms. More snowfall here than any other city in the US."

"I've heard."

"Snowbanks taller than you are," he continued. "Big as a building."

"That's a lot of snow," she said flatly.

"You bet it is. So you best not be thinking about leaving anytime soon. Your father sent you here for a reason, and you know what that reason is. You can leave in the spring. Start over then."

Valerie frowned slightly. *Does he know something?* "I haven't made any travel plans."

Frank turned and started down the steps. "Good. Let's keep it that way. I'll be back next week to see how you're doing. Call if you need anything."

"Will do," she replied, feeling more than a little bothered by the visit.

~

The dining room was fully booked for a large private birthday party that evening, so Angie arrived early to help set up tables. When she walked in, Valerie was in the kitchen helping Henry peel potatoes.

"That's a lot of potatoes," Angie said. "Want some help?"

"That would be nice," Valerie replied.

Angie tied an apron around her waist and reached for a vegetable peeler.

"Did you mail the letter?" Valerie whispered as they stood at the worktable, their backs to Henry.

"I sent it first thing this morning." Angie finished peeling one potato and reached for another.

Valerie reached for another as well. "Did you tell Joe about it?"

"No." Angie glanced at her. "Why?"

"Because his father was here this afternoon."

"Frank?" Angie's brow furrowed with concern. "What did he say?"

"He came to give me ten dollars and ask how I was doing, but he made it very clear that I shouldn't think about leaving anytime soon. He talked about the snow, but the main message was that I had to stay here until the spring and follow through with my father's plan for me."

"To give up your baby," Angie quietly said, glancing over her shoulder to make sure Henry was out of earshot.

Valerie spoke softly as well. "It seems kind of coincidental that he would come out here to say that after I sent that letter with you yesterday, don't you think?"

Angie lowered the potato and peeler. "You think I snitched on you?"

Valerie shrugged. "I don't know. Are you sure you didn't tell Joe? Because he might have shared that information with Frank."

"I told you I didn't say anything. Even though he's my husband and I don't like keeping secrets from him." Angie began to peel faster and more aggressively.

Valerie stopped what she was doing and faced Angie, who was obviously offended. "I'm sorry. I didn't mean to imply anything."

"It sounds like you did," Angie said. After a moment, she stopped peeling and exhaled heavily, as if she was too tired to be angry. Turning to face Valerie, she whispered, "I swear I didn't tell him, and he doesn't know anything about you being pregnant. I just told him that you left a boyfriend back home and you were missing him. That's all."

Valerie reached for another potato. "Okay. I believe you. But maybe that was enough to worry Mr. Brown."

"It's possible."

Later, Valerie couldn't help but wonder if Blaine had been the one to say something to Mr. Brown. Perhaps they were in cahoots to keep her here until spring. Maybe she had to be more careful about whom she trusted.

CHAPTER 15

Half the town showed up to celebrate Carol Brown's fiftieth birthday at the community hall that weekend. Joe had taken a rare night off, and Angie had bought a new cocktail dress. It was sleeveless, light purple with shiny silver threads and a crew neckline. When they walked through the door, a live band was playing a Perry Como hit, and streamers fluttered from the ceiling.

Angie and Joe found Carol by the punch bowl, which was the centerpiece on a long table with sandwiches, cookies, and cakes. Carol wore a yellow chiffon party dress with a bow at the waistline and a bouffant hairstyle.

"You look lovely," Angie said as she kissed her mother-in-law on the cheek. "Happy birthday."

"Thank you," she replied. "And you look stunning."

Joe kissed his mother on the cheek and asked her to dance. Angie poured herself a glass of punch and barely had a chance to take three sips before a friend named Rob approached. "Hey, Angie. Want to dance?"

"Sure." She set her punch glass on the table and followed him onto the floor for a jive.

~

Later that evening, after speeches were delivered and the birthday cake was sliced and shared, Angie was ready to go home. The hall was clearing out, so she looked around for Joe. There were still a few small groups of men chatting along the wall, but her husband was not among them. She asked around, but no one had seen him, not even Frank or Carol. She ventured outside to cool off in the crisp evening air, and after a moment, she heard voices in the back parking lot and moved to the corner of the building.

There was Joe, standing in the dim light spilling out of one of the hall windows. He stood between two parked cars and spoke to a woman in soft tones. Angie squinted to get a better look and recognized Mrs. Lassiter, who worked as a schoolteacher at the high school. Mrs. Lassiter smiled, laughed, and laid her hand on Joe's chest. Then she pressed her body up against his. He made no attempt to push her away. Instead, he let her pin him up against the car, where they kissed.

Stunned and sickened by what she was seeing, all Angie could do was stand and stare. Joe drew back, opened the car door, and helped Mrs. Lassiter into the driver's seat. He shut the door, stepped aside, and watched her drive off.

When he finally turned and started back toward the hall entrance, he spotted Angie standing under the overhang.

Joe halted. "What are you doing out here?"

"Looking for you," she replied, fighting tears.

She waited for him to tell her that it wasn't what it looked like. Perhaps Mrs. Lassiter had had too much to drink and had come onto him and he was only trying to be polite and get her into her car. But shouldn't he have taken her keys away instead of kissing her?

Joe turned and started walking. "We should go home," he said.

Angie couldn't make her feet move, but it was no longer shock that held her to the spot. It was rage.

"That's it?" She threw her hands into the air. "That's all you're going to say to me?"

"Don't start, Angie. Not now. Let's just go."

"No!" she contended. "I want you to tell me what I just saw."

Joe stopped and turned. "You didn't see anything. Ellen just needed someone to walk her to her car."

"Oh, she's 'Ellen' now, is she? I saw you kiss her."

He shook his head. "I don't want to talk about this here." Joe wrapped his hand around Angie's elbow. "Come on."

She shook herself free. "I'm not going anywhere with you."

He grabbed her again and tried to hurry her toward the car while she fought to pry his hand off.

"Let go of me," she ground out and stumbled in her high-heeled shoes. Angie fell and skinned the heels of her hands on the pavement.

"Oh, God," Joe said, quickly bending to help her. "Are you okay?"

"Get away from me."

"Please, just get in the car," he said. "We'll go home, and I'll run you a bath."

"I don't want a bath. I want you to tell me what I saw."

Joe's face turned red. "It was nothing."

She scoffed as she got to her feet and brushed dirt from her knees. There were two big runs in her pantyhose. "Nothing?" She stood up straight. "That's all you have to say?"

"I don't know what else to tell you," he replied, "except that I'm sorry. She was flirting with me all night. Maybe you would have noticed if you weren't dancing with Rob half the time."

She scoffed. "I only danced with him when you were already dancing with someone else."

Angie strode quickly around the front of the building, where their car was parked on the street, but she ran past it toward the waterfront.

"Angie, wait!"

The tears on her face turned cold in the late-night chill, and she realized she didn't have her coat, but she didn't care. All she wanted was to get away from Joe and be alone.

"Don't follow me!" she shouted, but the next thing she heard was the sound of the car door slamming and the engine roaring to life. She didn't want Joe to find her and sweet-talk her into going home with him, so she hid behind a delivery truck.

Joe drove slowly past. As soon as he turned the corner, she started running again, down the street toward the waterfront, onto the city dock, past the Village Morgue Bar and warehouses, all the way to the small-boat harbor, where she finally collapsed on a bench, breathing heavily and weeping miserably.

It was a dark night with low clouds and no moon, and the black water was calm. Angie sat for a moment, staring at the ground and shivering in the cold until she forced herself to stop crying and wipe the tears from her cheeks.

She shouldn't be surprised. Joe was charming and flirtatious. Women found him irresistible, and naturally he took pleasure in that. He milked it for all it was worth.

But she couldn't bear the thought of him desiring other women. It was worse than ten knives in her heart. And truth be told, she'd always feared he would cheat someday. He'd been unfaithful in high school—at least once that she knew of. For a week Angie had watched him flirt with a new girl in town, and when Angie had learned that they'd made out at a house party she hadn't been invited to, she'd broken up with him. Just like that. No hesitation. The next week, he had come knocking on her door, groveling and apologizing, promising that it would never happen again. She had forgiven him and taken him back because she'd been heartbroken and crying into her pillow for days.

But tonight, Joe had broken that promise. Was this the first time? She wasn't sure. It didn't matter. The trust was gone now.

There was a sudden rustling in one of the boats, and she stood up to peer through the darkness.

"Angie?"

At the sound of her name, she let out a breath of relief. "Jeremy?"

He stepped out of his skiff onto the small dock and walked slowly, tentatively, toward her.

"Are you okay?" he asked.

"What are you doing here?" she replied, without answering his question.

"Sleeping."

"In your boat?"

"Yeah. Under the tarp. But what are *you* doing here? And why are you crying?"

She sank onto the bench again and covered her face with her hands. "I saw Joe kissing Mrs. Lassiter in the parking lot behind the dance, and when I told him what I saw, he said it was nothing. He tried to drag me home, and I fell down." She showed Jeremy her skinned knees and the runs in her pantyhose and burst into tears again. "The worst part of it is . . . I don't think this was the first time. It's just the first time I caught him."

Jeremy sat down beside her and gathered her into his arms. "Joe should know better. You're too good for him, Angie. You deserve better. I always thought so."

She fought to pull herself together and wiped the back of her hand across her wet cheek.

"But did you say Mrs. Lassiter?" Jeremy asked, confused.

"Yes!" she sobbed.

"But she's old."

"I know!" Angie replied. "She's at least forty!"

Jeremy sat back and clenched his hands into fists. "I could knock his block off for making you cry like this."

Angie reached for Jeremy's hand and urged him to unclasp his fist. "That wouldn't help. He's twice your size." She sat back. "It's such a double standard. He likes to flirt, but I'm not allowed to be friends with you because it makes him jealous."

"He's jealous of *me*?" Jeremy scratched his head. "I thought he hated me because I'm always getting into trouble."

"Well, that too," she replied. "And the fact that you give him the slip. He hates that."

Angie shivered in the cold. Jeremy shrugged out of his jacket and wrapped it around her shoulders. Warmth from his body still lingered in the sleeves, and she gathered the garment tightly around her.

The long beams of car headlights swung across McKinley Street. Angie and Jeremy watched in tense silence as the car turned onto the causeway that led to the dock.

Angie quickly stood. "It's him. If he finds you here with me, I don't know what he'll do."

Jeremy leaped off the bench and grabbed her hand. "Come on."

She ran with him down the steps to the small floating dock, where he helped her into his skiff.

"Lie down. That's it." Jeremy stood over her, watching the car move slowly along the dock. When it got close, he dropped to his hands and knees and lay down beside her. He drew the canvas tarp over them.

Quietly, they lay in the silence and darkness while the boat bobbed up and down on the gentle swells and bumped against the dock. Angie turned her head to look at Jeremy, but it was too dark to see his face. She could only feel his breath on her forehead while they listened to the sound of Joe's car moving past the warehouse. Jeremy held her hand until they heard the car turn around at the end of the dock and drive slowly back toward town.

The night grew quiet again. Jeremy sat up and tossed the tarp aside.

Angie's heart raced as she looked around. Staying low, Jeremy moved to the transom seat, and she sat at the bow, facing him.

"That's a pretty dress," he said. "You look nice tonight. Joe must have a few screws loose in his brain if he'd rather be kissing Mrs. Lassiter than you."

Angie chuckled, and it felt good to laugh. "You always know exactly what I need to hear."

She became aware that he was looking at her with adoration. It was almost palpable in the air between them, as if he had finally given up the necessity of hiding it. He wanted her to see it, perhaps even acknowledge it, but they had never shared any romantic feelings for each other or longings before. They'd always been just friends.

But that night, Angie found herself staring back at Jeremy and seeing him as a man. A man she could rely on.

Eventually, he lowered his gaze. "What are you going to do now?"

"I'm not sure," she said. "All I know is that the last thing I want to do is go home. He'll apologize, but I don't trust that he won't do it again. And I'm so angry with him right now I can't talk to him. I need time to cool off."

"I could take you out to the lodge for the night," Jeremy suggested. "Valerie would probably let you stay with her."

"Would you mind?"

"It would be my pleasure, madam." Jeremy got up, untied the skiff, and then returned to his seat and picked up the oars. "I'll take us out a bit before I start the motor."

Angie was grateful for Jeremy's experience with escape tactics around her husband. She watched him row through the darkness and listened to the sound of the oars dipping into the water as he steered them away from the dock.

When they reached a safe distance, Angie felt a rush of unease. "I hope he doesn't go looking for me at the lodge."

Jeremy pulled the oars in long steady strokes. "Even if he does, Valerie won't tell on you. She's good like that."

"How would you know?"

He shrugged. "I just do. That girl knows how to keep a secret. And she'll find a good place for you to hide if he does show up."

"Especially after she hears what happened."

Jeremy rowed for half a mile until they reached the middle of the bay, where a cold breeze swept across the water's surface. Angie drew her knees together and hugged herself. Within seconds Jeremy was reaching for a scarf and hat behind him. He leaned forward, handed them to her, and said, "Put these on. It'll get colder once I start the motor and we pick up speed."

"Thank you."

Angie wrapped the scarf around her neck and kept her eyes on Jeremy as he set the oars into the oarlocks, switched on the engine, and steered the skiff masterfully across the dark water. Angie sat at the bow, watching him with the wind in his hair and his hand on the rudder.

They moved fast toward Wilderness Lodge, leaving a frothy trail behind them.

~

"The light's still on in her room," Jeremy said as they tramped up the sloping lawn toward the lodge.

"But it's past midnight," Angie replied as she walked. "The main door might be locked."

"If it is, we'll throw pebbles at her window." Jeremy led the way up the wooden steps and turned the knob, and the door clicked open. "No need for pebbles," he whispered, standing back to let Angie enter first.

She walked into the large rustic lobby, dimly lit by a single lamp behind the reception desk. Feeling the need to tiptoe, she started off toward Valerie's room but soon realized that Jeremy wasn't following. She stopped and whispered, "Aren't you coming?"

He made a face and shook his head.

"Are you sure?"

"Yeah. I gotta go."

Disappointed, Angie hesitated. "All right. But I should give your coat back to you." She slipped out of it and handed it to him.

He raised it to his face and sniffed it. "It smells nicer now." He grinned at her. "You always smell nice, Angie."

She basked in the compliment. "Thank you. And I owe you for looking after me tonight."

"You know I'd do anything for you." He donned the coat and fastened the buttons. Then his expression grew solemn. "I mean that, Angie. I'd do anything. Just say the word. Whatever you need, I'm here."

She had never seen him look so serious before. "I appreciate it."

He didn't leave, and she felt rooted to the spot. Then she couldn't help herself. She dashed forward and threw her arms around his neck. "I don't know what I would ever do without you."

They clung to each other in the open doorway, and Angie was aware of Jeremy's chest pressing against hers, his heart pounding, her breath—and his—coming short.

When she finally stepped back, his brow was furrowed with sadness and confusion. Angie was instantly overcome with guilt because she knew how he felt about her. He loved her. He always had, and she'd always loved him in return. But not in the same way that she loved Joe.

She didn't want to toy with Jeremy's feelings. But she *did* love him. There was no one more dear to her than Jeremy.

"I should knock on Valerie's door," she said apologetically.

He nodded, turned, and strode outside. She closed the door behind him and moved to the window. Jeremy jogged lightly down to the dock and stepped nimbly into his skiff. She remained at the window, watching as he picked up the oars and began to row. Almost instantly, he melted into the darkness, so she turned and ran quietly to Valerie's room.

CHAPTER 16

Valdez
1963

Valerie was sitting on her bed in her nightgown, strumming one of her own original tunes on her guitar, when a knock sounded at the door. It was past midnight, and she wasn't expecting anyone. She was alone, and there were very few guests in the hotel. With a flood of unease, she set her instrument aside and called out, "Who is it?"

"It's Angie. Can I come in?"

Valerie leaped off the bed and answered the door. Angie stood in the corridor wearing a sparkly lavender cocktail dress, but everything else about her looked windblown and wild. "What are you doing here? Is everything okay?"

"Not really," Angie replied.

Valerie reached out and pulled her inside. "What happened?"

Angie went straight to the bed, sat down, and flopped onto her back. "It was Carol's birthday party tonight at the community hall, and Joe and I had a fight. Jeremy brought me here in his skiff."

"What kind of fight?" Valerie asked. "And I didn't think Jeremy was invited to the party."

"He wasn't." Angie sat up. "I ran down to the dock to get away from Joe, and there he was, sleeping in his boat."

Valerie let out a sigh. "Oh, gosh. Does he not have anywhere else to go? I thought he was living with his parents these days."

Angie slowly shook her head. "Those people are rotten to the core, so he's better off sleeping in his boat, as long as it's not below freezing outside. When the snow comes, he puts up with them, or sometimes he disappears for a while, finds work in Seward."

Valerie placed her guitar back in the case, lowered the lid, and fastened the latches. "What was your fight about? With Joe."

"I can hardly bear to talk about it," Angie said. "I suppose I should start with me not being able to find him at the dance, so I went outside for some air, and there he was in the back parking lot with a woman. She's a teacher from the school, and she's older. She was laughing and flirting with him and then . . ." She paused. "Joe kissed her."

Valerie sat down on the edge of the bed. "He didn't. What did you do?"

"I waited for her to leave," Angie replied. "Then I confronted him and told him what I saw, but he tried to make it sound like it was nothing." Tears filled Angie's eyes. "He didn't even seem to care that I was upset or hurt. He just wanted me to get in the car and not make a scene."

"Was he drunk?" Valerie asked with disbelief.

"Probably. He's always drinking, even in the middle of the day, but no one seems to notice. He hides it pretty well most of the time." Angie stood up, walked to the window, and moved the curtain aside to peer into the night.

Valerie got up and hugged her. Angie cried briefly, then recovered and wiped away her tears. "Part of me wants to leave him tonight. That's what he deserves if he can't be faithful." She sat down on the bed again. "But where would I go? To Arizona, I suppose, to live with my parents. But I'd hate to disappoint them. They were so proud when I got married, and they're excited about the baby."

"I'm sure they'd understand," Valerie replied. "They'd want you to be happy." Valerie moved to her dresser, found a clean pair of pajamas, and handed them to Angie. "Put these on. You can sleep here tonight and figure things out in the morning."

"Thank you." Angie went to the bathroom and got changed.

Later, after Valerie switched off the lamp, they lay on their backs, beside each other under the covers, staring at the ceiling.

"I don't know what I would have done if Jeremy hadn't been there," Angie said.

"He's a good friend to you," Valerie replied.

"Yes, but I think . . ." She paused. "Valerie, I think he loves me. As more than just a friend."

Valerie turned her head on the pillow. "Really?"

"Yes. But I've never been able to see him that way. To me, he's always been just a poor little lost boy."

"Do you still feel that way?" Valerie asked.

Angie continued to stare at the ceiling. "I'm not sure. Sometimes I feel like I'd die if he wasn't in my life. Maybe that's why Joe keeps going after him."

There was a strange quivering sensation, and the bed began to shake. Suddenly anxious, Valerie sat up, her gaze shooting to meet Angie's. "Are you doing that?"

Angie calmly tossed her arm up under her head. "No, but don't worry. It's just an earthquake. We get them all the time."

The bed continued to vibrate. Fighting the urge to rise and flee from the room, Valerie held on to the mattress for dear life. "An earthquake? Are you sure?"

"I'm positive."

Valerie's perfume bottles bounced like jumping beans on top of her dresser. The talcum powder tipped over and fell to the floor in a cloud of white dust. Valerie held her breath until the shaking finally stopped.

"See?" Angie casually said. "It's over now. It was just a tremor."

Valerie took a moment to calm her frazzled nerves, then lay back down. "That was scary. I'm never going to fall asleep now. I'll be tossing and turning all night."

"It's no big deal," Angie said. "You'll get used to it."

"I don't know about that." Valerie's heart pounded for another full minute before she got out of bed and cleaned the talcum powder on the floor.

~

Valerie woke slowly, her eyes fluttering open before she remembered that Angie had gotten into a fight with Joe the night before and slept in her room. She rolled over but found the bed empty.

"Angie?"

She received no reply, not even from the bathroom, so Valerie rose and dressed quickly and made her way to the kitchen, where Henry was cracking eggs over a skillet. "You're late," he said.

"Sorry. I forgot to set my alarm. Did you feel that earthquake last night?"

"I heard about it, but I must have slept through it."

"How could you sleep through an earthquake?" she asked.

He merely shrugged and beat the eggs.

"Have you seen Angie?" Valerie asked.

"Angie doesn't usually work the breakfast shift."

"I know, but . . . never mind. I'll be right back." Valerie hurried to the lobby, looked out the front windows, and finally spotted Angie sitting on an Adirondack chair, staring out at the water.

Valerie joined her in the next chair. "You're up."

"I couldn't sleep," Angie replied. "Joe's on his way to get me now."

The news came as a surprise. "Did you talk to him about what happened?"

"Not really," Angie explained. "I just called him and told him where I was, and I asked him to come and get me." She let out a sigh of defeat. "I don't know what to expect after this. All I know is that I love him and he's the father of my baby. So I have to go home."

A car rolled into the parking lot, and Angie rose to her feet. As soon as Joe got out, she ran across the veranda and down the steps and collided with him in a passionate embrace. He took her face in his hands and kissed her, then drew her close and hugged her tight, rocking back and forth.

Valerie couldn't make out what they were saying to each other, but it was obvious they were apologizing and groveling in equal measures.

Valerie hoped that what happened the night before was a onetime thing and Joe wouldn't hurt Angie like that again.

He helped Angie into the car, shut the door, and looked up at Valerie, who was watching from the deck. He did not wave or acknowledge her. He simply got into the driver's seat, started the engine, and sped off.

Valerie sat for a while in the fresh morning air. When she finally stood to go back inside, she spotted Jeremy in his skiff, floating far from shore. He must have also been watching when Angie ran into Joe's arms.

Jeremy waved, and Valerie waved back. Then he started his noisy outboard motor, spun the boat in a circle, and roared off toward Shoup Bay. Valerie watched until he disappeared.

If it was true—that he loved Angie—he was probably miserable right now. Valerie decided that the next time she saw him, she would try to be more friendly.

Little did she know that it would be many months before she saw him again, and by then, she would rarely be seeing anyone.

CHAPTER 17

Valdez
February 1964

Wilderness Lodge had closed for the winter season on January 3. On that day, Valerie had moved into the Wilsons' cozy little house on the hill, where Maud kept a fire burning constantly in the hearth. Valerie had her own room on the second floor, where she spent many hours during the long days of darkness with her guitar, writing music. Years later, she would look back on those days with fondness and an awareness of a creative awakening, where melodies and lyrics poured out of her like a waterfall.

When she first moved in with the Wilsons, she wrote love songs about yearning and unrequited love.

She wrote more letters to Drew as well, always waiting longingly for a reply, but nothing ever came for her. By late February, when her belly was large and round and she could feel her baby kicking at night—as if he or she were dancing to the music she strummed on her guitar—she finally began to let go of her romantic dreams of a happily ever after with the man she loved. Drew had not responded to any of her letters, so she forced herself to accept that he would not be a part of her life.

In time, his importance began to fade. He was no longer the center of her world. Visions of her future lay elsewhere, in the love she felt for her unborn child.

Sometimes she lay in bed at night singing to him or her, rubbing her fingers in tiny circles around her belly button, imagining what it would feel like to finally hold her baby in her arms and look into his or her sweet eyes, offer comfort when there were tears. Dreams like that, day after day, changed something in Valerie, and it was a deep, internal transformation. By mid-February, she felt older and wiser and possessed a fierce ambition to defy her father's plans for her and keep this baby and raise it, somehow, on her own.

Her music changed as well. Her melodies became less melancholy, and her lyrics evoked images of the natural world, the change of seasons, and an acceptance of life's beautiful rhythm and flow.

She wasn't sure what she would do with all this music she had written. Perhaps she could find a way to support herself and her baby as a songwriter—though she had no idea how to make that happen, not in Valdez, Alaska, so far from cultural centers, theaters, and recording studios. It was a world she knew very little about, but she was nothing if not driven. She wanted to keep her baby, so she had the will, and by God, she would find a way.

~

At the end of February, snow fell for three days straight. On the third day, a raging wind swept down from the peaks of the Chugach Mountains like a hungry beast. In its wake, it left snowdrifts fifteen feet high.

The Wilson house stood strong and sturdy in the storm, though at times it creaked and groaned like an old ship in a gale. The windows rattled constantly in the cold gusts until Valerie feared they might shatter and explode out of their casings.

They lost power one afternoon, so Blaine hauled an extra load of firewood on a sled from the stack out behind the house. Maud prepared cold ham sandwiches and opened a can of beans, which she heated on the woodstove. They ate by candlelight in the kitchen at dinnertime.

About eight o'clock, the wind finally began to die down. Valerie went to the front window. The night sky was visible in patches behind shifting clouds, and the moon cast a bluish light on the fresh, clean snow.

"I think the storm has passed," she said to Maud, who sat contentedly on the sofa with a small glass of brandy, her usual habit before bed.

Then something caught Valerie's attention, something at the lodge—a flash of light in one of the back windows. She squinted through the distance and saw it again. A beam of light sweeping across the glass.

"Is anyone expected at the lodge tonight?" she asked.

"No. Why?" Maud replied, sitting forward.

Valerie frowned as she tried to focus and wondered if she was imagining things. "There it is again. Someone must be inside. I saw a flashlight swinging around in the kitchen."

Maud called out, "Blaine! Someone's down at the lodge!" She stood up and joined Valerie at the window.

Blaine stumbled out of the bedroom in his bathrobe and slippers and stood at the top of the stairs. "What's that? Are you sure?"

"Yes. Look."

He flew down the staircase and opened the front door. "Good God, you're right. I better get down there. You might want to put the kettle on."

"Put the kettle on?" Valerie said. "What if it's a burglar?"

"In a storm like this? It's most likely someone needing help. My guess is it's Jeremy. Who knows how long he's been hiding out down there? He's probably starving and chilled to the bone. Might want to warm up some soup as well."

Blaine hurried back upstairs to dress. A moment later, he ventured out the front door with his snowshoes and a flashlight. As soon as he reached the lodge, the power came back on.

~

"Look who'll be joining us for dinner," Blaine said magnanimously as he kicked the snow off his boots and walked through the front door.

Jeremy followed behind him, and Maud hurried to help him remove his coat. "Look at you. You dear boy, out there in the cold. Your nose is redder than Rudolph's. Let's get you warmed up by the fire." She took his snow-covered, red woolen mittens and laid them on a chair.

"Thank you, Mrs. Wilson." He spoke sheepishly as he bent to pull off his boots. He hopped as he lost his balance on the braided rug, and no one said a word about his big toe sticking out of a hole in his sock.

Valerie watched all this from the kitchen. When Jeremy finally noticed her standing there, his gaze fell to her pregnant belly. He pondered it for a few seconds, then raised a hand to say hello. "Hi, Valerie."

"Hi," she replied and stepped back. "Why don't you come into the kitchen and have some soup? It's beef noodle. Nice and hot."

He rubbed his hands together and blew into them. "That's kind of you."

He said nothing about the size of her belly but kept his eyes downcast as he ambled into the kitchen and took a seat at the table. Maud set out a bowl and spoon.

Valerie carried the pot to the table and used the tin ladle to fill Jeremy's bowl. He looked up at the ceiling and all around the room—anywhere to avoid looking at her stomach, which was next to him at eye level.

Maud placed a thick slice of fresh bread on his plate. "Why didn't you come to the door, Jeremy? There's no heat in the lodge this time of year."

"I didn't want to bother you," he replied.

When Valerie returned the pot to the stove, Jeremy reached for the bread and bit off a large chunk. He spoke with his mouth full. "This is very kind of you, Mrs. Wilson." He picked up his spoon and tasted the soup. "Oh, my goodness. This is delicious. I've never tasted anything like it. It's the best soup I've ever had. You're a magician."

Valerie, Maud, and Blaine puttered in the kitchen to give him a moment's peace to devour the soup, which was probably the first hot meal he'd had in days. Maybe even weeks.

When he emptied the bowl, Valerie offered him some more. She returned to the table and ladled a second helping into his bowl.

"Where's your boat?" Maud asked.

He swallowed heartily. "It's sheltered under your dock. It's a great place to hide things, you know. If I were to steal a boat, or even a small car, that's where I'd hide it until the coast was clear."

Maud and Valerie exchanged glances. Valerie wasn't sure if Jeremy was ridiculously brazen or just daft for admitting something like that.

"We haven't seen you in a while," she said.

"I hitched a ride to Fairbanks in October," he explained. "I found work hauling garbage, but it was boring after a while, so I figured I'd come home for Christmas."

"Your parents must have been pleased to see you," Maud said hopefully.

He kept his head down and slurped his soup. "I suppose. I don't know, really."

When he finished eating, Valerie cleared off the table, and Blaine said, "We'll make a bed for you on the sofa, Jeremy. Next to the fire. You'll sleep here tonight."

"I don't want to put you out, Mr. Wilson."

"It's no bother," he said. "Tomorrow, you can help me shovel the driveway and split some wood."

Jeremy considered it. "I'd be happy to help you out with that."

"Good," Blaine replied. "Now it's late, so we should all get some sleep."

Valerie started toward the stairs. "Good night, everyone. I'll see you in the morning."

She went up to her room, but before she got undressed, she dragged a chair across the floor and wedged it under the doorknob.

~

It was bright and sunny the next morning, and the snow sparkled like diamonds. Valerie heard Maud and Blaine speaking softly in the kitchen, so she ventured downstairs and glanced into the living room as she passed. The bedding was folded neatly on the sofa, and there was no sign of Jeremy.

"Good morning," she said, smelling fresh coffee in the percolator. She moved to the cupboard, found her favorite mug, and poured herself a cup. "So . . . ?"

Maud threw her hands up in the air. "He's gone. He didn't even say thank you or goodbye, and he made off with Blaine's favorite shotgun."

Valerie whirled around in surprise. "He stole it? After we gave him supper and a warm bed to sleep in?"

Blaine held up a hand. "Now, now. We don't know that for sure. Maybe he just borrowed it."

"His boat's gone too," Maud added. "How much would you like to bet that he's pawning that gun as we speak? He commented on it once. Do you remember? That time we drove him into town. He admired the fresh coat of varnish on it, looked it over in detail, and said it must be a family heirloom."

"It is," Blaine said. "It belonged to my grandfather."

"And he took it?" Valerie said with disbelief.

They heard a noise out front, and all turned as the door swung open.

Jeremy walked in. He smiled brightly and held up a dead hare. "Look what I caught." They stared at him with mouths agape. "I rowed my boat down to that clearing beyond the grove of alders and followed his tracks into the hemlocks. He'll make a nice stew, Mrs. Wilson. I can clean him for you too, if you like, after I help Mr. Wilson split that wood."

Blaine moved to greet Jeremy. "My word. Look at this. Well done!" He patted Jeremy on the back and took a closer look at the snow-white hare.

"I hope you don't mind that I borrowed your gun," Jeremy said. "I know it's special to you, but it was early, and I didn't want to wake anyone. But I had a funny feeling that the animals would be out looking for food this morning after the storm."

"You were right about that," Blaine jauntily replied. "And it's not a problem at all. I'm glad you took the initiative." Blaine clapped his hands together with relish. "How about some breakfast? Maud was just about to cook up some eggs and toast."

Jeremy's eyebrows lifted. "Eggs would be nice if you have enough to spare."

"We have plenty," Maud replied with warmth. "Blaine will help you take care of that rabbit, and then you can get cleaned up."

Valerie and Maud returned to the kitchen and fetched the eggs and butter out of the fridge.

"I'm relieved," Maud said quietly. "And happy he didn't steal that gun. It would have been very disappointing."

Valerie nodded. "It's nice when people surprise you in a good way. It's so much better than the other way around."

"Agreed," Maud replied. "Now let's beat these eggs and get some hot food on the table. Jeremy deserves a good breakfast after bringing home some fresh meat for dinner."

~

After breakfast, Valerie stood at the kitchen sink with her hands in the soapy dishwater and grimaced from a persistent dull ache in her lower back. Deciding she couldn't continue with the washing, she dried her hands and massaged the muscles at her hips, then moved to the table and carefully sank onto a chair. Her ankles were swollen, and she felt like a whale.

Savoring a moment of rest, she placed her hand on her belly and found the firm bump of her baby's bottom, or perhaps it was the baby's head. He or she rolled over, and the sensation distracted Valerie from her discomforts and filled her with anticipation. She loved this sweet little soul that was growing inside of her, and she couldn't wait to welcome him or her into the world.

As it so often did during times of joy or sadness, music flooded into Valerie's heart. She began to sing softly as she ran her fingers over her belly. She sang a ballad she had written in October after seeing the northern lights for the first time. The whole world seemed full of magic that evening, but it wasn't the whole world. It was just Alaska.

A loud crack outside caused her to look up. She rose heavily from her chair and moved to the window, where she saw Jeremy out back under the shed overhang. He placed a thick log upright on the ground, gripped the long axe handle, swung it in a wide arc, and split the log in two. Valerie leaned forward to keep him in her sights as he bent to pick up one of the split pieces and swung the axe again.

Eventually, Valerie resumed her washing, but her attention remained fixed on Jeremy. She thought about how Angie had never been able to see him as anything other than a little lost boy who had been her friend since childhood—a boy who had been bullied and pushed around because he was smaller than the others.

He didn't look small to Valerie that morning. He looked strong and capable. He was a fighter—a scrappy one—with enough agility and street smarts to escape the daily wrath of Joe Brown. Surely that counted for something.

~

Another blizzard began that afternoon. It blew down from the mountaintops and gusted through the fjord. Blaine insisted that Jeremy stay another night and sleep on the sofa, but he had to be cajoled. He was reluctant to be a bother. In the end, it was the delicious aroma of fresh rabbit stew that convinced him to accept the invitation.

After dinner, Maud suggested a game of cards. They played crazy eights, and Jeremy won all three hands. Valerie wondered whether he was lucky or a skilled cheater. Either way, he was delighted with his success, like a child with a new bicycle on Christmas morning.

Later, when the hour grew late, Maud served cookies and milk by the fire. Then she and Blaine announced they were heading to bed.

"Can I keep the fire going awhile?" Jeremy asked as Blaine stood up.

"You split enough wood today to keep it going until Easter," he replied. "I think you've earned it."

Valerie stood up as well and followed Maud to the kitchen. "I'm going to take a glass of hot milk upstairs, if that's okay?"

"Of course, dear. Help yourself to anything, and make a cup for Jeremy too."

Maud said good night and left Valerie standing at the stove, waiting for the burner to heat up.

When the milk was warm, she poured it into two mugs and carried them to the living room, where Jeremy was adding another log to the fire.

"That's kind of you." He picked up his cup, blew lightly on it, and took a careful sip. "It's delicious. Hits the spot."

"I'm glad," Valerie replied. "Now I'm heading off to bed. I'll see you in the morning."

She turned to go, but Jeremy stood up. "Wait a second, Valerie. Angie said you play the guitar. Would you play me a song or two?"

Her lips parted with uncertainty. "It's kind of late. And I haven't been playing much the past few weeks." She laid her hand on her belly, hoping he'd understand what she was trying to say. "It's not easy to hold the guitar. My back's been bothering me."

He glanced down at her belly. "Is this why you came to Alaska?"

"Yes," she answered honestly. "My father sent me here."

Jeremy nodded. "I know what it's like to be kicked out. You might be looking at the world-record holder, right here before your eyes."

Valerie laughed, then covered her mouth with her hand. "I'm sorry. That's not funny."

He shrugged it off. "It's just the way things are." Jeremy sat back down on the sofa. "I was thinking about getting a dog for company, and I'm working on a cabin in the woods. I don't have any money for lumber, but I'm good at scrounging up stuff."

Good at stealing too, she thought but kept her lips zipped about that.

"Does Angie know about your baby?" he asked.

Valerie's ankles were swollen again, so she moved to the rocking chair with her cup of milk and carefully lowered herself onto it. "Yes, but she's the only one except for Frank and Carol Brown. I told her when we first started working together because I had to tell someone. I needed a friend."

"She's a good friend," he replied. "I'd trust her with my life."

"Would you?" Valerie replied. "Even though she's married to the lawman who wants to lock you up?"

Jeremy waved that off. "What Angie and I have is special. We tell each other everything, and we keep each other's secrets. I'd never betray her, not in a million years, and she knows that."

Valerie regarded him curiously in the firelight. "She thinks the world of you."

His eyebrows lifted. "Did she tell you that?"

"Not in those exact words," Valerie replied, "but I know she trusts you and thinks you're a good person."

He looked down at his milk. "She's about the only one in Valdez who thinks that. She and her mom, who was the best person I ever met. I was sad when they moved back to the Lower Forty-Eight."

Valerie remembered the story Angie had told her about Jeremy getting caught for stealing a candy stick. Angie's mother had said it was a gift.

They sipped their hot milk and watched the fire burn, listened to it snap and hiss in the grate.

"Do you intend to marry the father?" Jeremy asked. "Or is that a rude question?"

"It's not rude," Valerie replied, rocking back and forth in the chair. "And the answer is no, I don't think so. He won't talk to me."

Jeremy chewed on his lower lip. "Well, if he doesn't want to do right by you, you're probably better off without him."

Valerie smiled warmly. "That's what Blaine says. And Angie. I've been trying to convince myself of it for months."

"But you still love him?"

She nodded. "I probably always will, in a way. He was my first love."

Jeremy sat back and rested his arm along the back of the sofa. "We're in the same boat, I guess."

A log shifted in the grate and sent a flurry of sparks up the chimney.

"Because you love Angie?" Valerie asked bluntly.

"Always will," he replied. "Even though she's married to Joe, I'll never leave her. *Especially* because she's married to Joe." He sat forward. "I hope it doesn't come to blows between him and me one of these days, but it might if he keeps on breaking her heart."

"Come to blows?"

Jeremy shrugged and finished the last of his milk. "If I ever saw him cheating on her, I don't know what I'd do. But it would be something."

Valerie studied his expression. "Let's hope that doesn't happen. Maybe after the baby comes, he'll stay home more."

"I doubt that." Jeremy set his cup aside and changed the subject. "So what are you gonna do after your baby comes? Will you stay here or go home?"

Valerie tipped her head back and continued rocking. "My father expects me to put the baby up for adoption and start over. But if Drew—that's the father's name—wanted to be with me, I never would have agreed to come here. I would have wanted to keep the baby. But . . ." She paused and let out a breath of frustration. "I wrote letters to him, but he's never replied. And after I came here, I started to change my mind about adoption, even if I don't have Drew. I've come to realize that I can take care of myself, and I want to keep my baby and raise him myself."

Jeremy wagged his finger at her. "If you can get through a Valdez winter, you can get through anything."

Valerie chuckled and looked at the window, where snow was piling up on the sill outside. "Being here has been good for me. There's so much beauty, even when we're buried in snow or there's only four hours of daylight. I've been happy here, and I've been able to focus on my music and getting ready for the baby. And Blaine and Maud have been incredibly supportive. Everything feels so right and comfortable here. I feel safe."

"Does that mean you're going to stay?" Jeremy asked.

Valerie experienced a feeling of weightlessness, as if the burden of the past was falling away. "I think so, yes. Maud and Blaine have agreed to keep me on at the lodge if that's what I want."

"It sounds like you have it all figured out," Jeremy said.

Valerie rubbed her belly and wondered what the future might hold. "It appears that way."

"Angie would be happy if you stayed," he added. "Your babies could be best friends."

Valerie smiled. "Wouldn't that be nice."

Jeremy moved to attend to the fire. He knelt, picked up the poker, and prodded a burning log to allow more oxygen to flow. The flames grew bright and lively and danced in the hearth.

"I suppose I should say good night now," Valerie said with a yawn.

Jeremy rose to his feet. "Thank you for the milk."

"You're welcome. And I enjoyed our chat."

She climbed the stairs, dressed for bed, and fell asleep to the sound of the wind singing through the snow-covered hemlocks.

~

When Valerie woke the next morning, she decided she would ask Blaine if he could offer Jeremy a regular job at Wilderness Lodge when the tourists returned. But when she walked into the kitchen and saw him and Maud eating breakfast alone, she knew. A brief glance at the sofa in the living room confirmed it. Jeremy had left.

"Did he say goodbye?" she asked.

Blaine shook his head. "That's not really his style."

"You're sure he didn't go hunting again?" She was surprised by how bereft she felt.

"His boots are gone, and the gun's still here. I don't expect we'll see him again. Maybe not even until the spring thaw."

Valerie was on the verge of tears. "But where will he go? Back to his parents' house? They don't treat him well. You know that, don't you?"

"We do. Maybe that's why he never likes to stay in one place for long. He has a hard time getting comfortable and settling in. He doesn't trust happiness, I suppose."

"If only he could meet a nice girl and settle down," Maud said. "I feel like that could be the making of him."

Valerie moved to serve herself some breakfast and wondered if Maud was suggesting that *she* might be that person—that she and Jeremy could somehow build a life together.

After pouring a glass of apple juice, she sat down at the table. It was a lovely thought but simply not possible. Jeremy was in love with Angie, and no matter how hard Valerie tried to tell herself she was over Drew, she wasn't sure she ever would be. She still dreamed of him, and every love song she wrote was about her love for him. Or the loss of him.

CHAPTER 18

Valdez
1964

Valerie stood at the end of the dock and watched wispy clouds float across the sky. It was nearly the end of March—a glorious time of year in Alaska, for it brought the return of the light. The sun rose at seven thirty, and dusk held off until nine o'clock at night. The extra hours of sunshine melted the snow, and enormous drifts were shrinking. Pleasure boats headed out for the first time since the fall. Soon, Wilderness Lodge would be open for the summer season, and by then Valerie would have delivered her baby. She would eventually be able to work evenings in the dining room and begin to navigate this new life.

Closing her eyes, she listened for the music of Valdez—waves lapping up against the rocks along the shoreline, a spring breeze whispering through the hemlocks, and the forest dripping constantly after a heavy spring rain.

Footsteps thumped on the wooden planks of the dock behind her. She turned and saw Blaine approaching, his hands in the pockets of his navy-blue parka.

"Beautiful morning," he said. "How would you like to take a ride into town with me and visit Angie?"

Valerie no longer felt that she was in hiding. She had decided weeks ago that she was here to stay. Soon, she would get to know the people of Valdez, and they would get to know her and her baby.

Her heart quickened with excitement. "Did she call?"

"Yes," Blaine replied. "She's home from the hospital and wants to introduce you to her little one. She asked if you could come by for lunch today."

Valerie was very near to her own due date and eager to talk to Angie about her labor and delivery.

"I'd love that. You won't mind driving me?"

"I have errands to run, which should take an hour or so. I'll drop you off and pick you up afterward."

"That sounds wonderful," Valerie said. "I'll get ready now."

~

"His name is Ethan."

Angie carefully passed her tiny newborn to Valerie, whose heart melted with love and anticipation for the moment when she would hold her own baby, just like this. "He's so precious." She tucked the blanket around him snugly.

"Isn't he? I can't believe how much I love him. I never imagined how strong the feelings would be. I'm completely infatuated."

Valerie swayed and bobbed at the knees, knowing instinctively how to soothe little Ethan when he fussed. "Aren't you a special little boy," she cooed. "So handsome. And smart. I can tell. You must take after your brilliant mommy."

Angie laughed. "Oh, stop."

Valerie met Angie's gaze and continued to bob at the knees. "I'm so happy for you."

Angie took a seat on the sofa and watched Valerie pace around the room with Ethan. "It'll be your turn soon."

"Yes. How was the labor?"

Angie made a face. "It seemed to go on forever, but now that it's over, it feels like nothing. You know how when you wake up in the morning and you remember a dream—then it fades from memory as the day goes on? It's like that. It doesn't matter at all, and all I want to do is have another one."

Valerie laughed. "You've found your calling?"

"Maybe so," Angie replied.

Ethan began to squirm in Valerie's arms, so she sat down on the sofa and handed him to Angie. "Maybe he's hungry?"

"I doubt it. I just gave him a bottle before you came. Maybe it's gas." Angie raised him over her shoulder and patted him gently on the back until he let out a loud, gurgled burp.

Valerie and Angie laughed.

"Well done." Angie turned him in her arms and cradled him on her lap. "How clever you are."

"That was the cutest burp I've ever heard." Valerie offered her finger to Ethan, and he gripped it tightly. "He's amazing."

"Yes," Angie replied. She kissed each of his soft cheeks.

Valerie sat back. "What does Joe think? He must be proud."

"Proud as a peacock, giving out cigars at the station as soon as the doctor told him it was a boy."

"He wasn't at the hospital with you?"

"No, he was working a shift. But it was fine. We talked about it beforehand. He hates hospitals, so I told him he didn't have to hang around in the waiting room." Angie ran her thumb lightly over Ethan's forehead. "He looks tired. I think I'll put him in his crib. Come and see his pretty mobile. It arrived last week, just in time."

Valerie rose from the sofa and followed Angie to the nursery. It was painted yellow with a wallpaper border and teddy bears on a red checkered background.

Angie bent to lay Ethan in the crib. She spun the mobile: more teddy bears on a train, going round and round. "Isn't it adorable?"

"Gorgeous," Valerie replied.

Angie sang a lullaby until Ethan drifted off. Then they backed away from the crib and tiptoed out of the room.

"How long will he sleep?" Valerie asked.

"At least an hour. Maybe more," Angie replied. "But Joe thinks I shouldn't let him sleep so much in the day."

"Why not?"

"Because the past two nights he woke up and cried to be fed, and it was exhausting. For Joe, at least, because he had to get up early for work. It doesn't bother me so much because I can sleep when Ethan does. That's what my mother told me to do."

"Maybe you should be sleeping now?" Valerie asked.

She linked her arm through Valerie's. "Not a chance. I haven't seen you in a dog's age, and there's so much to talk about. Come to the kitchen. I'll make tea."

She filled the kettle at the sink and turned on the stove, then dropped a couple of tea bags into the teapot. While they waited for the water to boil, Angie sat down at the table across from Valerie.

"I don't suppose you've heard from Drew?"

"Not a word. I finally gave up writing to him. I haven't written a letter in three months."

Angie sat back. "Are you okay? I remember how hopeful you were."

With a sigh of resignation, Valerie dropped her gaze to her lap. "I try to forget about him. But then at night I dream about him coming here and being a father to our child. It's difficult." Valerie fought to control her emotions. "I had to force myself to stop living for the mail delivery and just get on with my life, get through each day without feeling like someone died. Blaine and Maud have been wonderful. They're like a new set of parents. I love them, and I couldn't have gotten through any of this without them."

"They're good people," Angie replied.

"Yes, and they told me that after I have my baby, I can stay on and work at the lodge. Maud is willing to babysit in the evenings."

"That sounds ideal," Angie said. "But how do you feel about that? Your father won't be pleased."

"No, but I'm a grown woman. I can make my own decisions. Besides, he's not here. He can't force me to give up my baby."

"Have you spoken to him at all?"

"No. I think he's pretending I don't exist until I come home with all of this behind me, as if it never happened. I can see it now. He'll pick me up at the airport, and we won't speak a word about it. Ever."

Angie squeezed Valerie's hand.

A sense of calm settled over Valerie. "So there it is. Decision made. I'm going to keep my baby. There's no way in the world I could give him up—or her—especially after holding Ethan. Besides that, I love Alaska. I love going out on the tour boat and visiting the glaciers and teaching the tourists about the birds and whales and bears. I even love the snowstorms, and I don't mind the extra hours of darkness during the winter. I thought I would, but I wrote a ton of new music during that time. And the northern lights . . . I swear, it's like looking into the face of God. I wept the first time. I've never felt so inspired. And the love I feel for this sweet person in my belly helps ease my heartache over Drew. I'll be all right on my own, and I can't wait to be a mother."

Angie smiled. "You're going to be great at it."

"I hope so."

Joe arrived home, walked into the kitchen, and looked at Valerie with surprise. "I didn't know you were coming by."

He knew about the baby she was expecting. He had visited Blaine and Maud a few times, in recent months, to check on her. Always on behalf of his father.

"Blaine dropped me off," she explained. "I wanted to see Ethan. Congratulations. He's a beautiful baby."

Joe approached Angie, bent forward, and kissed her on the cheek. "Takes after his mother."

She smiled with an air of pleasure and watched Joe move to the fridge to get a beer. He used a bottle opener to snap off the cap, then leaned against the counter and took a swig.

"Are you sure you should be in town?" he asked Valerie. "I thought your dad wanted you to . . . you know." He paused, searching for the right words. "Keep things under wraps."

Valerie folded both hands over her belly. "Plans change sometimes."

"How so?"

She sat forward. "I just finished telling Angie that I've decided to stay in Valdez and raise my child here. So it won't be a secret much longer. I'll be coming out of hiding."

Joe frowned. "But your father already made arrangements for you to go home. And my father gave him his word. He promised he'd take you to the airport next month. I think the flight's already been purchased."

"I'm not going anywhere without my baby," she said.

Joe simply stared at her.

"I'm sorry about the plane ticket," she added, "but that's between my father and yours to work out if your dad paid for it."

"He won't be pleased," Joe replied. "Especially after he spent the past seven months making sure you were taken care of and providing for you."

Valerie gave him a cynical look. "That's a bit of an exaggeration. All he did was dump me on Blaine and Maud." But then she paused and considered Joe's reasoning. Something clicked in her mind suddenly as she began to understand.

"I think I'm getting it now," she said. "My father must have been sending money to your father to pay for my room and board. Was that the arrangement?"

Joe sipped his beer. "I have no idea."

Valerie narrowed her eyes and studied his expression.

Angie looked at him with disappointment. "Is that true, Joe? Were your parents taking money from Valerie's father? Is that why they got that new car?"

Joe held up a hand and spoke defensively. "Hey. I don't know what kind of arrangement they had. I only know that you're getting on a plane back to Nova Scotia next month. You will if you know what's good for you."

Valerie laughed defiantly. "You can't force me."

He bowed his head. "I'm sorry. That came out wrong. I just mean that the world isn't kind to single mothers. You should be thinking about your kid. What kind of life is he going to have, and how are you going to support him? Your father certainly won't help you, not if you disrespect his wishes. You have no family here. If you have that baby, you'll be up shit creek."

"I have Maud and Blaine," she argued.

"Oh, sure. They're helpful now, when you're working at the lodge. But they're not your family, and they're not going to take responsibility for you and that baby for the next eighteen years. You can't depend on them for that."

"I can depend on myself," she maintained.

He shook his head mockingly. "Sure. A single mother with no education. No husband. You'll do just great."

"Joe!" Angie said, scolding him.

He downed the rest of his beer and set the empty bottle on the table. "I'm just being realistic. You ought to give it some more thought, Valerie, and consider what you'll be giving up—a proper future where you can go to college, find a husband, and make your father proud. Why wouldn't you want that? And with all due respect, you're taking a lot for granted—like how fortunate you are to have a father who would pay for you to come here and let you go home with a clean slate."

Valerie watched him walk to the door and don his jacket. "I honestly don't think you care what I do with my life," she said. "I think you just want the money my father promised in exchange for my return next month—without my baby."

Angie sat forward. "Joe, tell me. Is it true? Because I never understood why you were always asking about Valerie. I was starting to think you had a thing for her, which wouldn't have been a big shock. You like other women."

"Please don't start that again, Angie," he said. "I've been making changes, and you know it."

"Do I?" Tears glistened in her eyes. "I'm not stupid. When I was in the hospital giving birth to your son, I know you were out gallivanting. I smelled the perfume on you when you came to the hospital—drunk."

He pinched his forehead, aggravated. "I wasn't out gallivanting. I was with my mother." He went to the door but stopped. "And you're a fine one to talk, going to the lodge with Jeremy that night after my mom's party and not coming home at all. He's obviously in love with you, but you won't see it, and you keep encouraging him." Joe opened the door. "I don't have time for this foolishness now. I need to get back to work. I'll see you at supper." He walked out.

Valerie sat in silence while Angie leaped to her feet and ran to the front window to watch. Joe got into his police cruiser and pulled out of the driveway. As soon as he was gone, Angie sank to her knees on the floor and gave in to her tears.

"Oh, Angie." Valerie knelt beside her and pulled her into her arms. "Everything's going to be okay."

"No, it's not," Angie replied, crying on Valerie's shoulder. "He says I shouldn't be friends with Jeremy, but he flirts with other women all the time. And I think he's sleeping with that schoolteacher. Sometimes I feel people whispering behind my back on the street. It's embarrassing. There are days I just want to take Ethan and leave this town."

Valerie sat back on her heels and wiped the tears from Angie's cheek. "Where would you go?"

"To my parents in Arizona. But I don't want to disappoint them. They've been through so much already, after Shana died. I just wanted to make them proud and happy, and Joe seemed like the best catch in Valdez. He was so handsome and popular in school. But I know he cheats on me, and I'm miserable."

Not knowing what to say to make Angie feel better, Valerie pulled her into her arms again. "It'll be all right," she said. "I'll help you. Whatever you need, I'm here."

Angie's body shuddered as she cried. Then she fought to recover and sat back, wiping furiously at her wet cheeks. "Remember when we talked about going to Hollywood and becoming famous? I used to dream about that all the time—about leaving Joe and making him regret looking at other women. He'd see me in the movies, and I'd be rich and famous, like Marilyn Monroe. I'd dye my hair blonde and everything. But now I have Ethan, and all I want is to be his mother."

The sound of Ethan's cries from the nursery brought Angie to her feet. "He's hungry."

Valerie was slower to rise and cupped her belly with her left arm while she pushed off the coffee table.

A moment later, she found Angie in the nursery, pacing slowly about while she cradled Ethan in her arms. "Someone needs to be changed," she said in a singsong voice.

To Valerie, the change in Angie was like night and day. Suddenly she was joyful and spellbound by her baby. She kissed him on the nose and cheeks.

Valerie watched while Angie changed Ethan's diaper. She imagined doing the same thing herself in a week or two. The baby kicked inside her belly just then, reading her thoughts, perhaps.

By now, Ethan had a clean diaper, but he continued to fuss.

"I need to warm up a bottle," Angie said. "Let's go to the kitchen."

Valerie followed and helped her fill a pot with water and set it on the stove.

"I have a bottle ready in the fridge," Angie said morosely, her voice trembling as if she were on the verge of tears again.

"Blaine is coming to get me soon," Valerie said. "But I hate to leave you like this. Maybe you could come with us. Maud would love to meet Ethan. That would cheer you up, wouldn't it?"

Angie set the bottle in the pot of water. Then she backed away and sat down on a chair at the table. "Joe will think I'm mad at him."

"You could leave a note and tell him what I just said—that Maud is dying to meet Ethan. Then you and I can talk more about all this."

Angie looked down at Ethan in her arms. "What's even left to talk about? Joe is my husband, and this is my home. I don't have any money of my own, so I can't leave him, even if I wanted to. Which I don't. I love him. I just wish I knew how to get him to stop flirting with other women. He always denies it and tells me I'm imagining things. He refuses to see how much it hurts me. Sometimes I think he needs to face the possibility of losing me before he'll smarten up."

"Maybe that's true," Valerie agreed.

Angie thought about it and spoke with resolve. "I'll take a frozen dinner out of the freezer for him. He can warm it in the oven."

"That's the spirit." Blaine's car pulled into the driveway, and Valerie went to the door to let him know that she and Angie were both coming back to the lodge with him.

CHAPTER 19

"I've been thinking about something," Valerie said to Angie as they walked into the Wilsons' kitchen.

"What's that?"

Strolling to the sink, Valerie looked out the window. The tidy woodpile reminded her of the morning when Jeremy had split wood and she had stood with her hands in the soapy water, watching him and seeing him in a new light. He hadn't come around in a while, and she hoped he was okay, wherever he was.

"Valerie?" Angie asked.

She jumped and turned, pushing thoughts of Jeremy from her mind. "Yes. I was going to say . . . all those letters I wrote to Drew . . . I never received a reply, but now I'm wondering if Joe's mother intercepted them. Carol is the postmistress. She sees everything that comes and goes out of Valdez. If she and Frank wanted me to stay here and do what my father wanted, she would have had reason to prevent me from contacting Drew. Do you think that's possible?"

Angie raised an eyebrow. "I wouldn't put it past her. She'd do anything for a new dress or a flashy car. I always wondered how they paid for that big birthday party at the hall."

Valerie moved to the table and sank onto a chair. "If that's true, it means that Drew might not even know I'm having his baby. He didn't know when I got on the plane to come here. As far as he's aware, I dropped off the face of the earth, and heaven knows what my father said to him if he ever came looking for me. He probably told Drew that I'd gone off to college abroad." Valerie felt a wave of frustration, but it was followed quickly by excitement at the possibility of changed circumstances. "What if he doesn't even know?"

"It's possible," Angie replied, "but please don't get your hopes up. If I've learned one thing lately, it's that men are rats. We can't depend on them." She paused. "I hate all of them. I think you and I should figure out a way to leave here together and go straight to Hollywood."

Valerie rested her hand on her belly. "That sounds like fun, but I can't let myself believe that all men are bad. Some are wonderful. Look at Blaine."

Angie let out a strange, weepy laugh and spoke apologetically. "I know. Oh, listen to me. I'm just angry with Joe. And maybe he's right. Maybe I'm imagining everything because of what I saw that night after Carol's party. Maybe I'm crazy."

"You're not crazy," Valerie said. "You saw him kiss another woman."

"Yes, but maybe that happened because he's so charming and handsome and women throw themselves at him. That's not *his* fault, and I know he loves me."

Valerie flicked her hair out of her eyes. "Even so, he needs to understand how he's hurting you. And if he can't . . . well, there's always Arizona."

Angie gave her a grudging nod. "At least I have you and Jeremy to depend on. You know—the former juvenile delinquent who steals power tools out of the mayor's shed?"

Valerie chuckled softly. "At least he's clever enough to get away with it, and he gives to those in need."

"A modern-day Robin Hood," Angie replied, rolling her eyes at the absurdity of it all.

Valerie sat back and watched Ethan kick his little legs under the flannel blanket. "How can I get a letter out of Valdez?" she asked. "Past all of Carol Brown's checkpoints."

Angie spoke lightly, as if it were no problem. "That's easy. You just need to give it to one of the men on the *Chena* next time it comes in. Any one of them would be happy to post it at the next port or when they return to Seattle."

"Brilliant," Valerie said. "That's exactly what I'll do. When is the *Chena* in town again?"

"They're due on the twenty-seventh, but that's Good Friday, so I'm not sure."

Valerie rubbed her hand over her belly. "I'll ask Blaine to find out, and then I'm going to try one more time. Just one more letter. And I swear if that doesn't work, I'll give up on Drew forever."

Angie's expression softened. "It won't be so hard once you hold your baby in your arms. Your heart will be so full of love the world will feel absolutely perfect." Her eyes grew wet. "Even when your head knows it isn't."

~

The phone rang at 5:15, and it was Joe asking for Angie. Maud answered and immediately gushed about baby Ethan. She kept him talking for at least five minutes before she handed the phone to Angie with a look of encouragement.

"Hello?" Angie faced the wall and spoke softly. "Yes, I know. It was spontaneous, but I wanted to visit Maud." She paused. "No, it wasn't about that. I just wanted to get out of the house." She twirled the phone cord around her finger. "Okay. Yes. I'll see you later."

She hung up and turned to meet Valerie's sympathetic gaze. "He's coming to get me at six. He said he wants to help me give Ethan a bath tonight. He refuses to change a diaper, so maybe he's feeling guilty about calling me foolish."

Maud watched Angie with understanding. "Don't hesitate to call us if you ever need anything."

"I appreciate that," Angie replied, "but I'm sure everything is going to be fine. Sometimes Joe and I just get under each other's skin, but we always manage to work it out."

~

The following day, Valerie woke at five thirty in the morning with a deep cramp in her belly. It didn't last long, but it was concerning, so she tossed the covers aside and swung her legs to the floor. She needed to use the bathroom, but it was chilly in the house, and the thought of leaving her warm bed made her want to crawl back under the covers until July. Unfortunately, her bladder was ready to burst, so she forced herself to push up off the mattress and pad across the plank floor.

Out in the hall, she paused at the top of the stairs, and suddenly there was a *splat*. She looked down at a puddle on the floor, between her bare feet, and realized her water had broken.

Valerie's heart began to race with trepidation, yet she was excited at the same time. It was happening. Today was the day.

"Maud?"

There was a squeaking of bedsprings, then a tapping of footsteps in the downstairs bedroom. Maud, while pulling on her terry cloth bathrobe, reached the bottom of the stairs and looked up. "What is it?"

"I think I'm in labor," Valerie said.

Maud's eyebrows lifted, and she laid a hand over her heart. "Are you sure?"

"Yes. My water just broke. I need a towel to wipe up the mess."

Maud quickly tied the belt on her robe. "Don't worry about that, sweetheart. I'll call the midwife. But should I call anyone else? What about your father?"

Valerie quickly shook her head. "No, please don't do that. And don't tell anyone else either, not even Angie, because I don't want to give up this baby. The last person I want to know about this is Frank Brown."

"You have my word. No one will know until you're ready. Except the midwife. We can't do without her."

Another labor pain squeezed at Valerie's insides, and she winced as she bent forward. Maud quickly turned and ran to the phone in the kitchen.

CHAPTER 20

Four hours later, Valerie lay in bed with her newborn child, spellbound as she hummed a pretty lullaby. Her body was weak with exhaustion from the labor, though it had progressed quickly and had been over in less than two hours. Afterward, the midwife had told Valerie that she'd been blessed with a body built for childbirth, as it was one of the easiest deliveries she could recall in recent years, especially from a first-time mother.

Valerie took it as a compliment. Now she was alone with her little one, a beautiful son she named Cameron. Cam for short. He had glassy eyes, a straight nose, and pudgy, long legs that would one day carry him into school on his first day. Or perhaps onto a soccer field.

She was thrilled at the thought of their future together, a whole life of new discoveries and love and affection. His hands were ever so small, and his fingers were long. She wondered if he had inherited her love of music. Perhaps he might become a piano player. She would probably teach him how to play guitar and read sheet music as soon as he was old enough, if he was interested. She certainly wasn't going to pressure him into doing things that didn't appeal to him. She wouldn't be like her father, controlling in that way.

As for a father figure, Blaine had expressed a desire to show him how to dribble a basketball. Maud couldn't wait to have him help her out in the kitchen as soon as he could walk. She would let him lick the bowl when she baked a cake.

They were lovely thoughts and dreams, and Valerie was awestruck by the notion that she had created a whole new person with her blood running through his little veins, feeding into his miniature heart. His flesh was her flesh, his bones had formed and grown inside her womb, and in this moment, he was completely dependent on her for his survival—for sustenance and love.

She couldn't wait to give him everything. She would treasure him and protect him, and she would love him forever.

~

That evening, a knock sounded on Valerie's bedroom door. Maud peered in to find Valerie on her feet with Cameron in her arms. His head rested on her shoulder while she slow danced with him and hummed "Moon River."

"We have a visitor," Maud said.

Valerie jolted with panic. She was constantly afraid that Frank Brown was going to burst through the door any moment and snatch her baby from her arms. "I thought we weren't going to tell anyone. Who is it?"

"It's only Jeremy," Maud replied. "He came with a cooler full of fresh trout. Lord knows where he got it. Blaine didn't see a fishing rod in his skiff. But we accepted the gift nonetheless, and Blaine is about to fry some up on the stove. Would you like to come down?"

Valerie considered it. "I'm still quite tired. I don't feel like getting dressed, but you could send Jeremy up. I'd like to see him, and this little man needs to be presented to at least one visitor on his first day in the world."

Maud smiled and backed out of the room. A moment later, Valerie heard Jeremy's footsteps up the stairs. He appeared in her open doorway and stood speechless. He wore a thick blue knit fisherman sweater and faded blue jeans with heavy wool socks.

Valerie wore a white cotton nightgown and blue bathrobe. She stood on the oval rug, uninhibited by her state of dress, and smiled at him.

"Hi," she said. "You must have a sixth sense. How did you know today was the right day for a visit?"

He entered her room tentatively, moved closer, and stared at Cameron with a mixture of apprehension and enchantment. "He's so tiny. I've never seen a newborn baby before."

Jeremy reached out, touched Cameron's soft head, and patted him like he would pat a kitten.

"How are you feeling?" he asked.

"Good," Valerie replied blithely. "Better than good. It's been a wonderful day. I'm so happy."

"You deserve to be happy," Jeremy said, "because you're a good person."

She could have wept at the compliment. Everything was making her feel weepy today, but it was joyful, not sad.

"Thank you." She shifted Cameron in her arms. "Would you like to hold him?"

Jeremy took a step back. "I don't know about that. I've never held a baby before."

"There's a first time for everything. Why don't you have a seat over there, and I'll pass him to you." She gestured toward the wooden chair against the wall.

Jeremy crossed to it and sat down. "What if he cries?"

"He probably won't. He's sleepy. But if he does, I'll take him." She bent to place her precious boy in Jeremy's waiting arms. He cradled Cameron gently and looked down at him with reverence.

"He's a miracle," Jeremy said. "Look at his hands. They're so small."

Valerie's heart was fully open. Her soul was content. "If you place your finger in his palm, he'll grab on to it. It's called the grasp reflex."

Jeremy gave it a try, and his eyes filled with laughter as Cameron took hold. "He likes me."

"He does."

She stood back and watched Jeremy interact with Cameron. She felt strangely buoyant. Life in that moment was pure rapture.

"I'd like to be a dad someday," Jeremy said, looking up at her.

"You'd be a good one."

His shoulders rose and fell with a sigh. "I wish Angie would come away with me. I'd treat her better than Joe, and I'd look after Ethan too. I'd get a job in Juneau, and I'd keep it."

Valerie didn't know what to say to Jeremy about that. She agreed with him, of course, that Joe didn't treat Angie well, but Valerie was quite certain that he would have to do a whole lot worse before Angie would ever leave him.

Cameron began to fuss, so Valerie took him from Jeremy. She bobbed up and down at the knees and rocked him in her arms until he settled. "I think he's sleepy."

She moved across the room, laid him in his cradle, and returned to her bed, where she sat up against the pillows.

Jeremy inched forward in his chair, elbows on knees, his hands clasped together. "Have you heard from the father? I forget his name."

"It's Drew. And no, I haven't. But I'm going to write him one more letter, because I think it's possible that he never received the others. I think Carol Brown might have stopped them from going out with the rest of the mail."

"Why would she do that?"

"Because my father has been sending money to the Browns for my upkeep, and he's probably paying them handsomely to make sure I come home with no baby. So please don't tell anyone that I've already given birth."

"Scout's honor."

"And this time," Valerie continued, "I want to give my letter to one of the men on the *Chena* next time she comes in. Angie thought it would be Friday, but that's a holiday. Do you know?"

Jeremy sat up straight, suddenly animated. "They're coming for sure on Friday. I could deliver the letter if you like. I know the cook. His name is Marcus, and he's trustworthy."

Valerie committed that name to memory. "I'd take you up on that, but I haven't written the letter yet. I'll probably ask Blaine to take me, because this time I want to hand deliver it myself and make sure it leaves town."

Jeremy looked across at little Cameron, sleeping soundly in the cradle. "I hope you can finally reach him with that letter, and I hope he's worthy of you. No woman should be with a man who doesn't treat her right." Jeremy sat back. "I wish I could convince Angie of that. If I could have it my way, I'd take her away from here, and I'd treat her like gold. I'd be a good father to her baby, and I'd never look at another woman. Not ever. Why would I? If I was married to Angie . . ." He stopped himself and shook his head. "I just don't understand Joe Brown. As far as I'm concerned, he's a bonehead who doesn't know how lucky he is."

Valerie watched Jeremy for a moment and realized she had misjudged him the first time she'd met him. It was no wonder Angie refused to give up his friendship, even though it made things worse with Joe.

Valerie let out a sigh and turned her eyes toward Cameron.

What she wouldn't give for her and Cameron to be loved like that.

CHAPTER 21

March 27, 1964

Jeremy steered his skiff around the stern of the supply ship *Chena*. The city dock was buzzing with locals, delivery trucks, and forklifts on the go, but Jeremy wasn't there to watch the unloading. He was searching for Angie.

He motored into the small-boat harbor and found a spot to tie up. Having secured his boat, he stepped onto the floating dock and started walking.

Head down, he passed the Village Morgue Bar and cast his mind back to the night of Carol Brown's fiftieth-birthday party when he'd heard Angie crying on the bench. How pretty she'd looked in her party dress, but she had been miserable and shivering in the cold, tears streaming down her face. The sound of her weeping had broken him apart. It made him remember all the times she and her mother had welcomed him into their warm, happy home after a nasty fight in his own dysfunctional one. Angie's mother must have kept a watchful eye on her backyard, because that was where he would run and hide whenever his father pulled out the strap. Jeremy would sneak behind her white snowberry hedge, and suddenly she would appear, as if by magic. She would offer comfort, a hug, and a glass of milk in her kitchen—which always smelled like cookies baking.

That was how Jeremy learned what love was supposed to look like. And he would never, ever take it for granted.

If not for Mrs. Hennessy, Jeremy might have grown up believing that all families were like his—that all grown men had scary tempers and enjoyed belittling others and that children feared their parents and hid in closets. He might have become a different person. Sure, he still had his problems. He had a hard time trusting people until they proved they were good hearted, and if they were, his loyalty knew no bounds. If they proved otherwise, good luck to them. He would treat them accordingly.

He paused and perused the end of the dock. At last, there she was. Sweet, lovely Angie, in a bright-red wool coat with a white scarf—a striking vision in a sea of longshoremen dressed in dull grays and faded browns. She was pushing her baby carriage from the end of the dock, where the *Chena* was tied up and unloading. She waved at him from a distance. Immediately, he began walking faster, in long sure strides toward her.

He reached the corner of one of the warehouses, and his knees nearly gave out under him when she smiled and said, "Hi, Jeremy." Her blue eyes glimmered, and she radiated a charm he'd never seen in her before. *It must be new motherhood,* he decided as she looked down at her baby and pulled the canopy back.

"I was hoping I'd run into you today," Angie said. "I've been dying for you to meet this little man."

Jeremy bent to look at the sleeping infant tucked warmly under a heavy red-and-white-checkered quilt. Angie drew the blanket back to reveal his face, cute and pudgy.

"He's wonderful," Jeremy said and met Angie's gaze. "How was it? Did it hurt much?"

"It hurt a lot," she replied, "but it was worth every second. I love him so much." She tucked Ethan back in and stood behind the carriage, both hands gripping the handle.

"What about you?" she asked. "How have you been?"

"I've been okay," he replied, shrugging.

"I heard you spent a few nights at the Wilsons' place last month. Valerie told me."

"That's right. I helped Mr. Wilson chop some wood."

"She said you played cards—and you won every hand."

"Lucky, I guess."

Angie looked toward the cannery dock, which ran parallel to the city dock. "Valerie said you caught a rabbit."

"I did. Maud used the meat for a stew."

Angie couldn't seem to look at him. Her eyes swung in every direction, except in his.

"Is everything okay?" His head dipped to try and catch her wandering gaze.

"I'm fine. I'm just . . ."

Jeremy kicked at a nail sticking out of the weathered plank at his feet. "Has Joe been kissing Mrs. Lassiter again?"

She exhaled with a groan. "Who knows? I never know what he's doing when he comes home late after work. Whenever I ask, he says something about you and turns the tables on me, puts me on the defensive."

Something caught in Jeremy's chest.

"Why would he mention me?"

She still couldn't meet his gaze. "Because he knows how close we are, and he's jealous. But I won't ever apologize for our friendship. I don't know what I'd do without you."

Jeremy looked around, scanning for people who might be watching them and report back to Joe. "If escape is what you want," he said in a quieter voice, "I'd take you anywhere. I could find a place for us to live in Juneau, and I'd get a job and marry you."

She laughed. "I'm already married."

"You could get a divorce." It wouldn't matter. He'd love her no matter what, under any circumstances.

"I can't do that," Angie said, suddenly bewildered and sounding a little shocked by Jeremy's offer. "Joe is Ethan's father."

"We could sneak away and hide," Jeremy said, taking her hand and leading her closer to the side of the warehouse. "We could go to a place where he would never find us."

"Like where?"

"Europe."

"Europe! How would we afford that?"

"I'd work. We could go to Norway. I'd get a fishing boat. Joe would never find us there."

Angie looked at him with a mixture of confusion and concern. "Why Norway?"

"It's like Alaska. It has fish and whales."

She stared at him for a moment, and he wondered if she would ever take him seriously. Then she reached for his hand.

His whole body caught fire.

"That's a lovely dream, Jeremy. But you know it's not possible."

The sky above them hung low with thick gray clouds. The winter chill touched his cheeks. "Why do you say that? You know I'd do anything for you. I'd protect you no matter what. Ethan too. As long as we're together, we'd be happy. If I had you, I'd never look at another woman."

He felt frantic with love and longing. Desperate to convince her to choose him over Joe. He wanted to hold her close and kiss her and feel her warm skin against his and make more babies with her.

Angie looked at him with affection but also with a note of apology. She never liked to see him hurt.

In that moment, he knew that she was never going to leave Joe. She wouldn't run away with him to Juneau or Norway. Like she'd said, it was a lovely dream, nothing more.

The cold seeped under his jacket, and he shivered.

Angie shivered too. Then she bent to check on Ethan in the carriage.

Jeremy watched her tuck the blanket around him. She was such a loving mother. He'd always known she would be.

How could he ever stop loving her?

Or maybe one day . . . if he waited long enough . . .

Anything could happen, couldn't it?

As Angie straightened, someone shouted on the dock. She turned toward the cars parked opposite the warehouse and said, "Oh no."

Joe was stalking toward them with a red face. "Angie!"

Jeremy's blood exploded with heat. "I gotta go!"

He ran in the other direction, sprinted down to the small floating dock, untied his skiff, and hopped in. It rocked back and forth as he started the motor, grabbed the rudder, and swerved wildly to circle around the enormous *Chena*.

Out on the open water, he was safe from Joe, who had chased him down to the small dock and watched him speed off.

Jeremy reached the middle of the bay, a quarter mile away from the dock, and cut the motor. Looking back, he saw Joe on the end of the main dock, pacing back and forth with fury.

"Take that, you knucklehead!" Jeremy shouted.

Joe pointed at him as if he was going to come after him somehow. But with a quarter mile of deep water between them, Jeremy started to laugh. He stood up in the boat and danced. He did the twist, turned around, and wiggled his rear end. "Come and get me, you big twat!" he shouted. "I'm right here! You can't catch me, though!"

Joe continued pacing, and Jeremy kept on dancing. He thought about bending over and pulling his pants down, but that didn't seem too mature, so he sat down and grabbed hold of the rudder, deciding it would be best to make himself scarce. He'd go hide out in his cabin for a while.

Suddenly a shot rang out. A bullet hit the water with a splash next to Jeremy's skiff.

"Shit!"

Joe fired at him again. This time, the bullet struck the bow.

Jeremy spun the skiff in a wide circle, keeping an eye on that bullet hole, which was thankfully above the waterline. He looked back at the dock and saw Joe's partner dragging him away.

At least someone has some sense in the Valdez Police Department, Jeremy thought. A crime of passion in town wouldn't be good for tourist season.

For a while he continued, speeding along. Then he slowed, cut the motor, and bobbed up and down on the swells. He thought about what had just happened. Slowly, in stages, he realized that he should have done a better job thinking this through. Angie was still back there, and Joe was fit to be tied. Heaven knew what he might do when he got her home. There'd be a fight, for sure.

With a flash of panic like fireworks in his gut, Jeremy scrambled toward the motor. He needed to take the skiff back to the dock and make sure Angie was going to be okay.

But then a loud rumbling began, somewhere in the distance, like never-ending thunder. A giant swell came out of nowhere and lifted his boat at least twenty feet. After he rode down the other side of the wave, he looked back toward town. People were running on the dock. Trees along the nearby shoreline started whipping back and forth, but there was no wind. The rumbling grew louder, and Jeremy knew it was an earthquake. Living in Alaska, he'd experienced many, but he'd never seen trees bend to the ground before.

The warehouses on the city dock began to break apart. Rafters and walls splintered and cracked. The dock beneath them crumbled and collapsed into the water, taking all the people and cars and buildings with it. A church bell in town began to ring loudly as the *Chena* was ripped away from the dock and lifted at least thirty feet on a massive wave that rose up from the depths. The ship's stern pointed toward the sky, and all Jeremy could do was watch in horror and disbelief as the ship came crashing down on top of the people and debris in the water.

Angie . . .

Fishing boats collided with the *Chena* as it slowly righted itself. The entire waterfront seemed to be washing out to sea. Jeremy didn't care about the docks or the cars or the buildings. All that mattered was Angie, who had been standing next to the small-boat harbor mere moments before disaster had struck.

He grabbed hold of the rudder and sped toward the *Chena* as fast as his skiff would take him.

CHAPTER 22

Juneau
2017

Gwen sat in a daze, waiting for Jeremy to continue his description of the events of March 27, 1964, when Valdez had been ravaged by the second-largest earthquake in world history. But he abruptly stopped talking and stared off into space. It was as if he had fallen into a trance.

"Jeremy?"

His eyes shot to hers. "I've said enough for today. I gotta go."

He shoved his chair back, stood, and reached for his jacket.

"Wait . . ." Gwen couldn't let him leave, not when she was so close to learning the answers to her questions. "Please stay."

"I can't." He shrugged into his jacket. "Nice meeting you." His face went pale as he headed for the door.

Gwen rose and made a move to follow him, but it was obvious he was reliving something traumatic, so she let him go. As soon as the door swung shut behind him, she locked eyes with Margie behind the bar, who glared at her for a few seconds, then began to aggressively wipe down the bar.

Gwen returned to her chair, feeling guilty for being the cause of Jeremy's apparent panic attack.

Peter approached. "What happened?"

"I'm not sure," she replied. "But we should probably go somewhere else where we can talk."

He waited for her to collect her jacket and purse, then led her outside. By now, it was pouring rain. Cars drove past with wipers whipping back and forth, their tires swishing through puddles on the street.

"Let's just go back into the hotel," Peter suggested, leading her to the separate entrance next to the bar.

He ushered Gwen inside, and they went immediately upstairs to her room. She unlocked the door and entered first. Peter followed and shut the door behind them. Gwen removed her coat and hung it inside the antique wardrobe.

"You were talking to him for quite a while," Peter said. "It looked like he had a lot to say."

"He did," she replied. "He held nothing back about Valerie's time in Valdez. He knew a lot from his friendship with her, but he also knew things he learned from her friend Angie. She was the wife of a local cop who didn't think too much of Jeremy. It's a complicated story, a bit of a love triangle between Jeremy, Angie, and her husband. Valerie seemed caught in the middle."

Peter sat down on one of the twin beds. "Did he tell you anything about the baby he rescued?"

Gwen pulled off her shoes, sat on the other twin bed, and slid back against the pillows. "We didn't quite get there. He was telling me about the earthquake and how he watched from his boat when the docks collapsed, but that's when he got the strangest look on his face and said he had to leave." She met Peter's gaze. "I think whatever happened was awful. He couldn't even talk about it."

"A lot of people died that day," Peter said. "He must have seen some terrible things."

"I believe so."

They sat in silence while Gwen strove to remember everything Jeremy had revealed in the bar. "He wouldn't let me take notes or record our conversation, so I should probably tell you everything right now before I forget the details."

Peter reached into the pocket of his jeans. "Do you mind if I record you with my phone?"

"Please do. And I'll record it as well. It's important information for the historical record. This will need to be transcribed for the museum."

"And for my book," he reminded her, his eyes lifting.

"Yes." She immediately recognized Peter's fear, his underlying mistrust. "I give you my word that I won't steal this from you."

He relaxed and set his phone to record.

Gwen spent the next half hour recounting everything Jeremy had disclosed in the bar. When she finished, they put away their phones and took a break, lying back on the two twin beds.

"He didn't look the way I expected him to," Peter said.

"How did you expect him to look?"

"I don't know. A little more rough around the edges. Like someone who's lived a hard life."

She folded her hands across her belly. "You're right. He didn't look like a prison convict. He looked like somebody's well-to-do granddad. His jacket was Patagonia. Did you notice that? And he was clean shaven and quite handsome for a man of his age."

They continued to lie there, each of them staring at the ceiling.

"Are you hungry?" Peter asked.

"I am. Maybe we should get some dinner."

They agreed it was a good idea and rose to their feet. They were just putting on their jackets when Gwen's cell phone rang. She picked it up and looked at the screen.

"It's Eric," she said, fighting to suppress a feeling of disappointment, because she wasn't in the mood to talk to him now.

Peter gestured toward the door. "I can leave you alone for a few minutes . . ."

"No, please don't go." She took hold of his arm. "I'm not going to answer it. I'll text him."

She quickly messaged that she was heading out for dinner and suggested they talk the following morning.

As she and Peter made their way downstairs, she said, "I just realized it's midnight in Nova Scotia. He's up late."

"He must really want to talk to you. Are you sure you don't want to call him back?"

"I'm sure," she replied. "I don't mind if he tosses and turns all night, thinking about me going out to dinner in Alaska with a handsome writer he knows nothing about."

Peter glanced over his shoulder at her. "Handsome?"

Gwen gave him a look. "Don't let it go to your head."

"I'll try not to. As long as you're not just using me to make him jealous."

"I can't make any promises."

They walked outside into the rain, and Peter raised the umbrella. Gwen linked her arm through his as they hopped across puddles on the way to a restaurant while discussing everything they'd learned from Jeremy.

They both understood the significance of the information, yet there were so many questions still unanswered.

~

Later that night, Gwen sat up in bed and scrolled through emails on her phone. She got sleepy and was about to switch off the lamp when a Facebook notification chimed. Her heart did a little flip when she saw Jeremy's name.

Hello Gwen. I apologize for walking out on you. It's hard to talk about that day. But I'm sure you want to know what happened with Valerie's baby. If you're free tomorrow, I'd be pleased to have you for lunch. My wife insists. And bring your friend, the guy in the bar. Margie told me you left with him. Margie, the bartender, is my daughter, BTW. Let me know if you can come and I'll send you the address.

Instantly wide awake, Gwen responded.

Hi Jeremy. Thank you for this message and yes, I would love to come for lunch tomorrow. My friend's name is Peter and I appreciate you including him. I look forward to meeting your wife.

Jeremy responded with the time and his address on Douglas Island.

Then Gwen texted Peter: Are you still up? Something amazing just happened. Jeremy messaged me and invited us to lunch tomorrow. He apologized for walking out. Are you up for that?

She pressed send and waited for a reply. The three dots floated, and then Peter responded.

Definitely! That's great. Well done. Thanks for getting me on the invitation list.

She typed a reply: It wasn't me. It was his daughter Margie who was working in the bar. She saw us leave together.

Peter texted: That was his daughter? I guess that explains why he chose that place.

Gwen quickly typed: Yes. And it makes me wonder . . . You don't suppose he's married to Angie?

Gwen waited for Peter's response.

I just had the same thought.

Gwen texted. I guess we'll find out tomorrow. Now we should both get some sleep. It's 4 AM in Nova Scotia. Past my bedtime.

Peter responded: Totally. Good night. Sleep well.

You too. :-)

He "liked" her final message with a heart, and she found herself smiling as she set her phone on the bedside table and switched off the light.

CHAPTER 23

Gwen and Peter stepped out of the cab and looked up at Jeremy's house—a well-maintained split-level home with blue vinyl siding and a shiny Ford Focus hatchback parked in the driveway.

"Looks like he upgraded from the hermit cabin in the woods," Gwen whispered, leaning close to Peter. "Freshly mowed lawn, well-tended spring garden. Friendly looking neighbors."

"It appears so."

They climbed the front steps and rang the doorbell. An older woman answered. "You must be Gwen and Peter," she said warmly. "I'm Jane. Please come in."

Peter discreetly nudged Gwen, because they'd come close, in the cab on the way there, to placing bets on whether Jeremy had ended up with Angie. But Jane was clearly too young. She looked to be in her midsixties. With dark eyes and silver hair, she was an attractive, elegant-looking woman.

Gwen entered first and locked eyes with Jeremy, who appeared on the landing. "You found us without any trouble?"

"Yes. Your directions were perfect." She felt strangely awestruck by the sight of him. "It's so nice of you to have us. This is Peter."

Jeremy said hello, and Jane took their coats, then led them upstairs to the living room.

"Something smells delicious," Peter said.

"I hope you like chicken potpie," Jane replied. "It's still in the oven."

"That sounds wonderful."

"Can I get anyone a drink?" Jeremy asked. "We have juice, Pepsi, ginger ale, or beer and wine, if you prefer."

Peter and Gwen asked for ginger ale, then sat down on the chintz sofa. Jane set a crystal plate of crackers and cheese on the Victorian-style coffee table and sat down in an upholstered chair across from them.

"Jeremy tells me you're a relative of Scarlett Fontaine," Jane said to Gwen.

"Yes. She was my mother's first cousin, and after Scarlett went to Hollywood, she kept in touch with my grandmother, who was her great-aunt."

Jeremy arrived with the drinks in tall crystal tumblers and handed them to Gwen and Peter.

"Are you originally from Alaska?" Gwen asked Jane.

"Yes, I grew up in Juneau. My parents owned a marina, and that's where I met Jeremy after the earthquake. My father hired him as captain on a whale-watching tour."

Jeremy reached for his ginger ale. "I might have embellished my résumé a bit."

"A bit?" Jane said with laughter in her eyes.

Jeremy shrugged. "I told her father I'd worked on the *Wanderer* in Valdez. As far as I know, he never called Blaine to check my references, but even if he had, Blaine would have vouched for me. He was good that way."

Gwen reached for her ginger ale as well. "Whatever happened to Blaine and Maud?"

"The Wilsons kept the lodge running for twenty years after the quake," Jeremy told her. "Then they sold it for a hefty profit and retired to Seattle to be closer to their grandchildren."

"Did you keep in touch with them after that?" Gwen asked.

"We exchanged Christmas cards."

Gwen did the math in her head and concluded that Maud and Blaine must both be gone by now.

"What about you, Peter?" Jane asked. "Are you also from Nova Scotia?"

Gwen reached for Peter's hand and held it. It wasn't her intention to pretend that they were a couple. She simply wanted him to know that she would support whatever he wished to tell them.

"No," Peter replied, rubbing the pad of his thumb over her knuckle. "I'm from the Lower Forty-Eight, as they say. I'm a writer, and I'm working on a book about Scarlett."

Jeremy drew back slightly. "A book."

"Yes," Gwen said. "I was going to tell you about that yesterday, but I didn't get the chance. Peter is the one who discovered the newspaper clipping and recognized Valerie. As a family member, I was grateful that he came to me with it."

"And you also run the museum. Isn't that right?" Jane asked, while a sudden chill from Jeremy cooled the warmth in the room.

Gwen cleared her throat uncomfortably. "Yes. I like to consider myself the guardian of her memory."

Jeremy spoke gruffly. "I need to check on the chicken pie." He stood up and walked out.

"Don't mind him," Jane said, waving a hand. "He also considers himself the guardian of Scarlett's memory. He's kept her secret for more than fifty years."

Gwen was grateful for Jane's understanding—although the word *secret* raised her curiosity to new heights. "I'm sure she was very appreciative of that."

"I believe she was," Jane replied. "But I also think he's kept his promise long enough, and it's time for the world to know what Scarlett went through in Alaska."

Gwen was fully aware that her desire to know the truth went far beyond professional curiosity. There was a hole in her own heart, a place of emptiness and sorrow, a void that had been left behind by Lily when she'd departed this world. Then Eric had left too, and the hole had only grown deeper. For a full year, Gwen had wanted Eric to come back and fill that hole—at least part of it—but perhaps that wasn't possible. Perhaps it could never be filled, only accepted and endured.

"I agree," she replied, putting her own issues away for the time being and thinking of Scarlett and the museum. "It sheds new light on her song lyrics and makes them worthy of an academic study, in my opinion."

"She deserves that," Jane said.

Gwen heard Jeremy puttering about in the kitchen. "I should go and talk to him. Would you excuse me?"

"Of course," Jane replied.

Gwen stood, went to the kitchen, and found Jeremy at the counter, tossing a salad.

"Hey there," she softly said. "You walked out on me again."

He kept his back to her while he poured bottled dressing onto the salad. "I told you I didn't want to talk to the press."

"Peter's not the press," she assured him. "He's a writer who cares about good research. And he's a decent person. I wasn't sure at first. I was skeptical, like you, because I know how much Valerie valued her privacy, especially at the end of her life. But I swear to you that Peter has good intentions. He recognizes her artistic talents. And I, for one, think Valerie deserves to be remembered not just as a fashion icon. She was so much more than that."

Jeremy set down the salad tongs. "She was."

"I assume you heard us talking out there," Gwen added, taking a seat at the table. "I believe her song lyrics will mean more to the world if people understand who she really was. The true meaning of her art can't die with her, Jeremy. It needs to be studied and celebrated."

He nodded. "She deserves that kind of recognition. That kind of respect."

"Yes. And I believe Peter's book will shine a light on her true genius. It's an incredible discovery, really, when you think about it."

Jeremy gazed out the window at the hemlocks blowing in the wind. "You probably want to know what happened that day, after the docks collapsed."

"I do," Gwen said. "We both do."

The timer beeped on the stove, and Jeremy moved to silence it. He donned a pair of oven mitts, removed the chicken potpie from the oven, and examined the golden pastry. "Looks done, but it needs to rest a bit." He pulled off the oven mitts, tossed them onto the counter, and turned to her. "Let's go back to the living room."

Gwen followed him and returned to the sofa, next to Peter. He looked up at Jeremy, who nodded. It was enough, between men, to communicate that the situation was resolved.

"I should tell you what happened to Angie," Jeremy said, and Jane rubbed his back supportively. "On the day the earthquake struck, I was sitting in my skiff, a long way out when the shaking started. I didn't know what it was at first until I heard it—the roar, like a freight train coming straight at me. I'll never forget the sound of the church bell clanging across the water. Then the trees started whipping back and forth. By the time I looked back toward town, the docks were breaking apart, and I was stunned, I tell ya. The *Chena* rose up on a wave that came out of nowhere." He used his arm to show the angle of the ship. "The stern was pointing straight up until it came crashing down on whatever was floating in the water, including the people."

He paused for a moment, and Jane rubbed his back again. When he was ready to continue, he bowed his head. "I sped back to town, but the retreating wave carried me out further and tossed my boat around. It wasn't easy to get control of it. I thought I was done for, and I was worried about Angie. By the time I made it back, the *Chena* was being carried out on the backwash, along with everything else—cars and buildings and wood pilings. It was an absolute horror show. I don't know how else to describe it. I looked for survivors but couldn't find anyone. And the water was freezing. No way anyone could have survived for long. But when the docks collapsed, people were sucked down into whirlpools and never surfaced."

Jeremy stopped. He took a few sips of soda before continuing. "I never felt misery like that."

"What about Angie?" Gwen gently inquired.

He shook his head and looked away, working hard to keep his emotions in check.

Gwen closed her eyes. "I'm so sorry."

He nodded and leaned back. A vein pulsed at his temple. They all sat in silence.

"After a while," Jeremy continued, "I went out to the *Chena* to help bring some longshoremen back to the town. They were worried about their loved ones."

"What about Valerie?" Gwen asked. "Did you see her?"

"Not then. But I heard from some folks that she was hurt and they took her to the nursing home to see the doctor there. They told me she was practically hysterical because she'd lost her baby in the flood. People were searching, but there wasn't much hope."

"How badly was she injured?" Peter asked.

"She fell into a crack that opened up in the road, and she broke her leg."

Gwen turned to Peter. "She had a bad scar on her leg. She'd always said she fell off a bicycle, but maybe it was from that." She returned her attention to Jeremy. "What happened next?"

Jeremy spoke with purpose. "Eventually, I got in my skiff and headed out to the cove where I'd built my cabin. No one knew about it—it was pretty secluded—and by then I was numb from the cold and everything I'd seen. I came close to shore, shut off my motor, and everything got really quiet. I sat there in a daze, just floating and thinking about the last moment I saw Angie on the dock in her red coat. And then I heard something."

"What did you hear?" Peter asked, sitting forward.

"A baby crying."

Gwen's pulse began to race. "Was it Valerie's?"

He looked at her directly but didn't answer the question. "I went back out on the water, hugging the shoreline, and saw the carriage parked on top of what looked like a giant raft, but it was a section of roofing. It must've come from one of the buildings that collapsed on the dock. So I went to fetch that baby in the carriage. I knew right then that it was a miracle, that God had sent that little soul straight into my hands for safekeeping."

He paused and clasped his hands together, pressed them to his forehead.

"What happened after that?" Gwen asked, barely able to contain her concern.

"I towed the whole rooftop to shore. Then I jumped out of my skiff and pushed the carriage onto the beach."

"And the baby was all right?" Gwen asked.

"He was fine," Jeremy replied. "Tucked up cozy and warm in a thick wool blanket. But he was fussing and crying for his mother."

Gwen pondered this. "That's the baby you took to Valerie in the hospital."

He turned toward Jane and seemed unsure about continuing.

"Let's go into the kitchen," she said, "and sit down for lunch." It was clear she wanted to give her husband a break from these painful memories. "Then he'll tell you the rest."

Gwen and Peter shared a look of amazement, got up from the sofa, and followed Jane and Jeremy into the kitchen.

CHAPTER 24

Valdez
1964

Harborview Nursing Home, built in 1961, suffered severe cracks during the earthquake. Frequent aftershocks in the subsequent hours rattled the building and put everyone—patients and staff alike—on edge.

Valerie sat up in her bed with a cast on her leg. Her shinbone had cracked when she had fallen into the fissure on Alaska Avenue, but a brave soul had pulled her out of the hole in the earth and sent her to see the doctor at Harborview, even though she had protested vehemently, begging not to be taken away. Not when Cameron was still missing.

Now here she was, waiting in a state of utter despair. Each time someone new walked into her room or was wheeled past her door on a gurney, she asked frantic, desperate questions.

"Do they know if anyone's found a baby?"

"Have there been any survivors at the waterfront?"

"Please, will someone help me?"

The answers were repeatedly *no*—there was nothing anyone could do for her at present. She had to be patient. Each time she heard that word, her hopes were shredded. Her broken shinbone was nothing compared to the agonizing distress and misery over the loss of her baby.

It was worse than losing a limb or dying. What could have happened to him? Her imagination ran wild, and her mind spun with horrific images of his carriage flipping over into the ice-cold water. He wouldn't understand what was happening to him. He would attempt to cry for her, but seawater would fill his tiny lungs and . . .

Oh, God! If only she could have held on to him, but the powerful wave had carried her away, and she had been no match for it—for the cruel and violent killing machine that nature had become when it shook the earth and sucked innocent human beings into its deathly vortex. She'd heard tales of people on the docks falling into swirling undertows that swallowed entire cars and buildings on top of them. The ocean had become a malevolent beast. It had stolen her baby, ripped him from her grasp, and pushed her into a frightening abyss. Her own private hell.

Grim, distressing memories of those tense moments ravaged Valerie's mind and filled her with regret. Why had she gone into town that day? Why was it so important to send the letter? She should have stayed home at the lodge instead of surrendering to her greed for love— love from a man who didn't even want her. Drew could have tracked her down if he had truly cared, but he never had. She should have purged him from her heart months ago. If she had, Cameron would be safe, sleeping in her arms, back at the lodge with Maud and Blaine.

A nurse came by and asked about her leg. Did she need more pain medication? But there was no pill for the agony that beset her and held her in its grip.

I'll find you, Cameron. I swear it. No matter where you are or how long it takes, I will never stop searching for you.

~

It was close to eleven o'clock at night when chaos erupted in the hospital corridor. The noise and commotion caused Valerie to sit up, alert, craving information about survivors and those who were still missing. She was not the only one desperate for news of loved ones.

A nurse burst through the door, her eyes bright with excitement. "They found your baby!"

A cry of relief broke from Valerie's lips. She gasped as someone walked through the door with a small bundle in his arms. *Jeremy!*

Indescribable happiness filled her heart as she held out her arms. *Cameron, my angel! You're safe. I'm here with you now.*

Jeremy approached, but before he had a chance to reach her bedside, a man with a camera followed him into the room and said, "Jeremy, look here!"

Startled, he turned to face the lens, and the flashbulb exploded as he grinned from ear to ear. The photographer said, "Thanks!" and ran off before the spots disappeared from Jeremy's blinking eyes. He turned to Valerie, still waiting anxiously with her arms held out.

"I found him," Jeremy said. "And he's okay."

She sobbed and shook with a barrage of different emotions. "Oh, thank you, Jeremy. Please give him to me. Yes, give him here. Right here. Oh, my sweet, sweet boy . . ."

Her need to hold her son was dizzying. All-consuming. She laughed and cried as Jeremy placed the sleeping infant in her waiting arms. Nurses and other members of the staff had crowded around the bed, eager to witness this happy reunion after so many tragic losses that day.

Valerie peeled back the blanket and looked at Cameron's face. Then a stabbing sensation, like a thousand knives all at once, pierced her heart. The shock of it took her breath away.

It's not you.

My darling angel, it isn't you.

A fresh, gaping hole opened inside her as she hugged the child to her breast and wept. Others began to cry as well, hugging each other, believing this was a happy, emotional reunion of the best kind. A mother, against all odds, had had her prayers answered that day. It was a miracle, surely.

Valerie reached out and squeezed Jeremy's forearm. She said to the others, the circle of strangers staring down at her, "Leave us alone, please?"

As they dispersed, some of them touched her shoulder, as if a part of this miracle might rub off on them. Others murmured with understanding and left the room.

As soon as they were gone, Valerie looked down at Ethan with tears in her eyes. "This isn't Cameron," she said. "This is Angie's baby."

Jeremy stared at Valerie with ferocious intensity. "No. This is Cameron. He's your baby."

For a flashing instant, she wanted to believe he was speaking the truth. She had been through a terrible ordeal, after all, and oh, how she wanted it to be true . . .

Doubting her own sanity and clinging to a narrow sliver of hope, she looked down at the infant again. He was peaceful. Innocent and unaware of the terrible disaster that had befallen Alaskans that day.

She touched his soft cheek with the pad of her thumb and bent to kiss his tender forehead. She let her lips linger there awhile, imagining that it was Cameron and dreaming of the happiness she would feel if it truly was, while tears streamed down her face.

"Was it you who found him?" she asked, finally looking up.

"Yes," Jeremy replied.

"Where?"

He shifted in the chair. "He was in the carriage, riding on a rooftop that floated away from the docks. The carriage must've rolled right onto it."

"A miracle, for sure," Valerie said with sadness, wishing it was her own miracle, not another's. "Where is Angie? She must be beside herself with worry."

A hush fell over the room, and Jeremy's body trembled before he spoke. "Angie's gone." His voice broke. Tears filled his eyes, but he wiped them away harshly—and with anger. "She went into the water when the docks collapsed. No one survived."

Valerie knew firsthand how dreadful it had been. She'd seen it all.

With grim, excruciating misery, she hugged Ethan closer to her heart and wept anew. "Oh, God. Not Angie."

Jeremy leaned forward and smothered his sobs on the edge of the mattress. Valerie laid her hand on the back of his head and ran her fingers through his hair, doing her best to offer comfort and love, for she understood his pain. She, too, was struggling through the worst kind of suffering.

After a moment, he sat up and wiped away his tears. "He's *your* baby," he insisted.

"Why do you keep saying that?" she asked. "I'm telling you it's not true. I would know my own son."

"But he needs you," Jeremy explained. "He needs a mother. I could be his dad if you wanted. We could go anywhere. We could keep him safe. You and me."

Valerie swallowed over a coarse lump in her throat. Her heart wept for her own loss but also for Jeremy's—for the loss of his beautiful dream with Angie. She reached out and held his hand. "I'm so sorry she's gone."

He looked away, his whole body full of grief.

"But I can't steal someone else's child," Valerie said. "I couldn't live with a lie like that."

Jeremy's eyes were downcast. He looked sullen. Ashamed.

Valerie touched Ethan's pudgy little nose, then placed her pinkie in his palm. He clasped her finger.

For a fleeting moment, she imagined running away with Jeremy and living abroad where no one would ever know that Ethan didn't belong to them. But *she* would know. And she would never stop grieving and longing for her own son. No child could ever replace Cameron. And she would always feel guilty—not just because it was wrong but because of what had happened mere hours before, when the town had been flooding and she'd thought she was going to die.

"Joe saved my life," she said to Jeremy.

His eyes lifted and grew wide with astonishment.

"When I was running after the wave that took Cameron," she continued, "a crack opened up in the road ahead of me. I fell into it, at least six feet, and broke my leg, and water started pouring in. I thought it was going to be my grave until Joe suddenly appeared. He jumped in and lifted me out. He almost didn't make it out himself, but others came to help, and we both survived. Another miracle, I suppose."

Jeremy looked down at his hands, and Valerie sensed that he didn't want to hear about Joe's act of heroism. His heart was still full of jealousy.

"He's in pain tonight," Valerie said, "just like you, knowing that his wife has died and believing that his son is also dead. He needs to know the truth. And you should be the one to deliver it since you're the one who saved Ethan."

Jeremy said nothing for a moment. Then at last he nodded.

A town official darted into the room and spoke quickly. "I don't want to alarm you, but the oil tanks on the waterfront have caught fire, and there's a tsunami warning. We need to evacuate the building. Someone will be here to help you in a few minutes." He ran off to continue spreading the news and organize the evacuation.

Would the misfortune never end? Valerie looked down at Ethan sleeping soundly in her arms. He was blessed to have survived the unthinkable events of the day, but he had lost his mother.

And where was Cameron? Stinging tears flooded Valerie's eyes, and her head throbbed from the weight of her anguish.

But perhaps there was still hope. If Ethan had been spared when everyone else on the docks had perished, anything was possible, wasn't it?

She squeezed Jeremy's hand. "Can you get the nurse? We need to tell her that this isn't my baby. We need to tell her that he belongs to Joe Brown."

Jeremy finally stood and left the room to find someone.

CHAPTER 25

Valdez
1964

Hot, riotous flames burned stubbornly on the waterfront, feeding off the spillage of oil at the Union Oil Tank Farm. The nearby Village Morgue Bar was also ablaze, surrendering quickly to the merciless will of the fire. The old, timeworn timbers sizzled and groaned as they fractured and came crashing down.

The sun had set over an hour ago, but the sky was brightly lit over the burning tanks. Joe backed away from the heat, squinting into the blinding glare and pressing his nose into the crook of his arm to shield his face from the smoke. Firefighters did their best, but it was a losing battle.

Joe's partner, Edwards, laid a hand on his shoulder. "There's nothing more we can do here."

Joe turned away from the inferno. Somehow, over the past few hours, he had kept his grief and sorrow at bay. He was operating on pure adrenaline—or perhaps shock and denial. "We need to evacuate the rest of the town," he said.

The village of Chenega, Kodiak Island, and Seward had been decimated by tsunamis, and Valdez was believed to be under threat.

Joe and Edwards split up, moving from one building to the next, knocking on doors, searching for anyone who might still be holding out, guarding property.

Houses near the water had been flooded during the first wave, but farther inland, the damage was mostly structural. Joe found a house leaning heavily to one side with the front door wide open. "Hello? Is anyone here?"

A faint cry reached his ears, so he stepped gingerly over a pile of books that had toppled out of a bookcase. He found his way across the slanted floor to the kitchen, where he heard another whimper. His gaze fell to a small white dog hiding beneath the table, backed up against the wall, trembling.

Joe approached and got down on his hands and knees, reached in, and scooped him out from under. With the dog in his arms, Joe stood up and rubbed the top of its head. "Everything's all right. You're okay now."

Joe carried the dog out of the crooked house and walked to the next home. With any luck it had been abandoned hours ago. He stood at the front door, staring into the ravaged entrance hall and kitchen beyond, where broken plates littered the floor.

Joe stood for a moment, absentmindedly rubbing the small dog's head while his thoughts drifted back to the moment when the shaking had begun and he'd taken too long to realize what was happening.

An earthquake. A major one.

He had just argued with Angie and fired three shots at Jeremy. Edwards had dragged him away and shouted at him to cool off and lower his weapon. Joe barely remembered discharging his sidearm. He mostly remembered Jeremy dancing in his skiff, laughing and taunting him.

When Joe finally let the gun fall from his grasp, Edwards bent to pick it up, and that was when the vibrations started. Joe stared at the ground outside the Village Morgue Bar, then turned and looked back at the town, where cars were rolling and crashing into each other. Utility poles swayed back and forth, and power lines snapped. Joe looked toward the far end of the dock, where Angie, in her bright-red coat, was running toward him, pushing Ethan as fast as she could in the carriage.

Joe's father, Frank, spilled out of the bar. "Carol! Get off the dock!" He ran in zigzag fashion toward the *Chena*, and Joe followed to reach Angie and Ethan.

At that moment, the entire dock started to collapse. The buildings broke apart, and everyone went down, sinking into the churning water. Joe was still on the earthen causeway and skidded to a halt when his father went down ahead of him and disappeared. Angie was farther out among the wreckage of the warehouses as they collapsed. He lost sight of her completely and ran forward, helplessly, just as an enormous wave rose up like a ten-story building and lifted the *Chena* to a vertical position. Joe knew, beyond doubt, that there was no chance of saving anyone. If he didn't turn around and run like hell, he'd be sucked under too.

So he ran. He sprinted up Alaska Avenue and barely made it off the causeway before he was knocked off his feet by the incoming wave and carried two blocks into town.

Gasping for air and flailing about in the current, he managed to stay above water until he grabbed on to the roof of a floating car. He held on until the wave slowed and began to retreat. Then his boots touched the ground, and he shook himself to regain his senses. A woman ran past him. He watched her stop and look around. Then the earth opened up, and she dropped into a giant fissure.

Joe had run to her.

Looking back on it, he realized he must have known he had half a chance of saving this person after failing to save Angie and Ethan. His parents too.

He'd reached the giant crack in the earth and looked down. It was Valerie, struggling to stand up on an injured leg, but water was flooding in, and the earth was still rolling and shaking. The fissure was already starting to close.

"Help me, please!" she cried.

Joe leaped into the chasm, lifted her up, and hoisted her high enough to crawl out. Incoming water knocked him onto his back, and he thought that was the end.

If it was, at least he would be with Angie and Ethan, and that would be okay. Better than okay. He'd disappointed Angie in this life. Maybe he could do better in the next . . .

Suddenly, strong hands had grabbed him under the arms and wrenched him to his feet, and more hands had reached down from above and pulled him out of the flooding abyss, which had closed seconds after he'd climbed out.

Now, Joe stood in the darkness, in the doorway of someone's house, with a little dog under his arm. All he saw was Angie in her red coat running toward him.

Joe's legs gave out. He dropped to his knees in a fit of despair, hugged the dog, and cried into its soft neck. Its tongue lapped at Joe's wet cheeks.

Angie. My love, Angie . . .

He was so sorry for all the times he'd hurt her. Why had he acted that way, getting drunk and going off with other women when he loved his wife and couldn't imagine his life without her? Why had he done things that caused her pain?

Now she was gone, and he could never make amends.

Their last words had been hostile and bitter, full of threats and accusations.

Joe cried and cried. If only he could go back and have one more chance . . .

There was a rumbling suddenly—an aftershock that caused him to open his eyes. Panic gripped him. The terrorized dog squirmed and leaped out of his arms and ran back to the house where Joe had found him.

Someone called out, "Joe!"

It was Edwards. Joe struggled to his feet and walked to meet him.

"What is it?" Joe's eyes burned from the ash floating in the air.

"Come to the station. There's good news."

How could there be good news? Joe wondered wearily as he picked his way over broken glass and rubble.

"What's happened?" he asked, following mindlessly.

Edwards stopped and turned. "Ethan was found. He's safe, and he's at the station."

All the blood in Joe's body slowed to a crawl through his veins. "What did you say?"

Edwards repeated himself, and Joe blinked a few times, fighting to wake from the nightmare that still held him in its cruel grasp.

"Who found him?" Joe asked.

"Jeremy Mikhailov. Ethan was floating on a rooftop in the bay, still in his carriage. It was pure luck. Or maybe a miracle."

Joe dropped to his knees in the middle of the street, cupped his hands together, and pressed them to his forehead. "Thank you," he whispered.

Edwards waited for Joe to get up. Then they ran to the station to meet Jeremy.

CHAPTER 26

Juneau
2017

Gwen paused with her fork hovering over Jane's chicken potpie. "It wasn't Valerie's baby in the newspaper photograph," she said, her pulse drumming a rapid beat. "It was Angie's baby."

"Yes," Jeremy replied.

"But what about Cameron? Was he ever found?"

Jeremy nodded soberly. "His body was recovered the next morning, inside one of the flooded buildings on Alaska Avenue. He must have washed in there when the wave took him."

Gwen sat in sorrow, imagining what Valerie must have suffered when she had learned the truth—the horrendous, devastating news that no mother ever wants to hear.

"Did she at least get to see him?" Gwen asked. "Did she get to hold him again to say goodbye?"

"Yes, she did."

Gwen felt the agony of her own loss two years ago, when she'd sat in the hospital bed and sobbed over Lily, wrapped in a small blanket in her arms. It was the worst moment of her life. A nightmare that wouldn't end. The best she could do was put the agony into a drawer and close it for a while. Lock it away until she was prepared to feel it again. To remember Lily. To accept that she was gone but to remember the love—the love that would always be there.

Peter reached for Gwen's hand and held it. She couldn't speak for fear of weeping. They all sat in silence, acknowledging the tragedy.

"How devastating for Valerie," she finally said when she was able to form words. "I know what it's like to lose a child."

Jane regarded her with sympathy. "I'm sorry to hear that."

Gwen didn't want to go into the details of her own loss, so she steered the conversation back to Valerie. "That's not what I imagined happened to her and her baby."

"What did you imagine?" Jeremy asked.

"That she'd put him up for adoption, like her father wanted. I thought maybe her child was out there in the world somewhere, still alive. I wanted to find him. I guess . . . in a way, I wanted a happy ending out of this. To learn that the baby survived and that I had a cousin." Her voice broke, but she pulled herself together and took a breath.

Jeremy poked at his food. "I learned a lot from that woman. She always did the right thing, and she was kind. Knowing her and the Wilsons changed my life."

Jane reached for his hand and kissed him lightly on the cheek.

"So what happened when you gave Ethan back to Joe?" Peter asked.

"He was grateful," Jeremy replied. "He thanked me and asked where I'd found him. I told him the story. He never mentioned trying to murder me with his gun, so I didn't mention it either. He asked if I knew about Angie, and I said I did. I told him I was sorry, and he said, 'I'm sorry too.' And that was all. I walked out, and the big tsunami everyone expected never came. But the next morning, the town was deemed unsafe, so all the residents were forced to evacuate. Valerie was sent to Fairbanks, but she didn't stay long. She caught a flight to California, and I took off to Juneau."

"What about Angie's baby?" Gwen asked. "Did Joe raise Ethan on his own?"

Jeremy picked up his fork and resumed eating. "Not on his own. He married a woman who came to help with the planning for the new town, which had to be relocated after the quake. That's the Valdez of today. Different from before but still the same in many ways. From what I heard, Joe quit drinking, cold turkey, after the quake, and he and his new wife had two kids together. They all turned out okay. I kept tabs on Ethan, just because. Blaine told me he went to college in Anchorage and still lives there, to this day. A civil engineer, married with three kids."

Gwen wondered if Valerie had kept tabs on Ethan as well, from a distance. "I'm sure Angie would have been proud of him," she said, relaxing at this welcome bit of good news.

Gwen helped Jane clear away the plates and serve a pecan pie with vanilla ice cream for dessert. While they lingered over coffee, Gwen brought the conversation back around to Valerie—and one remaining question.

"What about the father of her baby? You said his name was Drew. Did she ever see him again?"

Jeremy shrugged. "I don't know the answer to that. Valerie only wrote to me once after she left Alaska. It was when she was up for her first Oscar. She told me she was struggling with all the attention. She never really liked the spotlight. It was a different life from Valdez. She thought about walking away and leaving it all behind, before people found out about her private life, but I wrote back and promised I'd never share anything with the press, and I never did. Neither did the Wilsons. Or Joe because I called him on the telephone about it. I figured he owed me one. He never disappointed me."

"I'm relieved," Gwen said. "And it explains why her time in Alaska was never made public."

Jeremy nodded and sat back. "So that's everything. Nothing more I can tell you."

"No parting words of wisdom?" Peter asked, half joking.

Jeremy took him seriously and considered it. "Here's something. We should all be grateful for every day we get. Have fun and make hay while the sun shines."

Jane rose from her chair. "That deserves a toast, and I just happen to have some of that peanut butter whiskey the tourists are always raving about." She fetched four crystal shot glasses from the sideboard in the living room and set the bottle on the table. Jeremy poured for everyone.

"To Valerie," he said.

"To her music," Peter added. "May it live forever."

"And to her strength," Gwen replied.

Jane stood up and raised her glass even higher. "And to Angie's sensible decision not to run off to Norway with my future husband. Or I wouldn't be sitting here with you all right now."

They all laughed, and Gwen said, "Cheers to that."

"Bottoms up." Jeremy tossed back his shot and set the glass on the table. He then regaled them with a few wild stories about running from the cops in Juneau the previous summer, on the Fourth of July.

"It pays to keep fit in your golden years," he said, pouring himself another shot of whiskey.

Jane laughed and punched him in the arm.

~

That evening, Gwen and Peter walked to the cruise ship pier and bought tickets to ride the tram up Mount Roberts—a six-minute ascent to a height of 1,800 feet. It was a popular tourist destination with a restaurant, a nature center, a theater, and stunning views of Juneau and Douglas Island.

When they reached the top, snow covered the ground. It felt like a different world. Leisurely, they wandered through the displays and gift shop and watched a short film about Alaskan native culture. Afterward they ventured outside to the viewing deck and stood at the wooden rail, looking down at Juneau, where a cruise ship was just pulling away from the dock.

"It looks so small from here," Peter said as they watched the ship maneuver in the channel.

They stood among the alpine foliage, looking outward. "The air in Alaska smells different from home," Gwen said.

"It's different from LA too," he replied. "I quite like it."

They basked in the fresh air for a moment, and then she turned to him. "I'm still reeling from everything we learned today. I can't believe I knew nothing about the earthquake that happened here. And I wasn't sure we were ever going to learn the truth about what happened to Valerie and her baby. I thought that secret might have gone to the grave with her, but Jeremy knew everything. He answered all our questions. I honestly didn't expect that."

"He's a good man," Peter replied. "I'm glad things worked out for him in the end, but it's sad . . . what happened to Angie."

"And Cameron. And so many others." Gwen stared at the steep slope of the mountain below and felt another stirring of grief from within.

"Are you okay?" Peter asked, laying his hand on her back.

"I'm not sure. I can't stop thinking about the moment when the wave swept Valerie away, the second when she let go of the handle of the carriage. It must have been awful, losing her grip on it. And when she went back, and he was gone . . . it's a mother's worst nightmare. The guilt she must have felt over losing her grip . . . she would never have forgiven herself for that."

Peter rubbed his hand in small circles between Gwen's shoulder blades. He said nothing. He simply waited for her to express her feelings.

"At least I finally understand who she was," Gwen said, "and why she lived alone the rest of her life and never had any more children. It's hard to be brave enough to try again. Or maybe she didn't think she deserved a second chance after failing to protect Cameron that day. I've felt that way myself, even though I know, rationally, that it wasn't my fault."

Peter rubbed her back again.

"In the end," Gwen continued, "I think Valerie's career and her music was how she dealt with the memory of it. Writing music might have been therapeutic for her. Or perhaps it was the ultimate distraction."

Gwen knew all about distraction to avoid anguish. But by avoiding her own pain, she'd allowed herself to stay trapped in the past. All she'd wanted since Eric had left was to have her old life back—her life without the pain from losing Lily, when her heart had been whole.

But it was impossible to go back. You could only go forward. Gwen looked up at the sky.

I don't want to die alone like Valerie. I want to love and be loved.

A part of Gwen began to feel a new understanding about why Eric had felt the need to leave her. It wasn't just because of her grief and how she had shut him out. He'd wanted children, and he had feared she'd never be able to move on after what had happened. They hadn't been on the same path with their grief or what they'd wanted in the future. Their timing had been off.

But was she ready to move on now? Was she ready to dive into a new life on the other side of the loss?

Peter cupped her elbow in his hand. "Come here."

She turned to him, and he gathered her into his arms. She melted into the warmth and comfort of his embrace.

"I'm sorry for what happened to your daughter," he said. "No one should have to go through something like that. I don't know why bad things happen the way they do."

She rested her cheek on his shoulder. "It's part of life, I guess. It's painful sometimes. But thankfully, not always. I guess that's what

Jeremy was trying to tell us. That we need to cherish and enjoy the good days."

Peter spoke softly into her ear. "Make hay while the sun shines. At least when we're not running from the cops."

Gwen laughed and drew back, but there were fresh tears in her eyes. "I'm so glad you came to me with that newspaper clipping. I'll never be able to thank you enough for letting me be a part of your research. It changes everything I thought I knew about Valerie's life, and it's helped me to look more consciously at my own."

They both faced forward to take in the view again.

"And I have to confess something," Gwen said. "Part of the reason why I was so invested in the possibility that Valerie's child might be alive somewhere was so that I could relinquish some of her fortune. I wanted there to be other family members besides just me—because after Lily died, I didn't want the pressure of being solely responsible for the safekeeping of the Scarlett Fontaine legend and her financial estate. I'm the only heir, but I'm childless now. Who will I leave it to after I'm gone? Who will care enough to look after things and not let it become a soulless corporate machine?" She shook her head at herself. "That probably sounds so lame."

"Not at all."

The sun emerged from behind a cloud, and Gwen felt its warmth on her cheeks. As she stood in the changing light, she pondered what Valerie might have wanted.

"We've always taken on charitable causes," Gwen said, "but I think what I'd like to do now is start a foundation for single mothers who need help getting by on their own. In Valerie's name, of course."

"That sounds like a noble endeavor."

"I'll talk to my parents about it when I get home."

They stood for a while at the top of the mountain. Then Peter turned to her. "I think, after this, I should go to Valdez if I'm going to write about what happened. What about you? Will you go home now? And talk to your husband?"

Gwen inhaled the fresh scent of the pine forest. "I don't know if I'm ready for that. I still don't know what's going on with him and Keri—I don't even think Eric knows—and that needs to be resolved."

They stood side by side, looking over the rail.

"It would certainly be beneficial for me to see Valdez," Gwen said, "as the curator of Scarlett's museum."

"Yes," Peter replied. "But it's not the same as it used to be. Even if we go, we won't see the town that existed then. It's all gone."

"But Wilderness Lodge is still there." She glanced at him. "And the Columbia Glacier. And most importantly, the Valdez Museum. I'd love to spend some time going through the archives. They have an amazing collection of old photographs. Most of them are available online, but I'm sure Douglas could help us focus on the year of the quake."

A glint of hope came into Peter's eyes. "Does that mean you'll come with me?"

"I think it does." She felt a fresh flow of energy. "We should get going."

Not wanting to waste another second talking about it, they turned and headed toward the tram.

PART III

THE BEAUTY

CHAPTER 27

Gwen and Peter boarded a Boeing 737-700, and for nearly two hours in the window seat, Gwen looked down at rugged, snowcapped mountains, lush evergreen forests, and serpentine rivers.

Peter arranged for a rental car at the airport in Anchorage, as it seemed wise to travel in Valerie's footsteps. Frank Brown wouldn't come to chauffeur them to Valdez, but the route was the same. They drove northeast around Prince William Sound and the epicenter of the quake at the mouth of College Fjord, fifteen miles below the earth's surface.

With Peter behind the wheel, they made good time and stopped for lunch in Glenallen. They continued onward to Thompson Pass, a snowy gap in the Chugach Mountains, where they pulled over and stepped out of the car to marvel at the Worthington Glacier.

They both stood hushed and spellbound.

"I've never seen a glacier before," Peter said, watching it glisten in the bright sunshine. "Not in real life."

"Me neither," Gwen replied. "It's quite something, isn't it?"

They lingered awhile so that Peter could set up his tripod and telephoto lens and take photographs in the changing light.

Gwen was content with a few selfies on her phone.

When Peter was satisfied with the shots he'd taken, they got back into the car and continued their journey. Later, as they were nearing

Valdez, Gwen's phone vibrated in her pocket. She pulled it out and looked at it.

"This is the third time today."

"Another photo from Eric?" Peter asked as he steered around a gentle bend in the road.

"Yes, and this one is him holding the world's ugliest vase. It was a wedding gift from his eccentric aunt, and we laughed every time we pulled it out of the cupboard where we kept it hidden unless she was coming over." Gwen held the phone up, but Peter could only glance briefly as he drove.

"That's him?" Peter asked. "Your ex?"

"Yes. That's Eric."

She stared at the picture for a few seconds. It was odd to see him smiling at her—as if they were still best friends and nothing had ever gone wrong.

"He wants to remind you of happier times," Peter said.

"Yes," she agreed.

"Did you tell him you were going to Valdez?" Peter asked.

Gwen slid her phone back into her purse. "No. He thinks I'm still in Juneau." She gazed out the window at the passing forest on the outskirts of the town. "I'll tell him later when I feel like responding. I just don't want to get into anything now. I don't want to answer questions about when I'm coming home, because I have no idea." She turned to Peter. "There's probably a lot we need to discover here. We might want to stay awhile."

But was she doing it again? Looking for a distraction? Avoiding the difficult reality of the present?

They drove on, picking up speed on a downward slope toward Valdez and Wilderness Lodge, where they had two rooms booked and dinner reservations at seven.

~

Wilderness Lodge, by 2017, had become one of the premier excursions for every major cruise line that visited Prince William Sound. The new owners had retained the rustic charm of the original hotel facilities. The lobby still boasted the same floor-to-ceiling stone fireplace and golden pine timbers, but the red checkered upholstery had been refreshed and updated. The dining room also upheld its original style, but the kitchen had been expanded and modernized with stainless steel worktables; cutting-edge, energy-efficient appliances; and a zone-style configuration. In 2010, a new pub called Crab Cabin had been constructed as an expansion of the dock. It hosted crab feasts for the cruise ship visitors during the day, followed by a whale-watching-and-glacier tour on the *Wanderer II*—a 110-foot wheelchair-accessible vessel with heated cabins and multiple viewing decks.

Gwen and Peter pulled into the parking lot, got out of the car, and gazed up at the lodge with wonderment.

"It's exactly how I imagined it," Gwen said, feeling as if she'd walked into a dream.

"No wonder Valerie was so inspired here," Peter said. "Creatively, I mean."

They retrieved their suitcases from the trunk and wheeled them to the expansive wooden deck. The door to the lobby was thick knotty pine, aged to a warm, golden patina. Gwen entered first and approached the reception desk. A young woman in a sharp-looking navy blazer and white shirt greeted them.

"Welcome to Wilderness Lodge. Checking in?"

"Yes," Peter said. He gave her both their names.

She found them in the system and prepared electronic e-cards. "You're next to each other in the east wing. Both rooms have water views. Turn left on the far side of the fireplace, and it's all the way at the end of the hall."

"Thank you." Gwen started off across the lobby. "The end of the hall," she said over her shoulder to Peter. "Isn't that where Valerie stayed?"

"If so, this is very serendipitous."

They reached their rooms and tapped their cards on the touch pads.

"I'll see you in a bit," Gwen said and entered her room with a sense of nostalgia, though she'd never been there before. The decor was obviously contemporary. This twenty-first-century version of the room was pure luxury, with a king-size bed, a thick white duvet, and fluffy pillows. It faced a large flat-screen television on top of an entertainment unit with a black granite countertop. Gwen checked the drawers and cupboards and found a fully stocked minibar, a coffee maker, elegant wineglasses, and a corkscrew.

Next, she turned to the wide picture window, where ivory-colored sheers were closed but still let in the light. She drew them open and admired the view of the water and majestic Chugach Mountain range beyond.

A knock sounded at her door. She hurried to answer it.

Peter stood in the hall holding up a bottle of prosecco and two champagne flutes. "How's your room?"

"Perfect. How's yours?" She stood back and invited him in.

"Great. I thought this moment deserved a toast." He set the bottle on the desk.

"I didn't get a bottle of bubbly," she mentioned, feeling a little left out as she looked around.

"I called ahead and special ordered it," he explained. "I figured we deserved it after everything we managed to learn over the past few days." He peeled off the foil. "It's going to be great for the book and for your museum as well." He popped the cork and poured the fizzy wine into the flutes.

"I still can't believe it," she said, accepting the glass he offered. "It hardly seems real that we might be in the same room where Valerie lived and wrote her early music. And isn't it interesting that I'm calling her Valerie now when she was always Scarlett to me?"

Peter picked up his glass and held it up. "To Valerie. And to Cameron. And Jeremy. And you and me."

She clinked the tip of her glass against his. "To us."

They sipped the chilled prosecco and wandered to the window. Peter took note of the fancy new boat at the dock. "I wonder what happened to the original *Wanderer*."

"We could ask the owners," Gwen suggested. "But we probably shouldn't reveal why we're here. We can tell them later, of course, after the book comes out." She moved to sit on the edge of the bed. "So what's next? We have dinner reservations at seven. Should we book a spot on the glacier tour tomorrow?"

"That sounds good," Peter replied. "I'd also like to drive to the site of the Old Town and walk around a bit."

"We can probably do both of those things tomorrow," she said, sipping her drink.

Her phone rang in her purse, and she quickly stood to retrieve it. "It's Eric again." She stared at his number on the screen.

"Should I leave you alone?" Peter asked, gesturing toward the door. "We could meet up for supper later."

"No, please don't go," she responded. "Have a seat, and finish your drink. I'll see what he wants and try to make it quick." She tapped the little green button. "Hello?"

"How's it going?" Eric asked, overly cheerful. "Are you still in Alaska?"

Gwen turned away from Peter and wandered past the bed. "Yes, but I left Juneau this morning. I'm now in Valdez doing some extra research."

"Valdez? As in the *Exxon Valdez* oil spill?"

"That's right. It happened not far from here."

Eric was quiet for a few seconds. "Are you still with that guy?"

Gwen met Peter's gaze. "His name is Peter. And yes, we just arrived at the hotel."

There was another prolonged silence. "Are you in separate rooms or . . . ?"

Gwen turned away from Peter and spoke quietly. "I have my own room. But really . . . we've been over this. It's none of your business."

"I understand. But, Gwen . . ."

She waited for him to finish the thought and became aware of her heart hammering against her rib cage.

"I miss you," he said. "I can't stop thinking about us. We used to be soulmates, remember?"

"I remember," Gwen softly said.

"So . . . is there any hope for us?" he asked.

Wishing she felt more certain of her life and what she wanted, Gwen went into the bathroom and studied her reflection in the mirror. "I don't know."

Eric gave her a moment to ruminate. When he finally spoke, his voice reminded her of the way he used to talk when they were in bed together, when they were most intimate. "Till death do us part," he said. "When I spoke those words in church, I had no doubts about you. I was certain we'd be together forever."

"I was certain too," she replied.

He took his time posing the next question, because he knew her well. He understood that his words needed space and time to breathe, then relax into her consciousness.

"Can I pick you up at the airport when you get back?"

"Um . . ."

"I don't expect you to make any decisions right away," he said. "I just want to spend some time with you and see if maybe . . ." He paused.

"Maybe what?" she asked.

"If maybe we could talk about giving our marriage a second try. I've already ended things with Keri. It's over."

Gwen went a little weak in the knees. She sat down on the tub, and a memory drifted in. She recalled the weeks just after Eric had left her, when this was all that she had wanted—for him to come home and apologize and tell her that he didn't want to give up on their marriage, because he still loved her.

Their marriage had been a happy one. At least until tragedy had struck.

She'd been walking around like an automaton ever since.

Until recently.

Gwen stood, looked at herself in the mirror again, and combed her fingers through her hair. She didn't want to think about this now. She wanted to get dressed for dinner and have a nice evening.

But Eric had more to say. "I'm sorry for how I pressured you to get pregnant right away, after Lily. I should have been more patient. And I want you to know that I'd be okay with whatever you want. Children or no children. I just want to be with you and grow old with you. That was always our plan. But if you feel like you might be ready to have a baby someday, I'd be willing to do that too. Whatever you want, Gwen. All I want is you. Us. Together forever."

The walls felt like they were closing in around her. Gwen was in no place, emotionally, to make any split-second decisions. She honestly didn't know what she wanted. She was still angry with Eric, but she had once been so happy in their marriage. It felt wrong to simply throw it away, to not even try. What was the alternative? Divorce?

"Okay," she said hesitantly. "Pick me up at the airport, and we'll talk. But that doesn't mean I want to jump back into things with you. A lot's happened in the past two years, and we can't just pick up where we left off. Even if we could, I'm not sure that's what I'd want."

"I wouldn't want that either," he said encouragingly, "because we didn't leave off in a good place. And that's totally on me. It's my fault we didn't get through those rough times, and I'm sorry. I really am. If you're willing to give me another chance, I swear to you—I'll spend the rest of my life making it up to you."

She had to resist the inclination to melt into his apology and forget everything that had transpired over the past two years. Specifically, Keri. "Let's just start with dinner."

"I'll accept that like the good sport that I am," Eric said, sounding more jovial. "Let me know when your flight is coming in, and I'll be there to meet you."

"All right," she said. "We'll talk later."

Gwen ended the call and stood at the bathroom sink, staring down at the white porcelain and the shiny stainless steel drain. She washed her hands, dried them on the towel, and checked her face in the mirror.

When she finally emerged from the bathroom, Peter was at the window, gazing out at the water. He turned as she approached. "Everything okay?"

"Yes," she replied. "He says he wants to pick me up at the airport when I get back and talk." She glanced around the room. "Where's my prosecco? Oh, there it is." She moved to the bedside table, picked it up, and tried not to guzzle the whole glass in one gulp.

"Listen," Peter said. "I'll completely understand if you want to go home early. I can finish up the research here and share everything with you when I get back to LA."

Gwen whirled around to face him. "What? No. I'm not going home early. This is too important. I'm staying."

His shoulders relaxed slightly. "Okay. I'm glad to hear that."

She joined him at the window, where they stood side by side, watching the clouds float over the tall mountain peaks.

Gwen pointed. "Oh, look. There's an eagle."

The large bird of prey circled a few times over the water, then flew directly toward them, coasting low on the wind. He soared upward and over the lodge.

"How gorgeous was that?" Peter said.

"What an incredible wingspan."

They watched the sky for a moment, and then Gwen finished her prosecco. "Should we get dressed for dinner?"

Peter checked his watch. "Yes." He turned to go. "Come and knock on my door when you're ready."

"I will." He left her room and closed the door behind him, leaving Gwen alone with her thoughts.

They coasted to Valerie. Gwen wondered how many times she had enjoyed this view while waiting to give birth to her baby. She must have felt very alone when she'd first arrived. It must have been daunting, not knowing what her future would hold.

There were many things Gwen finally understood about Valerie, yet she still had questions—like how long it had taken her to feel at peace with her decision to pursue her career and her art and let go of the dream of motherhood. Or had she ever truly been at peace? Was that even possible? It was a question Gwen had asked herself many times over the past two years. She had yet to determine the answer.

CHAPTER 28

Cruising fast and steadily through the fjord, the *Wanderer II* delivered a vibrant and eclectic wilderness tour that included birds, animals, and marine life, as well as a narrative about geological events as far back as the Ice Age.

Gwen and Peter wore the hats and scarves they'd purchased in the gift shop the night before and stood at the rail on the upper deck for optimal viewing. They spotted two killer whales, scores of porpoises and sea otters, and white mountain goats high on the steep cliffs. Peter captured all of it with his Nikon camera, secure on a strap around his neck. He changed lenses often, clicking, then cocking the shutter to click again. He photographed Gwen as well, sometimes discreetly when she wasn't looking, although she was constantly aware of his movements. Other times he asked her to smile or look up at the sky or down at the water before he took her picture.

There were at least fifty other passengers on board, but at times Gwen felt as if they were the only ones. She found herself watching Peter when his attention was fixed on whatever he was seeing through his viewfinder. During those moments, she studied his hands and the breadth of his shoulders and the way his jeans pooled around his hiking boots.

Then she thought of her conversation with Eric, and she felt guilty for looking at another man like this, for admiring him physically and feeling a connection that seemed to be growing more obvious, and mutual, with every hour they spent together.

She'd wanted Eric back for more than a year, but now that it suddenly seemed possible, she felt only confusion and uncertainty.

The tour guide announced on the speaker system that they were approaching the Columbia Glacier. Gwen and Peter moved to the bow on the upper deck, watching as they drew near.

"Wow." Peter's gaze roamed across the magnificent sculpted wall of ice.

"It's so much bigger than I expected," Gwen said.

Looking down at the water below, she was mesmerized by hundreds of large and small chunks of ice floating past the *Wanderer II* as it forged its way closer to the glacier. The tour guide explained they were called *bergy bits*—fragments of larger icebergs that had broken off the glacier and fallen into the sea.

The captain slowed the boat to a crawl. About a quarter mile out, he cut the engine, and the tour guide ended her commentary and switched off the microphone. Suddenly it was quiet, and they floated peacefully in the fjord between steep granite mountains sculpted over the centuries by the relentless flowing of the ice.

The silence was broken only by "white thunder" as the glacier calved, and a block of ice the size of a car tumbled into the sea. It sank deep, and the displacement of water caused a monstrous wave to rise. The sunken iceberg floated to the surface and gradually rolled over before finally relaxing on the swells. Everyone on the boat exclaimed with awe, and Peter and Gwen reached for each other's hands.

The *Wanderer II* remained for a half hour in the shadow of the grand structure, and the glacier was active that morning. It entertained them with its noisy cracks and falling fragments. It was a while before

Peter raised his camera to snap pictures. He was more interested in the experience than in the effort to capture it on film.

Later, on the return journey, when the *Wanderer II* was cruising at full speed and the cold wind was in their faces, Gwen and Peter retreated to the heated cabin below. They found empty seats in the front row before the large viewing windows.

Gwen removed her mittens. "What we saw today makes me think of Valerie's song lyrics. *Rivers of ice flow from mountains to sea, and thunder resounds without rain.* Now I understand what she was alluding to—white thunder beneath a blue sky."

Peter removed his mittens as well. "I could have stayed there all day. It was better than television."

"By far," she agreed, crossing one leg over the other. "I've seen videos of glaciers on YouTube, but that can't compare to seeing them in real life. I'll never forget this. Not as long as I live."

Peter nodded. "Sometimes you just have to admit that this planet is something of a miracle."

Gwen rested her head on Peter's shoulder. She felt fortunate to be alive and immensely grateful for this beautiful day.

~

After the boat cruise, Gwen and Peter enjoyed a light lunch at Crab Cabin, then returned to their rooms for some downtime before heading out to the site of Old Town Valdez.

The drive took about twenty minutes, and they found a place to park on a dirt road that led to the water and the former location of the doomed city docks.

They got out and shut the car doors. Peter retrieved his camera case and tripod from the trunk, and they walked toward a concrete slab that turned out to be the original post office. It was now a memorial with information about the quake.

They read each panel while pondering the past and gazing around at the fields of grass and young spring flowers. The natural landscape made it difficult to imagine an entire town existing here a half century ago. It was all gone now, yet it was not forgotten.

Gwen and Peter walked on. The sky was clear blue, and the sun shone brightly. There was barely a breath of wind.

"It's so peaceful," Gwen said in a quiet voice. "But there's something somber about it." She gazed across the meadow. "It's beautiful, but it feels like . . . I don't know . . . a burial place."

"Yes."

Together, they continued, their sneakers crunching over bits of gravel on the road. Eventually they came to an intersection marked with road signs.

"McKinley Street," Peter said. "This is right about where the ground opened up in front of Valerie and the baby carriage got stuck."

They stared at the ground for a moment, and Gwen turned toward the water. "Then the wave came rushing in."

Today, the water was calm—like a looking glass reflecting the forest and mountains. No danger there. Only reflection.

Peter set up the tripod and camera and took some pictures. Gwen assisted by holding the camera case and light meter, passing it to him when he asked for it.

"Did you get some good shots?" she asked afterward when he folded up his tripod.

"Yes. Incredible. These will go in the book, next to images of the Old Town as it used to be. I hope the Valdez Museum will have something they'll be willing to share, along with permission to publish."

"I can help you with that," Gwen said. "I'm looking forward to meeting Douglas."

They soon reached the water's edge. The tide was out, and a few pilings from the old dock were visible, as well as what remained of the Village Morgue Bar.

"This is where Frank Brown was when the shaking started," Gwen said. "I hate to imagine him running out to save Carol, then going down with the dock."

"He couldn't have known he was going to die for her," Peter replied. "Or maybe it wouldn't have changed anything if he knew. Those are the moments when people show who they really are and what matters to them."

Gwen couldn't help herself. She reached for Peter's hand and held it as they looked out at the shallow water where the earth below had liquefied during the quake. The docks and everything else had slid into ice-cold whirlpools of death and doom.

"Let's go back," Gwen said. "I think I've seen enough."

"Me too," Peter replied.

They turned and took note of the markers along the way showing where businesses and homes used to be, then got into the car and drove back to Wilderness Lodge.

Their dinner reservations were set for seven, but Gwen was overcome by the events of the day—the highs of the magnificent Columbia Glacier followed by the lows of the Old Town and the shadow of all that death. She needed some time alone to rest and reflect.

~

That night, after dinner, the temperature dropped. Gwen and Peter sat in the main lobby in front of a hot fire. The restaurant manager brought rum cocktails on a tray, and they spent the evening skimming through a few research books they had purchased in the gift shop.

"Listen to this," Gwen said, stopping at a passage in John Muir's book *Travels in Alaska*, which began with a trip in 1879. "'When we contemplate the whole globe as one great dew drop, striped and dotted with continents and islands, flying through space with other stars all singing and shining together as one, the whole universe appears as an infinite storm of beauty.'"

"He wrote that in 1879?" Peter asked, leaning close to her on the sofa and looking at the printed words on the page.

"He certainly had a passion for the physical world," Gwen said.

"So did Valerie." Peter's eyes met Gwen's. His face was mere inches away, so close she could feel the beat of his breath on her lips.

There was an energy between them, a physical awareness that had been building all day. She'd seen it in his eyes, in the way he looked at her, and she'd felt it in his touch when he'd leaned close to tell her something on the boat and his hand had rested on her hip for a second or two. The memory of it caused a pleasant vibration in her body.

The fire danced and crackled in the grate, and sparks floated up the chimney. Gwen hadn't dated anyone since her separation. She'd been living a very quiet life. Whatever was happening here felt novel and exciting.

Peter didn't speak, but his gaze dipped to her mouth. Their eyes met again, and he smiled and touched his lips lightly to hers.

The kiss was soft and warm—and all too brief—but it was perfect for that moment in the lobby, next to the fire, in the company of other hotel guests seated not far away, on soft chairs arranged in intimate clusters.

Peter's eyes glimmered in the firelight, and Gwen had a memory of the first time she'd laid eyes on him when he had stepped out of his car in the parking lot at the museum. Perhaps even then, she'd felt an attraction, but she had decisively ignored it because of the work he did.

It still bothered her when she thought about it, but she couldn't ignore what was happening between them now, after days of constant togetherness and deep, stimulating conversations. And now that she knew him better, she didn't see him as a heartless or sleazy photographer, not when he had regrets and had chosen to leave that line of work behind.

"That was nice," she said, feeling suddenly shy. She lowered her gaze to the book on her lap.

"Yes."

It was mostly dark outside, except for the hint of dusk that seeped in through the sheer curtains of the lobby. Gwen still wasn't used to these late sunsets, but there was something magical about them, as if she and Peter were existing in an alternate universe.

Peter closed his eyes and touched his forehead to hers. Gwen closed her eyes as well, breathed in the musky scent of him, and everything grew calm.

"I didn't expect this," Peter said.

"Expect what?"

"To like you so much." His eyes lifted. "I'm afraid I have a bit of a crush."

Feeling flattered, Gwen smiled and placed her open palm on his chest. "I didn't expect this either."

He sat back and put his arm around her, and she set the book aside and snuggled into him.

~

The following morning, Gwen woke at six and couldn't go back to sleep. She took a long hot shower and asked herself if she regretted kissing and snuggling up against Peter on the sofa the night before.

The answer was a firm no. She may still be a married woman, but she was separated, and her husband had certainly enjoyed his freedom over the past year. Eric's texts and phone calls lately didn't change that. And the more she thought about it, the more she realized that she had never felt truly seen or understood by Eric. Even when he'd called and apologized and finally accepted some responsibility for their separation, he'd had no idea what she was feeling about "that guy" she was working with, and he hadn't seemed interested in probing deeper into her feelings about Peter. He just wanted her to come home and hear him out and give him a second chance. It was obvious that he was feeling some jealousy, but did he even care what *she* was feeling?

Gwen shut off the shower, got out of the tub, and toweled off in front of the steamed-up mirror.

No. She had no regrets. And she was certain there had been no element of getting even with Eric by kissing someone else. Honestly, that morning, she didn't care about Keri, and perhaps that spoke volumes about her state of mind and her vision of the future.

After she blew her hair dry and dressed for the day, she brewed coffee in her room. She had just taken the first sip when her cell phone chimed. Picking it up, she saw a text from Peter.

Hey. You up?

She quickly responded. Yes. I was awake at six. I just showered and I'm hungry for breakfast. Chop chop.

Peter sent a goofy-face emoji and followed up with: Jumping in the shower now.

Gwen pictured him leaping out of bed. She smiled at the image and continued to sip her hot and delicious coffee.

～

Gwen and Peter spent the entire day at the Valdez Museum. They met Douglas Warren at ten o'clock and spoke at length about the earthquake. Then he showed them the photography collection and left them alone to conduct their research.

At lunchtime, they ordered a pizza, and when the museum closed at the end of the day, Gwen and Peter went for supper in town and discussed their findings.

"I'm starting to feel like I have almost everything I need to finish the book," Peter said, "except for what happened with Drew."

"I'll put out some feelers," Gwen said.

"Great. I'll also need permissions from your museum and the Valdez Museum to publish copyrighted material. Otherwise, I think I'm ready to return to LA and get back to the manuscript."

Gwen sipped her wine and tried not to reveal how much she dreaded saying goodbye to him.

"I also have a favor to ask," Peter said.

"Fire away."

He hesitated, then set down his fork and knife. "I'm wondering if you'd be my first reader when the book is complete. I'd love your feedback. And I should mention that I'm a very insecure writer, so essentially, I'll be baring my soul to you and sweating about it. But I don't think there's anyone I would trust more than you to give me useful feedback and not totally gut me in the process."

Gwen looked up from her salad. "I'd be honored."

"And I have another favor to ask." He paused. "Would you consider writing a foreword? I'll need to talk to my editor about it. I have no idea how that works in terms of payment or . . ."

Gwen interrupted him. "I'd love to. And again, I'm honored that you're asking. If you like, we could discuss ideas about what you'd want me to say. We can talk about that after I read the book."

He reached for his wine, his expression grateful and touched with a hint of disbelief. "I don't know how to thank you, Gwen. None of this would have been possible without you."

"It's a two-way street." She reached across the table and took hold of his hand. "I'm grateful that you came to me with this—and to have been included in the discovery process."

He squeezed her hand. "It's been an incredible week."

She felt overcome. "Yes. In more ways than one."

Learning about Valerie's loss and knowing that she went on to live a full life was helping Gwen to better understand her own situation. She'd been living in such a state of denial these past two years, either trying to forget what happened or longing for her old life, wishing Eric would come back and make it like it was before. But today she felt as if she'd been plucked out of the muck. She was feeling light and mobile and looking outward, engaging with the world and seeing everything through a new lens.

Peter raised her hand to his lips and kissed the back of it. "I'm glad we met."

"Me too."

They both sat back and returned to their dinners. Peter cut into his steak and kept his eyes lowered. "I do have a question, though. But I don't want to make this awkward."

Not knowing what to expect, Gwen stopped chewing.

"I'm sorry," Peter said, "but I need to know. What's going to happen with us?"

The question caught Gwen off guard. What exactly did *he* want to happen?

"Like I told you," he continued, still cutting his steak, "I need to get back to LA and finish the manuscript if I'm going to meet my deadline. And you're going home to a husband who wants to get back together with you."

"It's complicated, isn't it," she said.

"Yes." He looked at her, his eyes sharp and assessing. "Which is why I'd like to get it out in the open and agree about where we stand so that there aren't any disappointments or misunderstandings about what's going on here. Between us. Romantically, I mean."

Oh, God. Gwen had no idea if he was worried about hearts getting broken—his or hers?—or if he was concerned about her withholding help on the book if she, at any point, felt like a spurned lover. Or perhaps he saw this as a potential "sexual harassment at work" issue?

She thought carefully about how she should respond. As far as she was concerned, there was nothing "harassy" about this. All they had done was kiss, and there was no power differential. They were equals, so no worries there. But could one of them get hurt? Was that what this was truly about?

"This is a bit awkward, isn't it," she said with a hint of a smile, hoping to add some lightness to this weighty conversation. "It's hard to answer without knowing what *your* thoughts are. Because if you're worried about me feeling jilted or hurt, that's not remotely close to the realm of possibilities here. We're both adults, and I've enjoyed every minute with you, and I understand that you need to go back to LA. And I'm in a . . . what's the right word for this? An uncertain situation."

"With Eric," he said.

"Yes." She reached for her wine and took a sip. "I honestly don't know what to expect when I get home and see him, and I probably shouldn't make any big decisions right now. You and I still have work to do at the museum tomorrow, and I don't want to put a stop to this— whatever this is—because I want to enjoy our time together, whatever's left of it. I haven't felt like this in a long time. Maybe never." It was a bold finish, but she didn't regret it.

Peter sat back, relaxing slightly. "Me neither. This has been amazing. I really like you, Gwen. I mean . . . I like you a lot."

His words swirled pleasantly around her, and the knots in her shoulders began to unwind. "I like you too," she replied indulgently.

"And I want to keep in touch," he added. "On a regular basis, if that's okay. I hope that won't be a problem."

"Why would it be?"

He reached for his wine and took a sip. "If you get back together with your husband, he might not like it."

"I see your point," she replied. "But this is a professional relationship."

Peter's earnest eyes sought hers. "I hope you can think of it as something more than that. I will, no matter what happens."

A group at a corner table erupted in laughter, and she and Peter glanced toward them. It was exactly what they needed to steer them out of the complicated analysis of where they stood personally. It would be best, she decided, to keep things light and open, at least for now. What the future held, she had no idea. She still needed to see Eric and discuss their relationship.

She and Peter returned to their meals, but Gwen felt a little wobbly on the inside. Their conversation had been candid and open, and now she found herself watching his lips and the strong line of his jaw and the movement of his hands. Her blood surged through her veins, and her heart shuddered as she became increasingly conscious of his virile appeal. Clearly her body was experiencing an aftershock from the kiss.

"Don't worry," he said, his blue eyes smiling at her. "It's all good. Everything's going to be fine."

Gwen refolded the napkin on her lap and tried to return to her dinner, but it was hard to eat when her emotions were bouncing off the walls.

CHAPTER 29

Three days later, Gwen flew business class from Anchorage to Halifax and was the first person off the plane. As she wheeled her carry-on suitcase from the gate to the baggage claim, where Eric would be waiting, she began to perspire. It had nothing to do with the temperature inside the terminal. The sudden suffocating heat stemmed from a confusing compulsion to keep the details of her relationship with Peter a secret. But this made no sense. She was not returning to her husband after a weekend affair with another man. She and Eric were separated, and he had been living with another woman for months. There was nothing for Gwen to feel guilty about nor any reason to lie or keep secrets.

Nevertheless, when she walked through the glass exit doors and spotted Eric in the crowd and he smiled and waved, she felt wary. She thought of Peter and wished she was back in Alaska at the Wilderness Lodge, sitting with him in front of a roaring fire and reading about the wildlife of Prince William Sound. That had been so much easier than this. And strangely, it was Peter she felt unfaithful to in this moment.

"There you are at last." Eric spread his arms wide for a hug. "How was the flight?"

She hugged him and muddled through the usual polite greetings—the thing you do when you get off a plane and say hello to the person who came to meet you. Eric asked about the food on the flight, and

Gwen responded appropriately as he pulled her suitcase for her. As they pushed through the revolving door and walked to the parking garage, they made weather comparisons between Alaska and Nova Scotia. He hoisted her suitcase into the trunk of his car.

It was clear they were struggling to find their footing, to reach familiar ground. At one time, they could talk about anything, or nothing at all, but this was painfully awkward.

They got into his swanky new BMW, and Gwen looked around at the dashboard and cream-colored leather seats. "Nice ride," she said. "When did you get this?"

"Last January. The lease was up on the old RAV4, so I splurged a bit."

It was mostly small talk for the first few miles of the journey, until Gwen couldn't take it anymore. If she'd learned anything in Alaska, it was that life was short and unpredictable. She was done wasting time by dancing around what needed to be said.

"So what's happening with you and Keri?" she asked. "Have you heard from her?"

Eric flicked the blinker and passed a slow-moving sedan. "Well, that's an interesting story." He glanced in his rearview mirror. "Last night she texted me, and I told her that you were coming home from Alaska today and that I was picking you up at the airport. Naturally, she had a conniption."

"But I thought you ended things with her."

"I did, but she's not very good at taking no for an answer. It might take a while to fully cut the cord."

Gwen observed him with intention. "Are you sure that's what you want? To cut the cord?"

"I'm positive," he replied matter-of-factly. "I just want you. I want to go back to how things used to be with us."

Funny, she used to want that too, but how could it ever be the same after everything they'd been through?

Her silence seemed to have a sobering effect on Eric. He lost most of his earlier bravado.

"I hope that doesn't scare you." He glanced briefly at her in the passenger seat. "I don't want to put pressure on you or anything."

"It's fine," she told him. "But I hope you didn't end things with Keri just for me, because it may surprise you to hear this, but I really don't know what I want. We've been apart for a long time, and I've gotten used to living without you."

He merged into the passing lane again. "I get that. I understand."

But Gwen was quite certain he didn't understand anything at all. Or he didn't truly believe it. He probably thought she was speaking from a place of pride or ego or just playing hard to get, but that wasn't the case. What she'd said was the truth.

She looked out the car window at the evergreens whizzing by.

Then she looked at Eric behind the wheel and felt as if she were looking at a stranger. Someone from her past with whom she no longer had anything in common.

He reached across the console and held her hand. "It's not my intention to push you into anything, and I understand that this isn't a done deal. I deserve to be raked over the coals, and I fully expect to be groveling and apologizing for however long it takes."

"It sounds like you have it all figured out," she said.

He looked at her with a small frown, as if he had only just spotted a detour sign on what he thought was an open road before him.

He slid his hand back to rest on the steering wheel, and Gwen thought of Peter again—about days of exhausting travel and challenging research, beautiful boat rides, and deep conversations. This moment in Eric's shiny new BMW was nothing like that. She felt quite fatigued.

"Talk to me," he said. "I want to know what you're thinking."

"Are you sure?"

"Yes."

"Okay, then. Here it is." She took a deep breath and let it out. "Ever since you walked out on us, you knew I was lost without you. And I was." She would never forget the devastating early days of their separation. The loneliness and the crushing sense of failure. "But things are different now. *I'm* different. And I'm not sure how I feel about you after you've been with someone else for the past six months and have looked completely happy and in love with her on social media. You weren't missing me then."

Eric stared straight ahead and nodded, but he looked slightly panicked. They were barely at the Fall River junction and still faced an hour of driving. Perhaps Gwen should have stuck to small talk.

But what had she just said to herself about not wasting time?

They drove in silence for a while. Then Eric spoke. "Let's not talk about that anymore. Let's change the subject, because I promised myself I wasn't going to pressure you, but it feels like we're rushing things. Rushing them in the wrong direction." He glanced briefly at her. "Can we take it slow? Can we at least get home and get comfortable around each other before we decide the fate of the universe?"

Gwen felt a little unnerved by his use of the word *home*, as if he'd never left it. Would he think he could move back in immediately and sleep in their bedroom tonight?

"I agree that we should take it slow," she said. "And if I was pushing too fast to resolve things, I guess I'm still a bit touchy about everything. But in my defense, you don't deserve for this to be easy."

"You're absolutely right," he replied. "And that's where I failed you before. I avoided the difficult stuff. But I want to try again and show you that I've changed. Or grown—whatever you want to call it. I hope you'll give me a second chance. Till death do us part, remember?"

"I do remember." By now, the distance to home seemed less daunting. Gwen turned on the radio. "Let's listen to some music, then."

She found the popular station she liked best, and one of Scarlett's songs came on. Gwen increased the volume. "Oh, my gosh. What are the odds? This is Scarlett."

Eric looked at her strangely. "No, it's not."

"Yes, it is. It's not her singing, but she wrote this."

Eric listened for a second. "No kidding. I never would have guessed."

"I know, right? This is a huge hit right now, and it feels brand new."

Eric was noticeably impressed. "It's amazing what producers can do in the studio to bring an old tune up to date." He leaned close as if he were about to share a secret. "Did you know the Bee Gees wrote 'Islands in the Stream,' sung by Kenny Rogers and Dolly Parton?"

"I did indeed," she replied.

They spent the rest of the drive talking about movies they'd watched recently, and it was a relief to talk about something other than their failed marriage.

~

Eric pulled into the driveway, shut off the engine, and leaned forward over the steering wheel. He peered up at the front of the house.

"She looks pretty good."

"She absolutely does," Gwen replied as she reached for her purse.

They got out of the car, and Eric retrieved Gwen's suitcase from the trunk. He carried it up the front steps and waited for her to unlock the door and cross the threshold.

Eric followed, set her suitcase down, and looked around. Gwen walked into the kitchen and set her keys on the center island.

"It smells so familiar," Eric said. "Like home."

There it was again—the assumption that this was where he was meant to be. But he'd built a different home with a different woman since he had been here last. Gwen wondered what that house smelled like to him.

Eric strolled into her den, where she'd spent most of her leisure time the previous winter. He perused her bookshelf and found a title that he remembered. He slid it out and flipped through the pages.

She recalled Peter doing the same thing in the same spot, quite recently.

"We both read this one," Eric said. "You read it first, and then you recommended it to me. You always had such great taste in books. Or maybe we were just on the same page." He smiled at her. "How'd you like that metaphor?"

Gwen chuckled. "Nice one." She leaned against the doorjamb and folded her arms, watching him.

"You look pensive," he said after a while as he moved to the love seat and sat down. He leaned back and continued to gaze about the room.

Gwen thought he looked sad and forlorn, which softened her heart a little. She moved out of the doorway and joined him on the sofa.

"It must be strange for you," she said, "being back here."

"It is. It's hard to look at everything. I think of the good times we had here. And of course, you being pregnant with Lily. We barely got the nursery painted before . . ." He couldn't finish.

They sat beside each other, leaning back and staring up at the ceiling.

"After you left," Gwen said, "I wanted to move. I couldn't bear to live here alone with that freshly painted empty room upstairs. But I didn't have the energy to call a real estate agent and put the house up for sale. Thank goodness."

"I'm glad."

"Me too. But the nursery hasn't been touched. The crib and baby stuff are still there. I keep the door closed."

Eric sat forward and bowed his head. She sat forward as well.

"What's wrong?" she asked.

He raked his fingers through his hair. "I'm sorry, Gwen. I know I have no right to ask this question, but I have to, or I'll go nuts."

"What question?"

He spoke hesitantly. "What's the story with you and the guy you went to Alaska with? Are you together?"

The guy . . .

Gwen stared at Eric. "I don't know. He lives in LA, and I live here."

"He's gone back there?"

"Yes."

"But is that the end of it?" Eric asked.

Gwen shrugged. "I'm not sure. We'll be in touch quite a bit over the next year because he's working on a project about Scarlett."

Eric leaned back and turned his attention to the ceiling again. He let out a dejected sigh. "I figured that's what you were working on. But why Alaska?"

Gwen scratched her nose. "I can't really say. I've been sworn to secrecy."

Eric made a face. "Fine." He folded his hands over his belt buckle.

A noisy motorcycle sped by on the road outside. Then it grew quiet again.

"I have to ask another question," Eric said, "and you can tell me it's none of my business if you want to."

"Duly noted. Go ahead and ask."

He met her gaze. "Have you been sleeping with him?"

Gwen laughed softly. "You were right when you said it was none of your business. Not after your big love affair with Keri."

He held both hands up in surrender. "I swear I'm not judging. I have no right to expect a double standard. I just need to know what's been going on in your life. I can't guarantee I won't feel jealous, because I will, but I don't want to be in the dark, because we always used to tell each other everything. Remember?"

Gwen stood and paced around the room. "Yes, but that was before you walked out on our marriage."

"Fair point."

She stopped and faced him. "We kissed. That's all. But there was an attraction. A connection. There still is."

Eric sat motionless for several seconds. Gwen started to wonder if he'd even heard what she'd said. The room was growing dark with the setting sun, so she turned to the desk and switched on the lamp.

Still, Eric kept his head bowed, his hands clasped together.

"Are you going to say something?" she finally asked. "You look gobsmacked."

Finally, he looked up, and his eyes were bloodshot and glistening, his forehead drawn with tension.

"This is my fault," he said. "It kills me to imagine you with someone else, but I failed you as a husband, so you had every right to forget about me and move on. But I hate it, Gwen. I hate all of it. I hate how I couldn't face the death of our child or your pain, so I took off like a coward. I'm so sorry for that. I can't believe that's what I did. I swear it's not who I am. You're the love of my life, and I abandoned you when you needed me most. When we needed each other."

He buried his face in his hands and wept.

Gwen moved forward. She sat down beside him and pulled him into her arms. "It was hard for both of us. I know that."

He held her tight, and his voice shook when he tried to speak. "I didn't even want to see her grave. I didn't want to get a headstone or deal with any of that. But only because I couldn't face it. I wanted to pretend it never happened and start over. Try again."

Gwen rubbed his back. "I understand. It was awful. When I think of those days, it feels like a bad dream, but it wasn't. It was real."

She was coming to realize that everyone dealt with grief in different ways. Some took longer than others to accept a loss. Some could never overcome their anger.

When at last Eric collected himself, he apologized and stood up. "I need a glass of water."

Gwen stood and walked with him to the kitchen. She fetched a glass from the cupboard, filled it at the cooler, and handed it to him.

"Thank you." He guzzled it, then set it down on the island. "I was supposed to take you to dinner and remind you of how good it used to be with us. But I just spent the past ten minutes crying like a baby."

Gwen pushed a lock of his hair away from his forehead. "Better that than a bunch of Casanova stuff."

Eric laughed woefully and sat on one of the stools while Gwen put his empty water glass in the dishwasher.

"Did you make a reservation?" she eventually asked.

"Yes. For our regular table."

Feeling a need to lighten the mood, she faced him. "Well, I don't know about you, but I'm hungry. We might as well go if you're up to it."

He was slouching. "I can't very well stay here and mope around your kitchen all night. I need to at least *try* to be debonair."

The beginning of a smile tipped the corners of Gwen's mouth. "Okay. But let's take it one day at a time, all right? No assumptions. No seductions."

"None," he replied, raising a hand. "All I want is to get to know you again and do better this time. Can we try that?"

She stared at him for a moment across the kitchen island. His face hadn't changed much since they'd first fallen in love. Everything about him was so very familiar.

"Let's just start with dinner," she suggested, moving around the island to give him a kiss on the cheek before heading upstairs to freshen up after the long flight across the country.

CHAPTER 30

One year later

Gwen drove into the museum parking lot on the first day of spring.
She got out of the car and reached back in for her travel mug, slung her
purse over her shoulder, and went around to the front door. Inside, she
passed Nora, who was on her way to the gift shop with the cash drawer
under one arm, balanced on her hip.

"Good morning," Gwen said. "Another gorgeous day."

"They say it's going to be a scorcher." Nora continued to the gift
shop to open the till.

Gwen arrived at her office and hurried to unlock the door because
her desk phone was ringing. She walked in and dropped her purse onto
the chair and lunged at her phone to answer it. It was a local independent bookstore owner.

"Good morning, Gwen," he said. "I'm sorry to bother you again, but
do you have any spare copies of the book? I sold out yesterday, and I don't
have a shipment coming until Tuesday, but there's a lady here who's eager
to read it. I thought I'd send her over there if you have copies?"

"I do," she replied. "They're in the gift shop. Tell her to come on
over. The museum doesn't open until ten, but I'll unlock the front door
for her."

"Thanks. You're a peach."

Gwen hung up and smiled. Peter's book was already in its second printing after only a few weeks and had topped bestseller lists worldwide. She and Peter had been in constant contact over the past year, and three days ago, he had texted to say there were nibbles about a movie deal, as well as discussions about a Broadway musical based on Scarlett's life—using her music, of course.

Gwen logged on to her computer and went through her email inbox. It was overflowing with unread messages. Many were from tour group operators asking for additional dates because of the sudden increase in demand for visits to the museum. Tourists were flying to Nova Scotia in droves, coming from across the world to see the house where Scarlett Fontaine had been born and raised.

Gwen took a sip of green tea and opened her scheduling app. With any luck, she'd get through all these messages and have every extra tour date confirmed by noon. That would leave her time for a break before job interviews that afternoon. She was hiring two additional full-time guides to start right away because the tour schedule was pure pandemonium, especially when a cruise ship docked in Halifax. Thankfully, today wasn't one of those days, so there was some semblance of sanity out there among the displays.

~

Around eleven o'clock, a knock sounded at Gwen's office door.

"Come in." Determined to finish an email, Gwen kept her eyes on her fingers, clicking across the keyboard, as the person walked in. She wrote one last sentence, rolled her chair to the center of her desk, and looked up.

Before her stood an older man she hadn't seen in many years: Mr. Thornby, her beloved music teacher from high school. Now retired, he still taught private piano lessons in the community. Gwen occasionally thought about giving him a call, because it was never too late to start a new hobby.

She smiled with delight and stood. "Mr. Thornby. How nice to see you." She moved around the desk and gave him a hug.

"It's good to see you too," he replied with a warmth that made everything seem right with the world.

Gwen drew back and took in his appearance. He had gained a few pounds over the years, and his hair was gray and thinning. Nevertheless, he looked youthful in loose-fitting blue jeans, a black fleece jacket, and a backpack slung over one shoulder.

"Have a seat." She gestured toward the wing chair that faced her desk and returned to her own chair.

"I thought it was time I paid you a visit," he said sheepishly.

She quirked an eyebrow. "Why is that?"

"Well . . ." His gaze roamed around her office, up to the ceiling, and down the wall of bookcases. "When your family opened the museum years ago, I thought about coming in and sharing what I knew about Valerie, but I felt it best to stay quiet. But I just read the book."

Gwen sat forward, her senses tingling with curiosity. "You knew Valerie?"

"I did. I knew her very well."

Gwen blinked a few times as her mind took hold of what was happening here. She slumped back in her chair and covered her mouth with her hand.

Mr. Thornby. Mr. Andrew Thornby.

A shallow breath escaped her, and she began to feel a surge of mental clarity—the kind of satisfaction that comes from seeing the whole story at last. She felt awe at the sight of him.

"Are you . . . are you Drew?"

He nodded, and Gwen sat in shock and amazement, barely able to form words.

"I thought I should come and talk to you," he said, "because you wrote the foreword in the book, which was pretty spot on for the most part. Mr. Miller captured everything very well. He's a good writer. It really took me back and helped me remember all those wonderful summer days with our guitars." He gazed out the window and seemed lost in thought for a moment before he returned his attention to Gwen. "How did you know about all that?"

Trying not to stumble over her words, she jostled to explain. "Valerie's friend Jeremy, in Alaska, had an excellent memory. They were quite close, and she shared a lot with him but also with Angie, who was close to Jeremy. He didn't want to be acknowledged as the chief source of the information, even though he let Peter write about his role in the events."

Mr. Thornby nodded. "Valerie told me about Jeremy and Angie. It was very sad, what happened to her."

Gwen pondered his reply as her thoughts picked up speed. She soon found herself sitting back with even more clarity, as if she were viewing everything from a great height, like a bird on the wind. "If she talked to you about Jeremy, that means you must have seen each other again, after the earthquake. We didn't know about that."

"I'm aware," Mr. Thornby replied. "I've read the book."

Gwen pressed her palm to her forehead. "You said we got it right for the most part. What did we get wrong? Will you tell me?"

He shifted to sit more comfortably in the chair. "That's why I came. And I brought you some things." He glanced down at his backpack. "They should be in the museum."

Gwen's heart started to pound like a jackhammer, and all she could think about was Peter and how she wished he was here.

While Mr. Thornby unzipped his backpack, she held up a hand. "Wait. If you're going to tell me things, would it be okay if I called Peter Miller, the author of the book, and set him up on speakerphone so he could listen in as well? Or maybe I could record what you say and share it with him later?"

"You can call him if you like," Mr. Thornby replied. "And feel free to record anything. I realize it probably has some historical value."

"It definitely does." Gwen's hands trembled as she dialed Peter's cell phone number.

He answered right away but groggily. "Hello?"

Gwen checked her watch. "Hi, it's me. Sorry to wake you. I know it's early there, but this is important. Can I put you on speakerphone?"

Peter cleared his throat, and she imagined him sitting up in bed, fighting to think clearly. "Sure. But I apologize in advance if I'm slow to keep up. I need coffee."

She pressed the speakerphone button and laid her device on the desk. "I promise this will be better than coffee." She smiled at Mr. Thornby. "It'll wake you right up. You might even levitate."

Peter spoke in a clearer voice. "This sounds interesting."

Gwen rested both arms on the desk and leaned over the phone. "Do you remember when you were at my house and you saw my yearbook with pictures of me in the high school musical?"

"I do," Peter replied.

"I told you about my favorite teacher, Mr. Thornby?"

"Yes."

"Well, he's here with me now, sitting in my office. He came to see me this morning because he read your book. He enjoyed it very much."

"Oh," Peter replied. "I'm honored. Gwen had such great things to say about you, Mr. Thornby."

Gwen's heart warmed at Peter's politeness, but she couldn't let him go on like this, thinking this was just a phone call from an admiring fan.

"Mr. Thornby has some important information for us," she told him. "It turns out he knew Valerie. More than knew her, actually. His first name is Andrew. Or Drew." Gwen paused and waited for Peter to connect the obvious dots.

He remained silent.

"Are you okay? Should I call 911?" she asked.

Peter chuckled. "You were right. This is better than coffee. I'm wide awake now."

Gwen smiled. "I told you. So all this time, Mr. Thornby has been living here in Wolfville, and he wants to tell us about his relationship with Valerie. I'm going to let him talk now. He's also given us permission to record him, so I'm going to set that up on my phone, and you can do the same thing if you like, as a backup. Is that all right, Mr. Thornby?"

"It's fine," he replied. "I'm still amazed by all this modern technology. If we had this in 1963, life would have been different. Scarlett Fontaine might never have existed."

Gwen couldn't disagree. If only Valerie had had Instagram in Alaska. Mr. Thornby might have been directing high school musicals in Valdez instead of the Annapolis Valley.

"What can you tell us?" Peter asked. "And I'm afraid to ask if I totally messed up the book."

"You didn't mess up anything," Mr. Thornby told him. "I was just saying to Gwen what a terrific job you did. It felt like a magic carpet ride back to that summer we spent together. You described everything perfectly."

"Thank you," Peter said. "I appreciate that more than you'll ever know."

"Can you tell us about that summer?" Gwen asked, interrupting. "And what happened afterward? I'm curious why you never responded to Valerie's letters."

"Because I never received them," he explained. "You wrote well and accurately about our breakup, which was one of those moments in life when you're young and foolish and do stupid things. But I did love Valerie, and I thought we'd work everything out. Then life got in the way."

"How so?" Peter asked.

Mr. Thornby folded his arms across his chest. "I shouldn't say *life* got in the way. It was her father and mine. When the summer ended and I finished my job in the apple orchard, I went back to Halifax but quickly realized my mistake in ending things with Valerie. I missed her and realized I didn't want to live without her, so I drove back to Wolfville and knocked on her door. Her father answered and told me that she had taken off to New York to become an actress and he had no contact information. He blamed me, of course, for breaking her heart and causing her to run away from home. He said nothing about a pregnancy."

Mr. Thornby shook his head with regret.

"What about the last letter she sent on the day of the earthquake? Did that one ever reach you?"

Gwen and Peter waited with bated breath for Mr. Thornby to respond, but he took his time. He looked out the window again.

"I don't know what happened to that letter from the time she handed it to the cook on the supply ship to the day it was finally delivered to her aunt in Nova Scotia. It was unopened, but it was dirty, and the ink was smudged in places and difficult to read, as if it had been stuck under a sack of potatoes or something. Anyway, by the time I read it, three years had passed. Valerie had just received her first Oscar, and I had moved on. Or at least I thought I had."

"What do you mean?" Gwen asked.

Mr. Thornby looked down at his hands on his lap and revealed that there had been a phone call—a long-distance call from a telephone booth on the main street of Wolfville to a private mansion in the Hollywood Hills. It hadn't been easy to reach "Ms. Fontaine," but with effort, he had finally gotten through. It was his name that had made it past the gatekeepers.

"I told the person who answered that my name was Drew Thornby. She left me waiting on the line for a second. Then she said, 'Yes, Ms. Fontaine is willing to take your call. Please hold on. Here she is.'"

Mr. Thornby paused before he was able to continue. "I could barely breathe while I waited. I wanted so badly to see her in person."

CHAPTER 31

1967

Scarlett Fontaine picked up the desk phone. She dragged the cord as she carried it to the large window that overlooked the swimming pool. The view from her living room looked out over the Hollywood Hills, where the setting sun splashed wide ribbons of pink across the sky.

"Drew," she said with aloofness. "How nice to hear from you."

Inside a telephone booth in the small town of Wolfville, Nova Scotia, Drew was dripping wet, drenched from running through the driving rain in the darkness. "I just read your letter," he said, still out of breath and panting. "Your aunt Mary came to see me tonight, and she gave it to me."

Dropping the mantle of Scarlett Fontaine, Valerie frowned as she comprehended this news. Why hadn't Aunt Mary told her?

Turning away from the window, she carried the phone with her and moved to a blue velvet chair. "You only just received it? Which letter?"

"What do you mean, *which letter?*" Drew asked. "There was more than one?"

"There were at least twenty," she told him. "But obviously they never reached you."

Drew felt suddenly sick to his stomach. "I never received anything. And I didn't know you were pregnant, Valerie. *God!* Why didn't you tell me? Why did you run off like you did?"

"Because you didn't want me!" she replied, exasperated. "Don't remember that?"

The anger in her voice was like a glass of ice water splashed in Drew's face. He fought to make sense of this and speak the truth. "It was a stupid fight, and God knows I regretted it. After I left the farm, I couldn't bear the thought of being without you, so I drove back to Wolfville and went to your house. But your father said you'd left for New York. He insisted he didn't have any contact information, and no one else seemed to know anything. None of your friends would tell me anything."

"That's because they didn't know," she said.

"Yes, but . . ."

He leaned back against the glass window while rain pelted the booth. "Please tell me what happened. I saw you in *The Last Castle*, and I thought you wanted to go to Hollywood to make all your dreams come true, that you had no regrets about leaving me. But tonight, when I read your letter, I couldn't believe it. It made me happy because you said you'd had our child and you still loved me. I thought I was dreaming. But now I'm wondering if it was just a cruel joke."

A man with an umbrella dashed by, and Drew watched him leap over a puddle on the sidewalk.

"It wasn't a joke," Valerie said at last, speaking softly.

She said nothing more, and Drew wondered if she was crying.

"Valerie . . ." With dread, he tapped his forehead lightly against the glass three times. "What happened to our baby?"

He was now certain that she was crying. She must have dropped the receiver and walked away a short distance. He could hear the sound of her breathing in shuddering gasps.

"Valerie . . . please come back. Talk to me."

Finally, she picked up the phone. "I'm here."

Drew stood utterly still. His gut was on fire. "What happened to our baby?"

"He died," she told him. "I'm so sorry. And I didn't run off to New York. My father sent me to Alaska. That's what happened to our son— he died in the earthquake. But it was all my fault."

Drew sank down to a squatting position on the floor of the phone booth and cupped his hands together over his eyes. "Please tell me what happened. Tell me everything."

For an unbearable moment, Valerie said nothing, and Drew feared she had dropped the phone again and gone off somewhere to cry. But finally, she began to describe everything about her life in Alaska, leading up to the day of the earthquake. She told him how she had pushed the baby carriage onto the city dock with hopes of her letter finally reaching him. But then the shaking had begun, and she had been knocked off her feet by a violent wave that had swept into town.

She described everything in horrific detail—her return to the place where Cameron's carriage had gotten stuck. Finding him gone. She told Drew about her tumble into the crack in the earth. Her broken leg. Joe Brown saving her at the last second.

Drew listened to the tale of her friend Jeremy rescuing Angie's baby from the floating rooftop and offering the child to Valerie as a gift to console her. And to console himself because he had lost the woman whom he loved. Jeremy had wanted to raise Angie's baby with Valerie, somewhere far away where no one would find them.

By the end of it all, Drew was numb with disbelief while cars drove past, splashing through puddles that doused the phone booth like a fire hose. The streetlight overhead blinked off and on, and Drew wondered if this was all part of the nightmare. The crushing weight of his sorrow made him dizzy.

"If I had known where you were," he told her, "I would have come. I would have come in a heartbeat, and I would have married you."

Valerie's voice was calmer now. Smooth and lovely, the way he remembered it. "Thank you for saying that. I wish I had known it back then, when I was missing you, and when I was trying so hard to hate you. But I never could. Whenever I played my guitar or wrote music, it was always about you. Every song of love is for you. And for Cameron."

Drew looked up at the small ceiling of the phone booth and spoke in a guttural voice. "It's your father I hate. If he was still alive, I'd go over there right now and strangle him with my bare hands."

Valerie did not respond to that. Drew wondered if she had forgiven her father before he had died or visited him on his deathbed. He asked her that question.

"No," she replied. "I never spoke to him again after I left Nova Scotia. At least he lived long enough to see me win the Oscar." She paused contemplatively. "I wonder if he was proud." Then she scoffed into the phone. "Knowing him, he was probably still ashamed of me. I don't think I ever could have pleased him, no matter what I did in my life."

Drew slipped a few more coins into the pay phone. "It doesn't matter. You should be proud of yourself," he said. "I was proud of you when I saw the movie and especially when I found out you'd written the theme song."

"Thank you," she said.

Drew looked out at the dark, wet street. He wished he had enough change to keep feeding the pay phone all night, even if they just remained on the line in silence.

But unfortunately, he was going to run out of change soon, so he hurried to say what needed to be said.

"Can I come and see you?"

"I don't think that's a good idea."

Of course it wasn't.

Nevertheless, he asked, "Why not?"

"You know why."

He fell silent. Did she know?

"I saw your engagement announcement in the local paper," she explained. "Aunt Mary sends it to me every week. Congratulations."

Valerie's words crashed into Drew like a moving train. A feeling of hopelessness followed, as if he were entertaining a ridiculous fantasy that would never be possible or real. What was he thinking? She was Scarlett Fontaine, movie star, goddess, Oscar winner.

Then came the guilt for wanting her. He imagined Kathleen at home with her parents, watching television, perhaps discussing flower arrangements for the wedding.

"How did you meet her?" Valerie asked gently.

Drew swallowed. "Her father owns an apple farm near Coldbrook. He's one of the biggest producers in the valley. I went to work for him a few summers ago, and Kathleen and I got to know each other. She's in the music program at Acadia."

"You must have a lot in common, then," Valerie said, sounding a touch jealous.

"I suppose."

Valerie paused. "Can I ask you something?"

"Of course. Anything."

She cleared her throat and spoke hesitantly. "Did you ever take her to our cabin in the woods?"

Drew straightened his shoulders. "Never."

She took her time before speaking again. "Have you been back there since . . . since we broke up?"

He tipped his head to let his temple rest on the cool glass and closed his eyes to dream about those idyllic days in the woods. "A few times, yes. I went out there with my guitar and tried to write, but I couldn't. I think you must have been my muse."

She laughed affectionately. "And you were mine."

"That's not true," he argued. "You've written brilliant music and lyrics without me. You just won an Oscar for one of those songs."

"But I was thinking of you when I wrote it," she told him.

Her words gave him more pleasure than they should have, considering he was engaged to Kathleen. He felt a sudden urgent need to change the subject.

"I'm going to Acadia this fall," he told her. "I've been accepted to the music program as a mature student."

"That's wonderful. Congratulations."

"Thanks. I'd like to teach someday."

"You'll be wonderful at it. Your students will be so lucky to have you."

"Now you're just being kind," he said.

She laughed softly. "Yes, but it's the truth. I'm happy for you, Drew. I really am."

He swung the telephone cord like a small skipping rope. "What about you? Are you seeing anyone? I saw you on television at the premiere for your movie. You were with your costar."

"Yes," she said, chuckling, "but that's just for publicity. There's nothing happening there. I'm quite happy on my own. I prefer it, actually. It's such a busy life, and I'm surrounded by people all the time. When I come home at night, I like to be alone and just play my guitar."

"It was always a joy for you, wasn't it?" he said.

"Yes. A joy and an escape. Mostly an escape from my father. But whatever the reason, I've always felt most comfortable when I'm writing songs. These days it's very calming and healing."

Another car drove past, its headlights on high beam, windshield wipers snapping back and forth in the rain. Water sluiced along the curb edge and flowed into the grate.

"I'm glad you called," Valerie said. "It was nice to hear your voice. And I'm sorry my letter took so long to reach you."

"I'm sorry too."

Drew wondered where they would be if he had received the first letter she'd sent. She almost certainly wouldn't be in Hollywood, nor would she have received an Oscar. She and Drew might be living out of his van, a couple of hippies with no fixed address, writing music, searching for open roads with their little boy.

"Take care, okay?" Valerie said.

"You too," he replied. "I can't wait to see your next movie. I'll be first in line to buy a ticket."

She spoke with affection. "Goodbye, Drew."

His insides clenched in protest because he didn't want to hang up. He wanted to stay on the phone with her forever, listening to the sweet sound of her voice. He choked back tears that threatened to fall and said, "Goodbye, Valerie."

He placed the receiver in the phone cradle and stood for a moment, in shock, inert, still gripping it tightly. Then he turned and slid the door open and stepped outside into the cold, punishing rain.

CHAPTER 32

2018

"Mr. Thornby . . ." His tale echoed in Gwen's mind, and she felt dazed. It was difficult to form words as she stared across her desk at him. "I had no idea. I didn't know you were acquainted with Valerie, let alone had such an intimate relationship with her. Why didn't you ever tell me?"

He shifted in the chair and cleared his throat. It was obvious that he needed a moment to recover from the memory of that rainy night in the telephone booth.

"It's not something a teacher says to a student," he finally explained. "You're supposed to forget that we have personal lives of our own."

He was correct about that. As a child, whenever Gwen had spotted one of her teachers in public, it was like seeing an alien from outer space.

"On top of that," he continued, "I didn't want to be in a position where a reporter might come to me for information about her. So I kept it secret from everyone I knew. Even my wife."

"She still doesn't know to this day?" Peter asked.

Mr. Thornby shook his head. "No, but it doesn't matter, because she's not my wife anymore. We divorced after eight years."

Gwen felt a pang of sympathy because she knew how it felt to accept defeat in a marriage.

"I'm sorry to hear that," Peter said. "Can I ask what happened?"

"I've told you quite a bit already," Mr. Thornby replied. "I'd prefer to respect my ex-wife's privacy."

Gwen admired his discretion, but she already knew what had happened. It was a small town and common knowledge that the music teacher's wife had left him for another man—a science teacher at the high school in the neighboring town.

"It wasn't anyone's fault," Mr. Thornby said. "After that phone call with Valerie, nothing was quite the same between Kathleen and me, and I don't think she ever felt truly loved. We went ahead with the wedding, but I still carried a torch for Valerie. Kathleen never understood what was wrong with me. I should have told her."

"Did you keep in touch with Valerie after that phone call?" Peter asked.

"Yes. We wrote letters a few times a year, just as friends. She shared her private thoughts with me, things she kept hidden from a world that only saw her as a public figure. She loved acting and singing and writing music, but she hated the fame. You captured that well in your book, Mr. Miller. I don't know how you managed to get it so right when she tried so hard to keep everything private."

"I'll admit it was a challenge," Peter replied. "But Gwen helped a lot, and I'm glad to hear that it rang true for you, because you probably knew the real Scarlett Fontaine better than anyone. You knew her before she was famous. When she was just Valerie."

"I did know her well," Mr. Thornby said. "And your book was the reason why I came to see Gwen today." He paused. "It's about something you got wrong."

Gwen sat up, her back ramrod straight.

"Shoot," Peter said. "Those are the last words a biographer ever wants to hear. But please . . . I'm listening."

"I'm listening as well." Gwen bit her lower lip.

Mr. Thornby reached into his backpack for a stack of letters and set them on the desk. "These are for you, Gwen, for the museum's archives. That's all our correspondence over the years, and there are personal anecdotes about her experiences on the sets of her films and her song-writing techniques. Valuable material, I think. It also includes the last letter she wrote from Switzerland, shortly after her cancer diagnosis." He slid the letters across the desk. "When you read that final letter, you'll see that she asked me to come and be with her at the end of her life. So that's what I did. I got on a plane, and we spent six months together, until she passed."

For a split second, Gwen's breathing was suspended. Slowly, she picked up the letters and stared at them.

"That's what you got wrong in the book," Mr. Thornby said. "Valerie didn't die alone. I was with her, and I was holding her hand." He met Gwen's wide eyes and spoke solemnly. "It was a peaceful passing. And I promise, she knew she was loved. She knew I never stopped."

Gwen made a sound, a small exhalation of breath that wasn't quite a word, but it was an expression of understanding.

Valerie's pain and her happiness—her frustrations and her fulfillments. It was all so pure. For better or worse, life was cruel. Gwen thought of her own daughter, Lily, slipping away when she had prayed so desperately for her to live. She thought of those glaciers breaking apart and falling into the sea, creating a thunderous explosion of water and ice, an incredible spectacle. Stars collided. Sparks exploded. Flames devoured. Embers lingered, then perished. It was all a journey of life and death, all of it a storm of infinite beauty. But always, months of darkness slowly gave way to light. How welcome it was, and how special, after a long cold winter.

"Did she have any last words?" Gwen asked, still partly searching for the path out of her own private struggles.

Mr. Thornby's expression warmed. His chin trembled, and his voice shook. "Yes. She said, 'Don't be sad. We'll be together again.'"

Gwen covered her eyes with a hand. She swiveled her chair to turn her face away. It was all too much. She cried softly, and Mr. Thornby waited in silence.

When at last she recovered her composure, she faced her desk, wiped away her tears, reached for a tissue, and blew her nose. "Peter, are you still there?"

"I'm here," he replied soberly.

She looked at Mr. Thornby. "Thank you for telling us this. I'm glad she wasn't alone and that you were together in the end."

She stood and moved around her desk. Mr. Thornby rose from his chair, and they embraced.

"I'm sorry I waited so long," he said as he stepped back. "But Valerie asked me to keep everything secret. Mostly, I believe, because she wanted to protect me from the attention if the world found out that I was with her in Switzerland."

"You were right to keep it to yourself," Peter said on the speakerphone. "It was your private, personal life, and Valerie deserved that privacy after giving so much of herself to the public."

Peter, better than most, knew how the media would have reacted.

"Thank you for the letters," Gwen said. "But I hope you understand that if I add them to the museum's collection, you might be hounded. People will be curious about you. So I hate to ask this, but something might help to keep the wolves at bay."

"What's that?"

"Could you give me a photograph of yourself around the time you were with her that summer? That might satisfy their appetite."

Mr. Thornby gestured toward the stack of letters on the table. "I've already given you a few pictures of the two of us together at the cabin. I had copies made. They're in one of those envelopes."

"Thank you."

"Yes, thank you," Peter added on the speakerphone. "I wish I was there. I'd love to meet you, Mr. Thornby. Gwen, could you handle a short-notice visit from me this week?"

Delighted, she returned to her chair and picked up her phone. "Of course. I'd love it. When can you get here?"

"I'm checking flights right now," he said. "Would tomorrow be too soon?"

"Not soon enough." Gwen smiled. "I can't wait to see you."

She ended the call, reached for her keys, and locked the letters in her desk drawer. Then she walked Mr. Thornby outside to his car. Before they said goodbye, she had one more question for him.

"May I ask you something?"

"Anything," he replied.

Momentarily distracted by the sound of a tennis ball being batted back and forth on the nearby court at the edge of the parking lot, Gwen glanced at the two players, a man and a woman, both dressed in white.

"It's something I've wondered for a long time." She returned her attention to Mr. Thornby. "I never thought I'd learn the answer, but maybe you know it."

"Maybe I do," he replied.

The sun was in Gwen's eyes, so she shaded them with the flat of her hand. "I guess my big question is if Valerie had any regrets about the choices she made. Specifically, about not having more children after Cameron."

Mr. Thornby nodded, as if he understood why Gwen was asking. "She did have some regrets, but it wasn't about how her life turned out or not having more children. She was proud of her work—the music and films—and she was fulfilled. What she regretted was feeling an obligation or pressure to get married and have children because that's what everyone expected her to do. But it wasn't what she wanted, so she regretted letting that pressure take such a toll on her emotionally."

"Pressure from whom?" Gwen asked.

"The public. Her adoring fans—and herself as well. Everyone was always speculating about when she would finally get engaged and to whom. When she was able, at the end of her short life, to look back on that, she wished she had just been open and decisive about it and pushed back against the pressure. Because deep down, she didn't want another child. She derived great joy from writing music with only Cameron in her heart."

"And you as well."

Gwen felt the warmth of the noonday sun on her face. She understood Valerie's struggle. She had been struggling with the same questions herself: Should she have another baby? If so, when? What if she never felt ready? Could she still live a full and happy life?

"So Valerie finally let go of her grief?" Gwen asked.

"I wouldn't say that exactly. She always carried that grief inside her, but she also recognized that what happened in Alaska had given her a profound appreciation of life, and for the rest of her days, she saw beauty everywhere. Maybe that's what made her music so inspiring."

Gwen stood in awe, basking in the comfort of knowing that life was a gift—horrendous at times but also beautiful in its everyday miracles.

She and Eric hadn't understood that when they'd lost Lily. Gwen had only seen eternal pain. But she understood things better now. Yes, there was pain, but there was also love. A love that would never die.

"Thank you," she said to Mr. Thornby and stepped forward to hug him again.

She waited for him to get into his car and open his window, and before he drove off, she promised to pay him a visit when Peter arrived.

～

Gwen returned to her office, closed the door, and called Peter.

"Hey," he said. "That was incredible."

"It certainly was. And I just had another conversation with him outside. I'll tell you about it when you get here."

"I'll look forward to it," he replied.

Gwen sat down at her desk. "I only wish we'd known about all this before you submitted your manuscript. Any chance you could publish an update?"

"I just emailed my editor," he told her. "We have a call scheduled for later today. I'm going to suggest that we add this new material to the paperback edition, which is scheduled to release early next year. Is it too much to ask for you to hold off on any big announcements or museum displays with the letters and photographs?"

"Not too much to ask at all," she replied, "considering I wouldn't even know about this if it weren't for your book. That's what brought Mr. Thornby in here today. Can you imagine if he hadn't shared this with us and one day, after he was gone, someone cleaned out his attic and threw those letters away, not recognizing their value?"

She couldn't wait to start reading them.

"Archival disaster averted," Peter said.

Gwen stood up and wandered leisurely in circles around her office. "Do you have a flight booked yet?"

"Yes. I'll be landing in Halifax at 5:05 p.m. tomorrow. I'll rent a car and get a room at the Old Orchard Inn again. It was good last time."

Gwen stopped pacing. "Peter, you don't have to stay in a hotel. You can stay at my place."

He was quiet for a few seconds. "Are you sure?"

"Of course I'm sure. I have a lovely guest room." She paused. "And I've missed you. I can't wait to see you."

"I feel the same. But what will Eric say?"

She looked at the framed photograph of her and Eric standing proudly in front of the house they'd restored together. Then she laid her hand on the wedding invitation she had just received from him and Keri. "I think he'll be happy."

With a rush of anticipation, Gwen said, "We'll talk more when you get here. I'll have a late dinner waiting for you. Do you need directions from the airport?"

"No. I remember everything," he said, and she smiled at that.

"I remember everything too. I'll see you tomorrow."

She ended the call, flopped onto her chair, and spun herself around in a full circle.

~

The following evening, Peter walked through her front door, straight into her arms for a hug. He lifted her off the floor and held her like that for a long time.

"It's so good to see you," he said, his breath warm at her neck.

When he finally set her down, she was full to bursting with happiness. "It's good to see you too. Please come in."

He closed the door behind him, and they chatted about his flight and drive from the airport as he followed her into the kitchen. She had a bottle of Tidal Bay wine chilling in the fridge, so she took it out and served it. They raised their glasses to Valerie and Drew. Then they enjoyed a delicious dinner of lobster linguine, by candlelight, at the kitchen island while catching up on everything, most notably the new book Peter was working on—another biography, this time about a famous mountain climber whose plane went missing in the 1990s.

Later, they sat on Gwen's front veranda in two white-painted rocking chairs, looking up at the stars over the Minas Basin.

"It's so beautiful here," Peter said. "I can't tell you how good it feels to be back. The peace and quiet has totally spoiled LA for me."

"Maybe you should move here," she casually suggested.

He turned his head to look at her. "I've certainly thought about it. Maybe I should think about it some more."

Gwen smiled. "Maybe you should."

They continued to rock in their chairs.

"I wonder what Eric is doing right now," Peter said.

"It's hard to say. Keri is obsessed with the wedding, so they might be practicing the choreography for their first dance, which we'll probably see on YouTube."

"That should be entertaining."

The crickets chirped in a steady rhythm, and a light breeze wafted through the weeping willow in the front yard.

"You know what finally ended it for Eric and me?" Gwen asked, turning her head slightly in the chair. "The thing that opened our eyes to the fact that we couldn't fix our marriage?"

"I'd like to know."

"Well, it wasn't just the problem of how we'd handled our grief differently or that I wasn't ready to have a baby before. We talked about that, and I told him I was finally open to having another child, but then things took a weird turn." Gwen paused as she gazed up at the Big Dipper. "First, we found out that the mother of an old college friend of mine had passed away. I suggested we go to the funeral to be there for her, and Eric said he preferred not to because funerals were depressing. I said, 'But this is a dear friend of mine, and she was incredibly close to her mother.' Eric wouldn't stop bellyaching about it, so I gave up trying to convince him, and I just went on my own."

"No one will ever say funerals are fun," Peter said, "but they are important."

"I agree," Gwen replied. "But there was no arguing with him. He said life's too short to spend it going to funerals. He hates hospitals too, by the way. Anyway, a half hour later, when I was looking at a video on my phone—one of the ones I shot in Alaska—he said, 'I don't think I could stare at a wall of ice for half an hour.' I said to him: 'I agree. You'd get bored. You'd start complaining about why the captain wasn't speeding back to town.'" Gwen let her gaze sweep across the enormous night sky. "I think that was the moment we both realized that we just didn't match up. And I'm still not sure if it was losing Lily that changed each of us in different ways or if we were always mismatched and didn't realize it. Maybe we got married because we felt the pressure to do that after so many years as a couple, just like Valerie felt a pressure to get married."

Peter mulled that over. "It didn't take him long to get back together with Keri. How did you feel about that?"

Gwen remembered the afternoon in her den when Eric had come by to ask for a divorce so that he could propose to Keri.

"I was surprisingly happy for him. Or maybe I was just selfishly relieved that he was motivated to get an uncontested divorce so that we could each move on as quickly as possible." She looked at Peter. "I have their wedding invitation on my desk at work. It's next weekend. I wasn't going to go, but now that you're here, you could be my plus-one."

Peter chuckled. "I'm pretty sure you'd rather stick needles in your eyes."

She joined him in laughter. "Correct. I'm not all that keen on going to my ex-husband's wedding, and I'm sure Keri would prefer it if I wasn't there. I'd much rather do something else with you."

"Like what?" he asked, reaching for her hand.

They rocked back and forth in perfect unison. "Oh, I don't know. Something boring."

"We could watch a documentary about Audrey Hepburn," he suggested.

"That wouldn't be boring at all."

"You're right. Hey. We could go dancing."

"That would be fun."

Gwen rubbed her thumb over the back of Peter's hand. "Thank you for the kind mention in the acknowledgments."

"I meant every word," he replied. "I couldn't have written the book without you."

Their chairs creaked as they rocked on the old wooden floorboards.

"Maybe I was your muse," she suggested, glancing at him with teasing affection.

"You were definitely something—something I don't ever want to be without."

He leaned across the armrest to invite her for a kiss, and she leaned into it with boundless pleasure and happiness.

The End

AUTHOR'S NOTE

The idea for this novel came about five years ago when I was inspired to write about a natural disaster that occurred in real life. I was browsing books online and stumbled across one that was just coming out in 2017 called *The Great Quake—How the Biggest Earthquake in North America Changed Our Understanding of the Planet*, by Henry Fountain.

I had never heard of the great Alaskan earthquake before, so I ordered the book, and my research began. The story slowly and gradually blossomed from there.

One of the things that made the book a pleasure to work on was the research element, which allowed me to take a trip to Alaska with my husband. We enjoyed a two-week cruise and numerous excursions to view glaciers, and we spent two separate days on breathtaking Glacier Bay, which was the experience of a lifetime.

Wilderness Lodge is a fictional hotel, but it was inspired by a few locations that we visited for crab feasts and boat cruises.

As for the historic Old Town of Valdez, which was condemned and relocated not long after the earthquake, it is still possible to visit the former townsite. It exists as I describe in the novel, and you can search for it on YouTube and take one of many virtual tours.

If you would like to see some of my personal photographs from the trip, including locations I used in the book such as the Alaskan Hotel, the Red Dog Saloon, the Mount Roberts Tramway in Juneau, and more, please visit my website blog at www.juliannemaclean.com. You can find a link to that post on the book-information page. Click on *A Storm of Infinite Beauty*.

Lastly, here is a list of books that were instrumental in my research, and I am indebted to the authors for their work. Any mistakes I have made in the pages of this novel are my own.

Valdez: A Brief Oral History, by Karen LaChance

Bad Friday: The Great and Terrible 1964 Alaska Earthquake, by Lew Freedman

An Observer's Guide to the Glaciers of Prince William Sound, Alaska, by Nancy R. Lethcoe

Travels in Alaska, by John Muir

Alaska's Prince William Sound: A Traveler's Guide, by Marybeth Holleman

This Is Chance!: The Great Alaska Earthquake, Genie Chance, and the Shattered City She Held Together, by Jon Mooallem

The Day Trees Bent to the Ground, compiled by Janet Boylan

For more information about the Alaska earthquake, I recommend the most excellent Valdez Museum website at www.valdezmuseum.org.

ACKNOWLEDGMENTS

Many thanks to the publishing team at Lake Union for taking such good care of me—in particular, my editor, Alicia Clancy, who is insightful and brilliant with her editorial suggestions. To the marketing team: you make me a very happy author, and I am eternally grateful for everything you've done for me and my books. Thanks also to Danielle Marshall for bringing me into the Lake Union family. I will always be grateful to you.

As always, I give thanks to my agent, Paige Wheeler, who has been working hard for me, behind the scenes, for more than twenty years. I love having you in my corner. To my cousin Michelle Killen (a.k.a. Michelle McMaster) for your lifelong friendship and critique of this novel. To Kimberly Dossett—thank you for taking care of the business side of my writing career. You make it possible for me to focus on the creative side, which I deeply appreciate.

To my mom, Noel—thank you for passing your love of reading on to me. Where would I be today without that passion for literature? And thank you for all our wonderful conversations each day. I treasure you.

To Stephen, the love of my life—you are a dream of a husband, and I am so lucky to be married to you. Sometimes I still pinch myself, wondering what I ever did to deserve such an incredible man. Thank you for making all my dreams come true.

BOOK CLUB DISCUSSION QUESTIONS

1. Early in the novel, Gwen misses her husband and wants him back. Under the circumstances of their separation, his subsequent relationship with another woman, and his admission of his mistakes, including apologies, did you believe he deserved a second chance?

2. If Gwen and Eric had not suffered the loss of their daughter, Lily, do you think their marriage would have lasted? Why or why not?

3. Jeremy is introduced as a dangerous character but proves himself to be a good man and intensely loyal to Angie. Joe is unfaithful to Angie, but she loves him. If the earthquake had not occurred and Joe had not experienced his epiphany after the death of his wife, do you think he would have stopped his philandering and become a faithful husband? If not, do you think Angie would have eventually left him for Jeremy? If Angie was your friend, what would be your advice to her?

4. Valerie lost her mother at a young age and did not feel loved or supported by her father. In what ways did these past experiences affect the way she handled her breakup with Drew and her willingness to go to Alaska?

5. When Drew uses a pay phone to call Valerie in Hollywood,

was she right or wrong to tell him not to come and visit her? How might things have been different in her life, and in others' lives, if Drew had gotten on a plane to California the next day?

6. Valerie chooses not to get married or have any more children. Why do you believe she made this choice? Was it a fear of abandonment? The appeal of her career? Or was it a devotion to Drew as the one and only true love of her life?

7. In chapter 29, Eric meets Gwen at the airport and drives her home. They talk in the kitchen, and he says, "All I want is to get to know you again and do better this time. Can we try that?" Gwen cautiously suggests they start with dinner. At that point in the novel, did you believe she would remain with Eric, or did you expect her to end up with Peter? What did you want for her? Explain your answer.

8. At the end of the novel, Peter expresses a desire to leave LA and relocate to Nova Scotia. What do you think the future holds for Gwen and Peter? Will they stay together and have a child? Is that what you believe Gwen will want for herself? Explain your opinion.

9. If you believe Gwen will choose to have a child with Peter, how would she become comfortable with that decision after learning about the choices that Valerie made? How would Gwen's choices differ from or resemble Valerie's choices?

ABOUT THE AUTHOR

Julianne MacLean is a *USA Today* bestselling author of more than thirty novels, including the popular Color of Heaven series. Readers have described her books as "breathtaking," "soulful," and "uplifting." MacLean is a four-time Romance Writers of America RITA finalist and has won numerous awards, including the Booksellers' Best Award and a Reviewers' Choice Award from the *Romantic Times*. Her novels have sold millions of copies worldwide and have been translated into more than a dozen languages.

MacLean has a degree in English literature from King's College in Halifax, Nova Scotia, and a business degree from Acadia University in Wolfville, Nova Scotia. She loves to travel and has lived in New

Zealand, Canada, and England. She currently resides on the east coast of Canada in a lakeside home with her husband and daughter. Readers can visit her website at www.juliannemaclean.com for more information about her books and writing life and to subscribe to her mailing list for all the latest news.